# ADAM ZAMEENZAD

## Pepsi and Maria

# ADAM ZAMEENZAD

## Pepsi and Maria

Published in 2004 by
The Maia Press Limited
82 Forest Road
London E8 3BH
www.maiapress.com

ISBN 1 904559 06 9

A CIP catalogue record for this book is available
from the British Library

Printed and bound in Great Britain by Thanet Press

*For Shammi*
*my wife*

The crow has given me the signal,
The crow has given me the signal.
When the crow makes me dance,
When the crow makes me dance,
He tells me (when) to stop,
He tells me (when) to stop.

## An escape

Maria was having her dream again. Her best dream. Her dream of Heaven. Of home. Of abundance and warmth and love. And food. She always did when she went to sleep hungry.

Her nose twitched in the drowsy night, like that of a curious little kitten entering its house after a walkabout, smelling the rich aroma of river-fresh fish frying on the old family stove.

In her dream Maria is going up the familiar hills of trash, swinging her mother's hand with her left and her little brother's with her right; and yet, with the strange logic of dreams, she has a hand free, with which she is eating a never-ending roll of her mother's freshly buttered, freshly baked oven-hot bread. Her two sisters are running ahead of her. Pumpkin the puppy – 'my little girl-dog', as Maria used to call her – is close behind, as always, sniffing at her heels, rubbing against her calves, her tail swishing back and forth with electric intensity. Papa is up at their section of the ridge already, sorting out the best from the rest. The really good stuff may have been taken before he got there, but still, there was always enough left to make a good enough living. Better than good enough, sometimes. After all, their colony was not called 'HEAVEN' for nothing, as her mother always said, laughing her mountain-clear laugh that resounded over the entire ups and downs of the mouldy terraces of the country's refuse.

Pepsi sat beside the sleeping girl, his back resting against the crumbling old wall of a half-burnt house. He imagined the wall was happy to have him there, felt the comfort of his back with thanks. Perhaps it was lonely and lost since the fire; an ever-present, dull ache in its half-charred belly, the kind of dull ache of loneliness he sometimes felt in his half-starved belly.

He took a deep breath, not bothered about the scent of urine in the cool night air, happy that he could breathe at all. He wanted to lift Maria's head from the cold, stony road up on to his lap, but was afraid it might wake her. Or break her dream. For he knew she was dreaming. He could tell by the smile of peace around her lips. Always when she woke up after that smile she would tell him of her dream. Her dream of Heaven and home, her brother and her sisters and her papa and her mother.

Pepsi was dreaming of his mother too. Only he was dreaming awake. And, unlike Maria, he did not want to think about what his mother used to say. That would put him to sleep too. He didn't want to sleep, tired though he was, so tired he could just lie down and die. And that was just what he was not prepared to do. Lie down and die.

He would put up a fight. With all his little might and all that was big in his mind and heart and soul, he would put up a fight. A fight to live. For as long as he could. It might not be for long. Nico Two went last week, from fever. And Paulo got shot in the head. But he wasn't going easy. It was different with Maria. She had just about given up. And he had to fight for her too. He had to be strong. Strong enough for two. And being strong meant being alert, being awake; at least until they could get to a place of relative safety. This was danger zone number one, and he was the prime target: he and Maria.

Caddy had always hated him more than the rest. Partly because Pepsi 'pretended to be better than he was', and claimed to be the son of Señor Romano, one of the most respected citizens of the country; but even more because Pepsi was never afraid of him, as the others were. He had spoken back to him more than once. Of course, it was in the daytime and in the open on a busy street. Even Caddy couldn't shoot him there. But did he burn up! Pepsi could see his very insides turning to char before his words and eyes. And since he had become friends with Maria, Caddy's hatred had multiplied itself with itself. Maria came from 'over there', across the border. That made her an outsider and so deserving of nothing but the worst. Together, they were *bad*, as Caddy would say in his understated way. All his passion went into action, his words were muted and dull, as were his thoughts. Perhaps that's why he had never risen above the rank of an ordinary police officer. Many of his colleagues were lieutenants or superintendents now, some moved to more prestigious precincts. But he had friends in the force, friends who agreed with him, shared his mission, and that was satisfying.

Pepsi had nearly dozed off when he could smell something. Something stronger than urine. It had to be Caddy. Like a dog an intruder, Pepsi had learnt to smell Caddy coming. Actually, it was a dog that alerted him first. Of the many strays roaming the area, one let out a loud yelp, as if kicked. That yelp had to be Caddy-induced! Pet dogs, accompanied by their owners, Caddy would stroke affectionately and even pick up and cuddle if the dog was small enough and the owner important enough. But stray dogs . . .

And then there was the smell, the unmistakable smell. The smell of Caddy.

It was too late for Pepsi to try and hide. He was far too close. No time to wake up Maria. Carrying her would be no good for both of them. Better to leave her there and make a run for it. Come back for her later. She was so small and stretched out on her back she almost looked a part of the pavement. Besides, seeing him run, Caddy was bound to shoot after him forgetting all else. And who knows, the sight of him running scared might please his vanity so much he might forget to fire. Long enough for him to have time to get away.

Whether or not Pepsi thought all this through in the split second he had to make a decision, he did leave Maria sleeping, and ran. Caddy saw him, pulled out his gun with lightning speed and fired three times, Maria woke up and screamed, Pepsi stumbled over a broken stone on the road and fell over, hitting his elbow hard on the road and letting out a cry.

Caddy thought he'd got him, and raising his fist in the air shouted, 'Got you, you son of a . . .' He stopped himself. He was against swearing, even strong language, 'Got you after all,' he began again, and then, looking at the screaming Maria, 'You can

11

wait little sister, wait your turn. Whoo whoo whoo!' He raised his fist again and jumped two feet in the air with joy.

This was the most passionate Pepsi had ever heard Caddy go. And it saved his life. For otherwise he would have got up and tried to make another dash, even knowing it was hopeless. He would never have let Caddy get him lying down. But his triumphant words made Pepsi realise Caddy believed he had hit him. The best thing to do then was to lie still, pretend to be dead or seriously wounded. If he so much as moved, Caddy would shoot again, and get him for sure. Now he would approach him without attack, and when he was close, well, then, he would see what he could do . . .

As Caddy, half-running, came to where he had fallen, Pepsi jerked his foot forwards, catching him in the shins. Taken completely by surprise, Caddy fell flat on his face, unable to utter even a cry. His gun slid out of his hand, rolled across the road and lay under a dimly lit street lamp, its metal glistening under the pale light.

Pepsi jumped and without thinking made straight for the gun.

Before Caddy could catch his breath Pepsi was standing over his head with the gun in his hand. He had never fired a gun in his life, yet he was perfectly sure he could. Caddy believed he would. His heart fluttered like a trapped bird, his mouth went dry and cold, hot urine spurted down his thighs.

Pepsi could feel the thick, quivering, stench of Caddy's fear – in some weird, confusing and inexplicable way, so very like his own fear. For no reason at all, he remembered his mother.

*Don't*, she was saying. *Don't, my son, don't*. It was about something different, someone different. About him cursing his father and swearing to kill him as soon as he was old enough to get a gun.

He bent low, glowered into Caddy's eyes, spat in them with streetwise precision, then, pocketing the gun, ran to where Maria was, now sitting upright against the wall and sobbing hysterically; eyes wide open, unblinking.

Lifting her in his arms he continued to run as fast he could. Caddy might well have a reserve gun tucked away somewhere on his person, he couldn't dare take a chance, slow down. For a skinny, gawky twelve-year-old, he showed amazing speed, in spite of being burnt out for the day and despite carrying Maria. But then, he had long legs; and at eight, Maria weighed no more than some five-year-olds. He could barely feel her in his arms as he vanished into the darkness of the night.

## A debt of honour

Caddy was in a daze. He felt like he never remembered feeling, and that was difficult for him. He was accustomed to being accustomed to things and situations. Any new experience was unsettling. This one was shatteringly so.

He scrambled on to his knees, grazing them like a schoolboy, and then, like a schoolboy, managed to get on his feet with an embarrassed, sheepish look on his smooth, hairless face – even though he was mocked by some of his colleagues, he refused to wear a 'manly' moustache – trying not to feel the wet running down his trouser legs. He was not much taller than Pepsi, though his heavily rubber-soled regulation boots gave him an extra, extra edge over the boy in his bare feet. Although a bit flabby around the waist, he had thick strong thighs and thick strong arms. The neck was more absent than present; the hair greasy and black; the face chubby and fresh, almost angelic, alarmingly like that of his four-year-old son. You could almost confuse the two if they were sleeping side by side, blanketed up to the chin – as they often did.

What was he going to say at his precinct, to his officers? About his gun! What happened to it . . . ?

He could say he was attacked. By two men, five, fifteen . . . But they would like to know the details. He was not good at making up details, not good at telling lies. He was always found out, since he was a child. He kept trying, though, coming up with more and more fanciful stories, whenever the need arose, or he felt like it, but it seldom worked. Except with Anna, and that not always, and only because she loved him . . . You had to be clever for telling lies, quick-witted. And he was neither. Never had been. His father had reminded him of that at every possible opportunity when he was growing up. They would trip him up at the precinct, he would flounder, it would end up worse than telling the truth.

He could keep the lie simple. Say he was burgled. Knew nothing about it until he got up in the morning . . . But that would make him look stupid. Besides, they would come over to check his house, look for signs of break-in, fingerprints, AND he would have to involve Anna, his wife, in the lie. But he wasn't sure if she would agree to that! She was always so d——d hot after the truth it was unnatural! And what would he tell *her* . . . That hadn't occurred to him before, and it started a new worry.

It was all *his* fault. And *hers*. That . . . that . . . Pepsi . . . and that . . . slutty girl of his. And now he had spared his life. He could never forgive him for that. He could never live with that . . . The full realisation of what had happened, what Pepsi had done to him, began slowly to dawn on him.

He could never kill him now. Not until he had got even with him first.

He would have to catch him, alive. Catch him, and punish him. Punish him like he had never punished anyone before, and the Lord knew he *had* punished people before, and punished them hard. But he would punish that Pepsi creature like he never punished anyone before. Punish him so bad he would beg to die. And then, when he had had enough, more than enough, then he would grant him his request. He would say, *OK, you did me a favour, by sparing my life; NOW, I will return the favour, so we are equal before God. You did me the favour of sparing my life, even though I didn't ask for it, I will do you the favour of taking your life, like you beg me to. So now we are even. And to make it more than even, I will do the same to that little . . . girl of yours. So I will do you* two *favours in place of one . . .*

But first he had to catch them. Alive. In a public place, in open daylight, in front of everyone, or somewhere secret, in the dark – in a church even – but alive.

What about his police precinct, the officers, the gun . . . ? And his wife . . . what would he tell her? Admit to being tricked by a sewer rat! And then, then have his life spared by the sewer rat . . . and the wet trousers . . . He had been holding for a long time and it was more than half a day's supply! How would he explain *that* to her??? Thank God his mother would be sleeping. And more thanks to God his father was dead. He was glad when he died, and now gladder than ever. He said a quick prayer to God to ask forgiveness for being happy that his father was dead before getting back to his predicament.

There was only one solution.

He wouldn't go back. He *couldn't*. Home, or the precinct. Not until he had got the boy first, and that little . . .

Yes, he had to redeem his honour before he could face anybody he knew ever again.

And retrieve his gun.

But . . . he would need a gun to get his gun!

He would have to go back home. To get his father's gun. His lucky gun, he always called it. Maybe it would be lucky for him too. He would sneak in, and then . . . Or perhaps he should break in. Yes, that's what he would do. Break in. A real break-in. Then, when he was nowhere to be found, everyone would think he was kidnapped or something. That would explain his missing gun as well, though, of course, if he was not there, they wouldn't know the gun was missing.

It was all getting a bit too complicated and involved, the more he thought about it. So he was not going to think about it. Like he did any time things got too involved, he would just do what had to be done, and everything else would take care of itself.

He would miss Anna, though. And she would miss him. More than that. She would need him, need money. He could leave her a note, so she shouldn't worry. But if he did, she would tell his mother. He knew she would. And *she* would tell it to her sister. And *she* to her son. And *he* to everyone else and then they would all be out looking for him and soon everything would be out in the open and the shame and the disgrace of it all . . . There, he was thinking again, when he had made up his mind not to. No, he just wouldn't think. He would just break into his house, get his father's gun, leave some money for Anna, yes, he must leave some money for Anna, kiss Juan goodbye . . . what about Juan? He would cry for him . . . No, he mustn't think about Juan. Mustn't think about anything. He was never very good at it.

## Heaven is the answer

Pepsi kept running, carrying Maria even though she was awake now and wanting to be set down on her feet.

It was only when he reached an open field behind an abandoned industrial site that he stopped. There was a huge old tree some way into the field. It had a large hole in it. Sheltering in it in the dark they would be completely invisible. The only give-away might be if some dogs gathered round them expecting love or food. But even so, anyone coming their way would be an easy target in the light of the stars. And this time he would use the gun, if he had to.

Going into the sewer by the old town and meeting some of his friends would have been first option, talk the new situation over with them, show off his gun; but Maria was terrified of sewers and Pepsi had had to spend more and more time outside because of her. 'You should be used to the smell and the rats,' he tried to tell her, 'after all. You were brought up on the largest rubbish dump on earth.' But it was no good. That rubbish dump was her Heaven, and its smells and rats were out in the open, in God's fresh air, not in dark tunnels made by man.

Once within the warmth and safety of the tree's welcoming lap, he began muttering to himself, softly so Maria wouldn't hear, *I am a dead man, I am a dead man, I am a dead man. Caddy is not going to let me live now. Even if he has to get the whole force to hunt me out.*

The only thing to do was to get out of Caddy's sphere, out of the city.

Maybe now was the time to look for Maria's Heaven. It was in the north of the country to the south, as far as he could make out from what Maria remembered. It would be safe there, if they could get there in the first place.

They would need some money, some food, some clothes.

*I must break into my home and steal from my father.* He said this out loud before realising that he had said 'my home' and 'my father', when *he* had told him over and over again that *he* was not his father, *that* was not his home, and he was never to come anywhere near the house or him again. He would have him lynched if he so much as saw him, hand him over to the police, he was a man of influence . . . The police, that was all he needed now. But he had to take the risk. Without some money and some warm clothes – nights could get really cold, even in July, especially out in the open – it would be impossible for Maria to survive the journey, even if he managed.

## One more less

Caddy started to walk back in the general direction of home, slowly, planning his break-in. Planning was different from thinking and he was happy with it. It was a long walk, but in his wet condition he couldn't go to the main road and hail a taxi. He could do that for free, almost as a favour to the cab driver, as he often did. And he was not the only policeman to do so. But not tonight. Tonight he had to make a manly virtue of being stoic about the urine and the stink and consider it no more no less than a part of his duty. One had to suffer for one's duties, and this was one of those occasions.

He had walked about three miles and, after a long day – he had done a double shift to make some extra money – and now well into the night, he was beginning to feel a bit sleepy, and very tired, when he heard a sudden familiar stir. His senses alerted and body getting back into gear, he stiffened himself and simply turning his neck this way and that began to survey his surroundings. And yes, there it was! In the bleary light of a street lamp on the opposite side, a small bundle by the side of the road about thirty feet away; and from that bundle, a head sticking out, the face turned towards the wall, body covered in a blanket which Caddy was sure would be greasy, smelly and tattered. And so it was, when he got near it. An old shoebox peeped guiltily from under the blanket, pressed close to the stomach of whoever was in it.

He stood looking down at the small sleeping body. Either becoming aware of the presence, warned by the pavement, or simply by coincidence, the sleeping child turned and a face appeared with round sleep-soaked eyes in the process of opening. But before they could fully register what they saw, Caddy jumped forward with a fresh burst of energy and squatted firmly on the face, pressing down upon the mouth and the nose with his wet crotch and squeezing the cheeks between his well-muscled thighs. The child's body convulsed, convulsed with such strength that it almost dislodged him. He cursed, then crossed himself for this lapse, and pushed his bottom down on the face with his full strength. He was not to bend over and throttle the neck or generally hold down the rest of the body with his hands for that would be cheating. Of course, since he was the one making up the rules as he went along, he *could* change them – but it wouldn't be fair!

He was in charge of the situation here, in control; unlike in any other area of his life, since as long as he could remember. Either playing third or fourth fiddle to his brothers where his father was concerned, or made fun of by schoolmates for having a 'girlie' face, or remaining at the bottom of the pile in his job for not being clever enough or forceful enough. Even his wife read books he found hard to follow. But here, with street kids, he was the master. He could do what he liked, play the game according to his own rules: and if he kept the rules fair, he was proud of himself – though occasionally he had to play foul to match the foulness of his prey.

The child continued to convulse and squirm and flail and it reminded Caddy of the time he used to go fishing with his father and he caught a fish and it gasped for breath and twisted and flapped about fighting for life. This ritual for survival fascinated him and he loved to fish simply to watch it, even though he did not like eating fish and hated being with his father.

The fish always lost, and so did the child. But Caddy remained seated on the face for quite some time, just to make sure, and to think. He had to . . . think, sometimes, whether he liked it or not. He couldn't leave the poor kid half-dead. That would be cruel. He had to make sure he was gone. To a better world where he would be happier. Or she. And leave *this* world a better place too. For he, or she, would only have caught diseases, bad ones, to do with sex, then infected others. Done drugs, sold drugs. Very likely grown to be a killer. Or at the very least, stolen from honest folk and burgled homes. Yes, the world would be a better place without him, or her, and Caddy was happy to have made another small contribution towards that end. And the child would go to the arms of Jesus who would forgive him or her, for his, or her, sins; for Jesus was good at that.

This 'him or her' thing was bothering him and he had to make sure, just for the record. It was a police habit, but also for himself.

He got up from the face and looked down at it to make sure it wasn't breathing or anything. It looked so different from the last time he saw it. Piss wet, blotchy, swollen – and genderless. Hard to tell if a boy or a girl. Sticky collar-length hair gave no definite clue. He had seen some such faces in the morgue, but never created one himself. He pulled the blanket off the body. The legs had shorts on, so a boy. But he couldn't be sure. Their kind wore anything they could lay their hands on, or steal, regardless of propriety. Bending over he yanked the shorts off the chicken legs. Yes, a boy. Like Pepsi. The thought sent him into a sudden rage and he laid a strong kick between the boy's legs.

It felt good. He walked back, ran forward like in a game of football and threw another kick, this time sending the boy hurtling across the road. On its way the body overturned the shoebox, spilling out its contents: an old browned-off photograph of a man in a suit and a woman in a white wedding gown; a tiny lace handkerchief which might have been pink or white, once; seven black, shiny stones, smooth and round, or oval, the largest as big as a duck's egg; a key ring without any keys; and a few coins.

Caddy picked up the photograph, gave it a quick look, tore it in half and let it fall; rolled a couple of the stones under his feet without actually thinking about it, and jacket-pocketed the handkerchief and the coins.

He was about to stamp on the key ring when he noticed it had a finger-length wooden cross on a chain linked to the ring. He stooped to pick it up, reverentially kissed the cross and put it in his trouser pocket, only to feel the urine with his fingers. Aghast at what he had done he quickly pulled it out, kissed the cross again, washed it with his spit not sure if spit was the right cleaner for it . . . but in the circumstances, what else could he do! Rubbing it against the side of his jacket to dry, he placed it in his breast pocket, close to his heart.

His tiredness now almost gone, he began walking home at a much brisker pace.

The slabs of concrete on the pavement where the child was squatted upon, killed and kicked, which had remained petrified during the entire episode, now began to breathe again at Caddy's departure. But they did not complain. There was no one to complain to. Besides, they had long since learnt not to question the ways of men, their creator-gods. *They* built and *they* broke, made and destroyed, each other, and all else. *Their* will be done!

## The next morning

The sun slanted its way into the cave of the tree and tickled Pepsi's eyelids. He stirred, then reached out a sleepy arm to feel for Maria. He couldn't. Jolted fully awake, he looked to make sure. She wasn't there.

'Maria, Maria,' he ran out shouting, 'Mareeeaaa . . .' the bare earth tickling his bare feet good-naturedly, 'Marrrrreeeaaa . . .'

'Here,' she called back from behind him, sitting on a stone, with one hand eating what looked like a pizza and holding a can of Coke in her other hand, three dogs wagging their tails beside her. But she had learnt to hold on to her food, unless a dog really looked sad, looked starved, or looked like Pumpkin! These didn't. In the early days she would call out to every dog, feed it whatever she had; but since much of the time there were more dogs around than food, she had begun to discriminate.

'Here, have some,' she beckoned Pepsi and held out a piece of soggy pizza, 'it's really nice. And this, this was nearly full,' she waived the Coke can in the air.

'Where did you get all this?' said Pepsi angrily, mouth salivating, 'and I have told you a hundred times never to leave like that without asking me!' If he was sounding like his mother he did not think of it.

'You were sleeping. I didn't want to wake you. From there,' she answered both questions in the wrong order, pointing to a heap of rubbish bags lying somewhere in the distance on the other side of the field. Maria had a knack of locating garbage and finding 'things' like no one else Pepsi knew. He was proud of her for this, though more often than not he pretended to be angry at her wandering off, well aware that without wandering off she wouldn't find anything.

But it was different now. More dangerous than ever before. He would have to be more strict now.

He kept his serious, angry face on as he took the can, stretched out his neck and took a bite at the pizza while still in Maria's hands.

He would soon be getting enough food for the both of them, one way or another.

He felt the gun in his pocket with his free hand.

'It's not nearly full!' he said testily, taking a sip from the can, 'It's not even nearly half-full.'

Sometimes you had to show who was the boss.

'It was when I found it,' said Maria, unperturbed.

## Ruses and disguises

For as long as they were in the city, it was necessary to disguise themselves, not be as readily recognisable to Caddy as they previously were. Almost by choice, at least in public, just to taunt him.

Pepsi managed to pick up a baseball cap from a market stall and wore it the right way round so that the flap came over his eyes. Dark glasses would have been too obvious and brought suspicion. Some of his mates already wore caps, but he'd wanted to show off his head of thick, curly hair. With that out of the way he had to take care of his feet. He was always known to be barefoot, hot or cold. He took two left-foot white trainers from a basket outside a shoe shop. With hundreds of tourists and locals and beggars and jugglers and musicians and artists and entertainers of all sorts and varieties, and dogs, trampling all over the place in a jumbled mass of individual entities lost in a weird sort of organised chaos, it was easy to slip between legs and make away with this or that from the equally numberless little stalls and kiosks and shops that littered the square and the surrounding streets. They were cheap sneakers, and so soft it wasn't difficult to get his right foot into the left, especially as it was a size bigger than the other.

The next, and the most important – also the most difficult – thing was to change his walk. Anyone who knew him could tell him by his walk from miles away. He had this jaunty, springy way of walking on the balls of his feet, his shoulders lifting up at every step. He would now try to walk on his full feet, evenly, in a dull, flat manner. Trouble was, he kept forgetting and getting back to his old rhythm. It was Maria's job to tug at his shorts to remind him. She kept forgetting too! So it was going to take some time, and practice, before he got used to it. Besides, Maria was having walking problems of her own.

She had been fitted with two left, four-inch-heeled sandals – a piece of string tied round her feet and the sandals to keep them from slipping off. She could barely stand up, much less walk. Also, to hide the sandals so that her height should look 'natural' and not heel-related, she was wearing something that dragged down to the ground and kept tripping her up. It was from a charity shop basket and probably a grown woman's mini-dress. She looked so ridiculous in it she cried, but Pepsi was adamant. *You will get us both in trouble if you looked like yourself. So we have to . . . etc. etc. etc . . .* With a straw hat found floating about on the road and now on her head she felt like a circus midget on the run, but Pepsi said it was either that or a head shave; and she had to agree to the hat.

Looking weird had the advantage that they could beg for a while before 'the regulars' realised their territory was being invaded and chased them out. Pepsi hadn't dared to go to any of his usual haunts. With some food in their bellies – bought with money begged from tourists, fruit provided 'free' by market stalls – and disguises complete, they relaxed back in the shade of a wall, Pepsi planning his break-in into his father's home that night.

*Maria will have to ditch those shoes, poor girl, she cannot possibly carry on in them,* he said to himself as he played with her straw hat, moving it up and down her face.

And he thought of his sister. She died . . . he couldn't even remember how long ago it was that Maria died. She was Maria too. Was it two years? Eighteen months? Perhaps more than two years . . . He felt ashamed of himself that he couldn't remember when she died. It was cold. He remembered the cold. Of course no one knew the exact date she died. Giving birth. In the alleyway behind the church with the green door as big as a house and a large golden knob in its centre with Jesus crucified upon it. He couldn't remember what it was called, the church. The child died, too. A boy, he might have been, they said. Didn't find them till days after. And that because of the dogs.

She would have been ten that month. Ah! That reminded him.

27

She would have been ten, and she was less than a year younger than him . . . yes, he began to remember. It was one year and eleven months exactly – as exactly as it could be, not knowing exactly the day of her death.

Their mother was found in the river about three months later. Some said she was thrown; others, that she killed herself. But Pepsi knew she would never do that. She was a sinner, he knew, and she knew, but she would never commit that last sin. She would never take the life that God had given her. Nothing though that life was, and nothing though she was herself, she would not do something like that. Never.

It was his father. His father who got her killed. He was sure of that. As sure as he could be, or make himself be. For that was what he wanted to believe, so that when he killed him, he would know that he had a good reason to do so. Not just because he turned him out after taking him in, and treated his mother worse than the whore she became, but that he actually killed her; finally and with violence, not just slowly and with shame. Or got her killed, which was the same thing. Maybe it was wrong to want to kill him when she was alive, and maybe she was right to want to stop him. But once she was dead, by his hands, then, surely . . . and he felt a surge of anger and shame at himself for not having killed him all this time. Not having avenged his mother's death, his mother's shame . . .

Nothing, she may have been – she did not deserve a death that was worse than nothing, worse than her life.

He could hear her voice as if she was sitting next to him and Maria. *You are nothing, my son. Remember that, my son. Nothing. You are nothing. I am nothing. We are nothing. Keep saying to yourself, 'I am nothing. I am nothing. I am nothing'. There is great comfort in those words. 'I am nothing. I am nothing. I am nothing.' Once you accept that you are nothing, then every-thing becomes acceptable. You expect nothing, you get nothing, and nothing matters – once you know you are nothing. That is all that matters.*

As nothing she lived, and as nothing she was when they dragged her out of the river.

Pepsi didn't like to believe he was nothing. Not on good days. And even if he was nothing, he was not going to go as nothing, like his mother. He would fight, fight to the bitter end, fight for his life, nothing though it was. But on bad days, like today, he wasn't so sure. He was nothing. And that's all there was to it. It didn't matter how he went.

But Maria. She was different. She was not nothing.

He pulled the hat off her head so he could see the light of the sun filtering through her soft auburn hair.

*You are not nothing, little Maria, you are something. Something good. Something important. Remember that. You deserve your Heaven. And I will get you there. I promise you that. If it is the last thing in my life that I do, I will get you to your Heaven. Your Heaven, with all its rich garbage and fresh-air rats and friendly filth. As sure as I am nothing, I will get you to your Heaven, if it is the last thing I do . . . I am only sorry I didn't try before, when it would have been easier. But now, now I have to. And I will. I promise you that, if it is the last thing I do . . .*

Maria smiled and looked up at him, as if she had heard every word he said, even though he had not said a word.

But he was good with words. Liked words. Unlike Caddy.

He remembered his time in school.

He'd enjoyed it so much. He was not nothing there. Learnt faster than any other boy in class. Loved to write stories. Made poems too. Wanted to be a famous writer, a great poet, when he grew up. Or an astronaut. Or if all that was 'too ambitious', as his teacher said, at least a police officer.

That was before he met the police, and Caddy.

Now he'd be happy if he just lived to grow up, even as a sewer rat. 'Fat chance,' he said to himself at the thought, and then began to laugh out loud, even though it wasn't really funny. He recalled the look on Caddy's face when he held the gun over him, to keep himself laughing.

'You're silly, laughing like that for *nothing,*' said Maria, and began to laugh with him. Pepsi laughed even louder at that, and together they kept on laughing while some passers-by stopped to look at them and said what happy little children they were . . . probably going to a fancy-dress party.

## Back to the night before

The night was a lot older now with a tired feel about her, even the twinkle in the eyes of the stars was getting duller by the minute, their weary 'had enough' light gradually fading away. A dazed-looking half-moon seemed lost in a distant bend of the sky. Caddy stood in front of his house scratching his crotch. He was wondering how best to break in, causing the least damage to the house.

The window. That would be best. One piece of shattered glass was easy to replace and wouldn't cost much. In fact, the glazier on the third street from theirs would do it for free. He could even do it himself. He liked doing odd jobs around the house. But then he remembered he wouldn't be here. He would have been kidnapped or something, and it made him feel sorry for himself. He would have liked to mend that window.

But first, he had to break it.

Caddy went close to the window and tried to remember where the catch was, that's where he should punch it. He would put his hand, fat but small, in the empty holster of the gun so as not to hurt himself. After hesitating and moving backward and forward for some time, he finally made a running dash for it. But just as he was about to lunge at it with his holster-enclosed fist, the window flew open and caught him on the side of his head, sending him sprawling back. His head spinning with pain, he tottered back quite a few steps until, unable to maintain his balance, he fell flat on his back in the middle of the road, the holster slipping from over his hand and slithering across the street like his gun.

'I am so sorry, sooo sorry, honey,' screamed Anna as she ran out of the house in her underwear without bothering to put a robe on, 'I am so sorry. I was just wondering what you were doing out there and opened the window . . .' by this time she was on her knees on the road with Caddy's head in her lap. There was a longish but not deep cut across his left temple, tiny beads of blood starting to form an arc above it.

The house was in a street with a row of houses cheek by jowl. A couple of windows in the nearby houses opened, with lights coming on and heads popping out.

'Are you all right, Anna? That is Anna, isn't it?' came a gruff voice from the top window of the house next door. It was Mr Anders who it was rumoured had not slept for the last thirty-five years, ever since his wife was killed by an intruder. Whether it was the loss of the wife or the fear of an intruder, no one was quite sure.

'Yes, yes. I'm fine. It was an accident. A . . . mistake. I am fine. We are both fine. Go back to sleep,' she added. Not sure if that was the right thing to say to Mr Anders.

'Speak for yourself,' groaned Caddy, steadying himself on his feet as Anna supported him up, 'You may be fine. I am not! I have just been . . .' he nearly blurted out the facts but fortunately for him Anna interrupted him.

'What's this? You are wet, all down your . . . front, and legs. And what were you doing, just standing outside . . .'

'It's nothing. Water, it's water. Yes. I had a bottle of water in my pocket. Yes. Must have broken when I fell. It . . .'

'I have told you before. Don't get glass bottles just because you can get a few pennies back for them. They are dangerous. Heavy too. Let me see. The glass must have cut you, let me . . .'

'Leave me alone,' he pushed her aside roughly, then grabbed at her again as his head swam, 'I can take care of myself. I am not Juan. There is no broken glass. The bottle must have . . . just opened. Not broken.' He pushed her aside again and this time managed to stay steady by himself. 'Let's go inside. You are making a spectacle of yourself in these . . . these undies in the middle of the street.'

'You smell!' Anna sniffed the air round him. 'Are you sure you haven't . . .'

'Of course not! Who do you think I am, Juan? Go ahead and . . . and . . . and make some coffee or something. Coffee. I could do with some coffee. Stop fussing about me like my mother. And don't tell her about this. She will only laugh. About me being hit on the head, I mean you hitting me on the head, with the window, I mean she will get angry with you for doing it, angry, not laughing, that's what I meant. Not laugh. Go, go, go ahead. I will follow by myself. I am perfectly capable of walking. Make some coffee. I will go to the bathroom and get cleaned up . . . clean this cut, I mean, put some aftershave on it or something, some sticking plaster. Change my pants, get into my pyjamas I mean. You go, go, make some coffee. Leave me alone. I can take care of myself. I am not Juan. Even he can take care of himself now. He is four, not a baby any more. You insist on treating him as if he was a baby. And I, I am a grown man, your husband, I can take care of myself . . . And you! I take care of you, don't I? Don't I? So go, go . . .'

Anna looked at him with raised eyebrows through the dim light of the street mingling with the hazy glow of approaching dawn. He never talked much, except when he had something to hide. Then he talked and talked. She was also sure he had wet himself. She didn't know whether to smile or feel sorry for him or to get angry for not trusting her with whatever was bothering him, for something surely was, much more than the knock on his head. Normally, if a pin pricked him he hollered the house down and wanted to be pampered. Now, with a bleeding cut across his temple he was pushing her away!

But she said nothing and went into the house ahead of him, and into the kitchen to light the cooker.

Windows began to close in the street and lights went out again.

By the time Anna made the coffee and took it up to the bathroom, Caddy was already asleep, back resting against the left wall, legs stretched out on the floor, naked from the waist down, mouth open, penis erect.

If his head fell forward he would swallow it, thought Anna. She was half-tempted to take off her knickers, go over and straddle him, but resisted. She also resisted the urge to wake him up and get him to bed. Walking across to the bedroom she brought a blanket and draped it carefully over him.

He would come to bed whenever he woke up.

It was just when she was getting into bed herself that she happened to look out of the window again, as she often did when on her own – that's how she had spotted Caddy hovering outside the house. There, on the other side of the street, in the decreasing darkness, she could see something, something that was not there before, something that had a familiar look about it, though she couldn't be sure what it was.

Once again she went downstairs and out, this time putting on her nightgown. Rather gingerly she went up to the object. It was a holster, *the* holster, the holster of her husband's gun. She recognised it immediately, she had held it in her hands so often she could tell just by the feel of it, even without looking at it.

Caddy's holster was never without his gun. Except when he was cleaning and polishing it.

Something was really wrong here, much more than she had originally imagined.

She walked back to her house and up to the bedroom, clutching the empty holster, lost in thought with a worried frown on her face. She almost felt like waking Caddy up there and then and asking him. But she knew she would never get a straight answer. And he looked so tired. Better let him sleep. Better wait till the morning. And then too, she would have to be careful, very careful, and try to work her way round the little tales he made up to get at the facts. In the end she usually got it, or got at it, the truth. But never sure, at least not always, that the final 'confession' she got was not a lie too. Sometimes even over meaningless little things, like what he had for lunch.

She went into the bathroom to see if the gun was there. It wasn't. He hadn't been anywhere else in the house, but still, she looked in all the possible places. Nothing.

She decided to bring him out of the bathroom and to bed, hoping, if he woke up enough along the way, to ask him about the gun and how the holster came to be on the road. If someone had taken the gun from there, he would surely not have left the holster behind. But something told her that's what she would get from him if she said the holster was on the road. So she changed her mind and decided she wouldn't tell him that. She would say she found it by his pants, and it was empty. That's what she would say, and see what he had to say.

But she didn't get the chance. Not that night. Caddy sleepwalked with her to the bed and fell on it more asleep than he was before.

She was lucky that Mother didn't wake up, and luckier that Juan slept through all this. She couldn't have coped dealing with two babies at the same time. Not that she wasn't used to it, most of the time.

## Of sex and guns and sweets

They must have fallen asleep laughing, Pepsi and Maria.

The market had closed down for the night. More than closed down, it seemed to have disappeared altogether. It was like being in a different place, a different space.

The sound of crunching on the pavement and a shadow across the moon, or just instinct, caused Pepsi to wake up.

A uniformed figure with big, heavy boots was towering above their bodies, looking down at their faces.

*Caddy!* thought Pepsi and his heart went to his newly acquired trainers while his hand went for the gun in his pocket. But the smell was different. And even through sleep-drenched eyes he could tell the man was much taller, and thinner, and he had a stringy moustache; the uniform was that of a security guard or something, *and* there was a smile on the face. A pleasant smile. Perhaps it was a dream!

He rubbed his eyes to make sure that he was seeing and not dreaming.

He was not dreaming.

The man bent his knees and squatted beside them.

Pepsi couldn't be sure who the man was or what his intentions. He couldn't make up his mind how to react. The best thing was to remain quiet, look innocent, wait and see. All keyed up and geared for action inside. All relaxed and passive on the outside.

And pray to Lord Jesus! Not that that did any good to Mama . . . But maybe she was in Heaven now, supping with the Lord, angels attending the feast – in the *real* Heaven and *not* Maria's Heaven of trash – and Maria, his sister, was one of the angels . . . The thought comforted him and he felt braver, more able to cope with the situation.

'Haven't you kids got a home to go to?' said the man in a voice that sounded very strange, out of place. It was a happy voice. Angry, Pepsi would have understood; righteous and rebuking would have fitted the occasion perfectly; concerned even, a shock though that would have been – but happy!

And what was he to reply? If he said, 'Yes, we have a home,' and the man replied, 'OK, I will take you there,' in the hope of getting a reward from the family, or just because he was happy, what would they do then? And if he said, 'No, we haven't,' the man could take them to a police station – and that could be the end of them, even without a police gun in his pocket.

But he didn't have to worry for long. Seeing him hesitate, the man broadened his smile and said, 'It's OK. You don't have to tell me if you don't want to. But I will take you anywhere if you wish. My home is close by, and I have a car.' There was pride mingled with happy here. 'I can take you anywhere you want, in my car. It's only an old one, but works perfectly. Never gave me a day's trouble since I bought it, only last year. And now I have a . . . but first, hold out your hand,' he stretched his own right hand towards Pepsi at the same time, thrusting his left hand into his left trouser pocket. It was then that Pepsi noticed he had a bulge in his trousers.

So that was it! Pepsi knew now. The man was after sex. No wonder he was happy, trying to impress him with his car. He must have taken one look at us and said, *Ah, free sex.* Whether he liked boys or girls, better still, if both, here was one of each . . .

Blood rushed into Pepsi's face and his mind went into over-spin. He had always managed to avoid sex, but many of the other kids on the street had not. Some even looked for it now, to make some money and, and . . . But they seldom got money out of anybody in uniform. Money came from the others, the . . . But he didn't want to think about that now.

He had to decide what to do. Money or no money, he couldn't let that happen. Not to Maria. She would die. Just like his sister.

She got a baby through sex, and that was what killed her. He couldn't let it happen to Maria, he wouldn't . . .

If he was alone he could have got up and run. Would have. But running now would be leaving Maria to the man's mercy, or rather, to his lust.

But, if there was no way out, the bastard could have *him*, if he wanted. He could deal with it. He was a boy. A man almost. Girls get babies. They die. He could get it over with and forget about it, if only Maria was left out of it.

But the man was looking at Maria even though his hand was stretched out towards him.

With trying to run away ruled out as an option, Pepsi had three choices left. To scream and shout for help; fight it out; or to beg and plead to be left alone, at least for Maria to be left alone. Screaming and shouting might fall on deaf ears, especially as there didn't seem to be many ears around: it was a market square with a church, houses started a little further on. It was more likely to attract the police than anyone else. Fighting it out: well, the man was big and a security guard. They were well-trained for combat, knew all the moves and martial arts and stuff like that. He would get more aggressive and do it even worse. That left begging and pleading. For Maria's sake if not for himself. But try as he might, he couldn't bring himself to do so; words froze, mouth dried up, tongue turned to leather.

And then, suddenly, he realised he didn't need to!

He remembered the gun.

He shoved his hand in his pocket, hoping to pull it out with the speed of a cinema hood and knock the man's brains out, but the nozzle of the gun got stuck in a tear of his pocket and he nearly pulled the trigger on himself in an attempt to jerk it out.

Just then the man pulled his hand out of his trousers bringing out the bulge with it. It was a large packet of sweets.

'I have had . . . my wife has had, *we* have had, a girl, a daughter. Born today, after three sons. I've always wanted a little girl. Like your sister, there. I was looking at her. So pretty. I would like my daughter to look like her, when she is . . . how old is your sister?' And when Pepsi, too stunned to reply, remained speechless, the man continued, 'Anyway, today is the happiest day of my life. Here,' he held out the sweets, 'I have been out giving bags of sweets the whole evening. This was the last left and I put in my pocket for my boys, but then I saw you here and thought I'll give it to you. I was returning home. I just live over there, by the corner, blue house . . . !'

Pepsi beat his head with the palm of his other hand. He had come so close to killing the man. Or himself. At least shooting his right leg off.

All of a sudden, without warning, tears welled up in his eyes. Pulling his gun hand out of the pocket he held his face in both hands, crumpled on the road and began to sob. Pent-up fear and anger and despair of the last twenty seconds, twenty-four hours, of the past many months, catching up on him with abrupt ferocity.

The man recoiled, embarrassed, unsure; then, inching forward, put his arms around Pepsi, 'There, there, don't worry. It will be all right. Whatever is going on with you, I promise. Don't worry . . . No! But, no. No, no!

'No. I can't promise that. I can't promise everything will be all right.

'I can't promise *anything* will be all right. But . . . maybe something I can do???'

Pepsi hardly heard him, just put his arms around him and held him, like he would have liked to hold his father, body convulsing with sobs.

The man stayed with him, silently.

Then gradually, releasing himself from Pepsi's arms, said, 'I have to go now. Sylvie will be worried. My wife. It was a home birth. I told her I'd be . . .

'Can I take you anywhere?'

Pepsi shook his head.

The man hesitated again, wondering whether to take the children home, but he had heard stories about street children conning their way into homes and . . . and . . . and he didn't want to take any risks, not with his wife just recovering from childbirth.

'I live just round the corner. Blue house. If you need anything, come and see me during the day. Any day. Wait outside if I am not there. My name is Marcos. Marcos Pollini.'

He stood up and looked all set to go, yet hovered uncomfortably, 'Here, have this. Keep it,' He leant over and shoved a slim wad of paper money in Pepsi's hands, 'It is not much. I spent all I had today. Most of it anyway. But remember, you can always come to me, and if there is something I can do for you, try to find someone who knows more about children like you, can do something . . . I don't know what, something . . . anything . . . ?'

He again looked expectantly at Pepsi, but when he didn't respond to that either, he said with finality,

'Look after yourself, and your little sister. I must go now. I only live round the corner. Next corner, actually. Blue house. Number 11. May the Holy Mother bless you both, take care of you.'

He hesitated again, for a moment, then, 'Come and see me when . . . whenever!'

And with that, he turned and walked away, disappearing round the corner.

Maria slept through all this.

## Remembrance of things past, plans for those to come

Pepsi couldn't believe his life. He had nearly killed twice in two nights. And if he had killed, he too would have become like . . . like *them*, like killers, or worse, like Caddy. That's what his mother would have said. Perhaps he had already become a little like Caddy by carrying a gun, *his* gun!

He almost threw it away, but then decided against it. He would keep it till he had dealt with his father. Even if he didn't kill him, to avenge his mother, he would hold the gun to his head and make him confess to killing her. And then scare him to death till he begged and begged for his life . . . Pepsi imagined the whole scene in his mind's eye, and it gave him great joy to imagine it.

But that would have to wait. Wait till after he had taken Maria to her Heaven. And he might need the gun for that too. Just in case.

It would have to be a Saturday night. The night after to-morrow. To break into Señor Romano's house. Not to kill this time, but to steal.

The man always spent Saturday night with his mother in another part of the city. His mother – she was nastier to Pepsi than Romano was; but then, she was nasty to everybody, perhaps more so to those she liked than those she didn't – had been born in that old house and said she would die in it. She would have nothing to do with her son's grand new ways and grand new house. So Romano went and spent every Saturday night there in her house – unless there was an election going on or a very important conference outside the city or the country – and attended Mass with her in the morning in 'her' church. He resented it like hell, but he did it.

Sometimes his wife and sons – 'other' sons, both four now – accompanied him, sometimes not. Pepsi didn't know what or how to feel about those other sons. In a way they were his brothers,

41

and he was supposed to love them, as his mother said. But it was because of them that he was where he was.

Romano had been married for thirteen years, and was childless. As a good Catholic there was no question of a divorce or another marriage. That was when, hungering for a son and heir, he decided to acknowledge Pepsi – Andrés – as a Romano, and his son. But only privately, saying he would make a public announcement in 'due course'. Sent him to a good school, as a 'distant nephew', gave a good monthly allowance to his mother and sister.

However, life moves as it moves, and through some new fertility treatment Tania, Romano's wife, became pregnant. Seven babies in her belly. But it wasn't certain how many, if any, would survive. And then she had the babies, all seven of them, three girls and four boys. One by one they started to die, but two lived, two boys. And when it was certain those two would be all right and grow up to be healthy and strong, Romano declared Andrés to be an impostor, his mother worse than a common whore, and threw them all out into the street. May be it was because of Tania – even though she pretended to like him – but it was his decision as sure as he was his child . . .

Pepsi tried not to think of the past. Best . . . not to think at all. Except about the absolutely essential. About Saturday night.

That was the night Pepsi would break in. He was afraid that if he went when his father was home, and he ran into him, *and* he had the gun, as he would, he might forget the real purpose of his break-in . . .

Perhaps he should steal from another house altogether. Just so as to have no chance of a confrontation with his father. He thought about it, but said, no! Why *steal* from an innocent person when he could *take* what rightly belonged to him. Now that he *needed* it, not because of greed. And he had the gun to help him, though if that was a good thing or a bad, he wasn't sure.

Saturday night it would have to be.

And what next!

Take Maria to her Heaven.

And what next!

If there was a next.

If he lived long enough for a next.

But he didn't *want* to think that far!

He didn't feel he had the energy left to breathe any more, much less think.

To not think was even more difficult.

Flopping flat on his back on the road, he pretended to be dead.

Might as well get some practice in, he said to himself, and started to laugh. It was either that, or cry. But it was no fun crying without a shoulder to cry on. And he would never worry Maria by crying on her shoulder, though there were times when he so wanted to.

## Another house another night

It was Friday, and Señor Romano was having his highs and lows. He always did on Fridays.

His lows, because tomorrow he would have to and go see his mother. AND stay the night there. Waste his Saturday, *and* have to wake up at dawn on Sunday. Mama insisted on attending the first Mass of the holy day!

Other people looked forward to Fridays so they could enjoy their weekends. Go out and have a binge on Saturdays, sleep till noon on Sundays . . . How he envied other people! But still, in other *countries* some politicians had to *work* at weekends. He did as well, occasionally, and it was a relief from his mother. Especially if it was a conference abroad or something interesting like that. But not very often, unfortunately; and he was stuck with her. He loved her dearly, of course . . . But not at weekends!

If only she came and lived with them. It was such a comfortable house. Luxurious. An acre of garden with flowers all the year round. A bathroom with every bedroom, one down in the hallway, another upstairs. Separate quarters for the servants. Televisions everywhere, almost. And computers, not that Mama approved of computers. *If the Lord had wanted computers HE would have created them Himself! On the fifth day. Or not at all.* But it was not just the computers. She liked nothing about that beautiful, great house of his. *It is more like a public building than a house. Doesn't feel like home at all. I feel as if one of your security guards will come any minute and say, 'Sorry, closing time, now. Get home you old goat . . .' Can't dream of spending* one *whole day here, much less live here . . .*

She wanted to live in that spooky little poky little public toilet-sized *thing* squashed between hundreds of other things of its kind. If it was in a little village or something, he could understand.

Some men of eminence who came from villages quite enjoyed going back to their places in the countryside, even if they were poor then. At least there was fresh air and greenery and rivers and mountains and chickens. But in the filth-ridden guts of the poor part of a great big dirty city! If only someone could drill some sense into that woman's head he would make the best President of the land, sort out all its many ills . . . And he, Señor Augusto Romano, would give up his own ambition to be President for such a man's sake! Perhaps not, but it was a thought.

There was pleasure on Fridays too!

On Fridays he put away his polished accent and spoke like his mother, like he did when he was a child; washed down his moustache instead of waxing it up, put on huge black-framed spectacles with brown-tinted lenses, removed his toupée – the hardest part – and went to some hotel or other and sent for girls. He chose as many different hotels as he could find: sometimes seedy little ones, sometimes discreet and expensive, depending on his whim, or by pure coincidence if his car happened to pass one he would say, *Ah, this looks OK for next Friday.* No one anywhere could recognise him without his head of lush black curls. Of course, some knew it was a toupée – he could never bring himself to acknowledge that everyone knew – but still, they had never seen him without it, so how could they tell what he looked like without it. And his moustache was always so up and perky, his spectacles so chic and slim and modern you could hardly tell they were there at all. All anyone saw in the hotels was a huge bald pate, a drooping, apologetic moustache, and thick black spectacles. That's what the girls saw. Probably remembered nothing about him except those huge black spectacles and that huge shiny head and his 'common' voice. He didn't like to be remembered like that, but rather that than be remembered as he was, like by the mother of that bastard boy . . .

However, even as he thought of her and the boy with anger and resentment, a wave of nostalgic sadness and burdensome guilt crept into his heart and swept through his blood. She was kind and gentle and beautiful. So beautiful, like the Holy Mother herself, and may God forgive him for thinking that about a whore. Well, she wasn't a whore, not always. And the boy, he had such a head of thick black curls. Just like he always wanted for himself. It would be nice to have a boy of one's own with such a head of thick black curls. Tania's sons had such mousy brown hair. Just like her. He was less sure *they* were his than the other boy. Who knew whose sperm these bloody doctors who played God injected into that mousy brown womb of that mousy brown wife of his! Of course she'd coloured her hair fiery red, but all *he* could see was mousy brown. Nothing like the rich black of his family! And that bastard boy. His eyes were so beautiful too, so big and black, and with a soul; like that of his father when he was young. Tania's sons had mousy brown eyes, like her . . . Even their souls were mousy brown, he was sure – just like hers, if she had a soul. But she was his wife, in the eyes of God and the Holy Church and his mother, and those sons were born to her in a state of holy matrimony. They were sanctified – baptised and confirmed by a Bishop from Rome itself; and he could walk with them with pride, in public, whatever he thought of them in private.

He did not like street whores, rather some servant girls working in big houses, often helping their servant mothers and needing some extra cash for themselves or their mothers. They could sometimes get a Friday night off instead of a Saturday night, or the Sunday. Now and then one could even get a virgin – like Camelia, the mother of that bastard boy – but harder and harder in these days of promiscuity and porn. Even the thirteen- and fourteen-year-olds had been split open, unlike Camelia at thirteen: poor thing, had to die before twenty-five . . . He felt sorry for her, but there was nothing he could do. It was not his fault.

He never went for anyone above seventeen, if he could help it. Still, one had to make the best of what was available. That was the first lesson life had taught him, and he had never forgotten it. That was why he had to settle for whores more and more these days when there were fewer servants in houses and more whores on streets. Such was life, and if he, as a politician, could not be pragmatic, who else would be!

Just as he was about to make his way to the car, still looking like 'himself', Tania came in, fiery red hair sitting uncomfortably over a mousy brown face and mousy brown eyes.

Romano always made 'the changes' later on. He would go to the Juarez Park between the Museum of Anthropology and the Marine Aquarium. Take off his toupée and put on his black spectacles in the car. Then go into the public toilet to wash down his moustache and change his clothes from whatever expensive business suit that he was wearing to some more casual gear, but still expensive. He had to show that he had money, whatever he looked like or however he spoke. He exchanged his discreet silver Rolex for a more violent gold Rolex, one large signet ring with a blue stone for a different sort of large signet ring with a very recognisable very large very red stone, and, as an extra touch, put a heavy gold chain round his neck, something he would never do in his public life. He kept his wedding ring on. It would be sacrilegious to take that off. And it looked no different from most wedding rings, so no danger there. Another thing he always kept was his gun. You never knew in such places with such people. And he'd rather be found out than found dead! Life was sweeter than politics. Certainly sexier. Leaving his car in the park, he would take a taxi.

'What do you want?' said Romano irritably to his wife, 'I am already getting late for my Lodge as it is.'

'There is a call for you. The man says it is urgent. Or important. Something like that. Says he must speak to you. Cadez, or Caddy, I think, Police Inspector or something. I am not . . . I think he's been here, sort of short, stou . . .'

'Yes, yes, yes, I know, I know. Don't go on.' Romano had just been on the verge of interrupting Tania and telling her to go tell the caller to . . . to . . . well, to call another time, when she mentioned Caddy.

Caddy would not call for nothing. Not on a Friday night. He knew he went to the Lodge on a Friday night. In fact, Caddy was such a damn, ass-licking asshole, such a cringing, creepy son of a toilet seat, he would not dare call any night for nothing unless it *was* something urgent, important.

He had to take the call.

'Get me the phone here,' he said to Tania, pointing to the phone sitting at a table next to where he was standing while she was at the far end of his study-cum-library, the size of a small concert hall, the walls lined with all the best books in the world he had never read. Pepsi loved this room the best in the house when he was here. Used to spend hours looking at books, trying to read the most difficult ones.

Tania got up to get the phone, but not before she gave Romano a look. A look that was not mousy brown at all. But Romano was too preoccupied with himself to notice. Not just then, but all the time. Otherwise he would have known long since that there was something deep inside Tania that was not at all mousy brown.

After handing him the phone she knew he would want to talk in private, but kept standing there pretending to admire a painting she hated so as to *make* him tell her to leave. He would think he had ordered her out. But *she* would know that *she* had made him do so.

One day she would hide his gold Rolex and his pimpish gold chain and his ruby red signet ring and his ridiculous black spectacles and hear him scream.

She'd throw them in the river, or in the fire; or, better still, give them to the first beggar who came her way, or to that bastard boy of his. Then she would jump up and down on his toupée while he was still wearing it and tell him about it.

How he adored her when he married her, when she was fourteen – for about three years! Then ten years of hell and hospitals; and then, then nothing . . . Nothing at all. Not even a goodnight kiss. Which was fine, in a way, for she was none too fond of bodily contact. Disliked sex. Would have disliked it even with a dashing Zorro type, much less that potbellied, baldy husband of hers, whose heart was uglier than the rest of him.

In the beginning, because Romano was so romantic and attentive, and had more hair and less blubber, she had accepted it. Not really enjoyed it, but accepted it. But then, after years of Romano's desperate and planned attempts to impregnate her and hospitals and internal examinations and fertility treatments, she had begun to loathe the very thought of it.

However, now that Romano never even tried it with her, she really wanted him to, so she could say no. Or agree, but reluctantly, making it clear she did not like it. Worse than that. Was disgusted by every caress, repelled by every thrust. Would rather him puke over her than ejaculate inside her. But he never gave her the opportunity to show him how she felt, and she hated him for it, hated him with all her heart and soul. She would have forgiven him his Friday nights out and his teeny prostitutes and teenier servant girls, his lies and subterfuges, his ugliness of appearance and character, his bad breath and baldness and toupée, everything, if only he had wanted her, at least now and then, so she could show her lack of desire, her distaste for sex, of him . . . Humiliate him with her contempt for his body.

But she never had the chance. All she had was that monster of a house and his pompous friends and that idiot mother of his and his Fridays at *the Lodge*. She could dislodge all that if she chose. She was just waiting for the right moment. That was one thing she was good at. Better than anyone she knew. Waiting!

She had waited for her children to be born, and then she had waited for them to die. But two remained, and now she was waiting for them to grow up and get out of her life. They couldn't give her back her firm stomach again, but they could give her some peace and quiet when they left. Most of all she was waiting to see what happened to Romano's political future.

It was just the thought that he might one day become

President that kept her from jumping on his toupée while he was wearing it, or doing something equally exciting, now. She was hooked on the idea of being First Lady, like that Jackie Kennedy woman.

But time was running out. If he didn't make it by the next election, he never would. And then he'd have hell to pay. That was for sure.

## The phone call

Romano ordered Tania away, played with the receiver till she was out of the door, then heard what Caddy had to say.

A few minutes later he pressed his finger on the security button and kept it there until Julio, the chief security officer, came running in, out of breath, gun poised for action, followed by two more men.

## Of lies and truth and warnings and fears

Anna finally got the truth out of Caddy.

She got many different stories to begin with.

He had been held up by two to fifteen men, big as giants and black as ravens.

He had been hit unconscious from behind by who knows who, and when he came to, someone had stolen his gun and pissed all over him.

He had tripped, fallen, hit his head on a big stone, large as the heating boiler, and then remembered nothing except being wet and without his gun.

But then, gradually, the truth began to emerge. He started talking about this boy. Pepsi. He had briefly mentioned him before, sometimes, as the boy who claimed to be the son of Señor Romano, but never said much else. He did today. And he talked of a little girl always hanging out with him, using crude simple words, but there was passion in them. A ring of truth. He could certainly not be making it all up. She was sure of it.

She pictured the children in her imagination. The boy with his head of thick curly hair, black as a starless night, his strong, weather-hardened feet, always bare; and his walk as if he owned the world when he had nothing but a saucy tongue and a mouth big enough to house it but not strong enough to hold it. And this little girl he was always with. Just a waif, with rich auburn hair that danced in the sun like a log fire at Christmas.

Anna loved children, had a special soft corner for poor street kids. She often prayed for a fairy godmother to descend on them, transform them like Cinderella, and help them find their Prince or Princess Charming so they lived happily ever after.

Of course Caddy was very angry with these kids. Especially the boy. He had tricked him out of his gun. Caddy had felt sorry for

52

them. Befriended them. The boy wanted to see his gun, to touch it, feel how it felt, said he wanted to become a policeman when he grew up. Caddy had let him have it. Just then the girl screamed, only to distract his attention, momentarily of course, but long enough to give the boy an opportunity to scram off. He ran after him, but these street kids know of alleyways no one has ever heard of. He got lost despite all his attempts to find him. It was while he was running after him that he tripped and fell into a puddle by a deserted old wall where people piss on their way home from bars.

Anna was not so sure of this last bit. But by and large she knew she had got the truth.

The point was, what to do now. He had to get his gun back somehow. He was not just worried for himself, but Señor Romano as well. The boy might do something silly with that gun, hot-headed and impetuous that he was.

It was then that Anna had a flash of inspiration.

Why not use Romano to find the boy. He had hordes of guards and servants and other yes-men at his disposal. They could scour the streets to get this boy. He might be on the lookout for Caddy, or other police officers, but he wouldn't be wary of other 'ordinary-looking men', the type Romano could employ.

But she was afraid Romano might harm the boy. Romano was not a favourite of hers and she had never voted for him. There was something about him that gave her the creeps. And it was not just that ridiculous toupée of his!

Another flash of inspiration. 'Don't tell Romano about the gun. Just say the boy has some proof that he really is his father. Some hospital . . .'

Caddy could have jumped for joy. Actually, the boy had often threatened to get some proof: to him, and to Señor Romano. Señor Romano could easily fall for that!

Anna carried on with her train of thoughts, ' . . . records, blood tests, something, anything, just to scare him into getting the boy. But tell him he doesn't have it on his person. That he has hidden it somewhere, and that if he brought or sent the boy to *you*,

you will be able to get it from him. Tell him the boy is a friend of yours, trusts you . . .

'And once you get the boy, you will surely get the gun. He will certainly have it somewhere. He wouldn't have bothered to go to all that trouble of tricking you out of it, and then throw it away! Even if he has sold it, you could find out to whom and get it from whoever. Once they know it is police property they wouldn't dare keep it.

'Only be gentle with the boy. I know he has done an awful thing, and I can see that you are real mad at him, but don't hurt him. I know you want to punish him. I can see that in your eyes. Do so. Put him in a cell for the night. That would scare the daylights out of him. Two nights if you want to be harsh. But no more. And feed him well. Promise me that. They have a hard life, these kids. No home to go to, nobody to love them. Imagine if our Juan . . . .'

Caddy had stopped listening.

Anna had come up with a wonderful scheme. Only Señor Romano would laugh his head off if Caddy told him Pepsi was a friend of his. But he could tell him that he would get the truth, the proof, if he had any, out of Pepsi, one way or another. Señor Romano would believe *that*.

But, in the mean time, what would he say to his Superintendent at the precinct, about his gun?

'You don't have to say anything. Put your father's gun in your holster. No one will know. Now if the holster was missing, that would have been a problem. But if that is there, any old gun would do until you get yours. At least it buys you time, doesn't it?'

Caddy was so relieved he nearly wet himself again.

Anna saw the relief in his eyes, held his face in her hands and gave him a big sumptuous kiss on the lips. He was such a little boy, that husband of hers. But kind, and gentle as a bumble bee. He did look quite angry now . . . well, more hurt then angry. But he wouldn't hurt the boy. Couldn't hurt a fly! Couldn't even bring himself to swear, the shy little man. If only he wouldn't . . . well

. . . lie, sometimes, make up stories. But it was only because he was afraid, afraid to be . . . be rejected. Laughed at, scorned, something like that. That father of his had a lot to answer for. And his mother wasn't much good to him either. But still, she was glad that he was what he was, in spite of his little follies.

She heaved a deep sigh and wished that Juan grew up to be like him. Just a little more . . . a little less . . . less afraid to . . . to hide . . . the facts, some facts . . .

At least he was the dead spitting image of his father to look at. She felt happy about that and gave Caddy another big sumptuous kiss.

Caddy gave her a quick peck back and hurried to where the telephone was to make that call to Señor Romano.

He knew it was Friday, and he always went to his Lodge on Fridays and didn't like being disturbed.

But this was important. His life could be at stake. His own certainly was.

He worried about whether to tell Romano about the gun, but decided against it. He wasn't sure how Romano's men would react if they thought the boy had a gun.

He wanted the boy alive.

He must make that clear to Señor Romano. Otherwise he might not get his hands on the proof. The boy could have given it to an accomplice. In fact, he *knew* he had. That accomplice, or rather accomplices, a horde of street kids, would take it to the police if something happened to him. Then his death, if he got killed that is, too could be blamed on Romano . . . and then . . . and then . . .

Caddy began building up on what Anna had told him to say, got into the spirit of it.

Anna twirled the pink lace handkerchief round her fingers. How sweet of him to have got her that. And he had given extra money for sweets to Juan, even though he was short of money these days!

## At the paupers' graveyard

*The dead are everywhere,*
*from end to end,*
*this way and that way and up and down and all around,*
*dancing in jungles and sleeping in deserts,*
*walking above the ground and below,*
*and across the sky,*
*going up hills and coming down hills,*
*growing in fields and swimming in all the seas.*

So Pepsi had once written about the graveyard where his sister and mother were buried.

Many of the graves were surprisingly well kept with marble headstones and real flowers growing all around, statuettes of the Holy Mother and ornate crosses with all sorts of Jesus figures being crucified on varied surfaces in varied styles.

Others were dug upon other graves and would soon be dug upon themselves, mere mounds of earth or grass, pathetic in their insignificance and the insignificance of those lying within their raw, churned wombs.

Pepsi came there about mid Saturday morning to say goodbye to his mother, and to his sister.

He had bought some food and drink with the money from Marcos, given that and most of the rest of the money to Maria, and left her in the hollow of their tree in the field behind the derelict industrial site.

'Don't go anywhere. Just wait for me. I may be back in a couple of hours, or not until tomorrow morning. But I will come back. I promise. I WILL come back. Just wait for me.

'Remember. Wait for me. I will come back. No matter what.

'Say after me, *I'll wait for you no matter what, I'll wait for you no matter what, I'll wait . . .*'

He had to keep that promise. No matter what . . .

But he needed to be alone first. To visit his mother and sister before he took off on his journey to Maria's Heaven. Before he went to his father's house to take some of what was rightfully his. He wouldn't take much, but still, his mother would have called it wrong, a sin even. He had to explain to her why he was doing it. For little Maria's sake. And also for little Maria. Ask for her forgiveness. Her understanding. Her blessings.

Then he would either go back to the tree and see Maria for a while before starting for his father's house, or go direct from the graveyard; depending on how he felt, or what his mother advised, if she spoke to him: which she sometimes did, quite a lot – and sometimes not at all.

His father had had his house built a long way away, so he had to leave early-ish. The K27 bus dropped you off at Santa Rosa, more than an hour and a half's ride, after which it was a good few miles of uphill walking before you even got sight of the house. He wanted to do the walk in the dark, but get to Santa Rosa while there was still some light left in the day.

A tired old black dog was limping his way through some distant graves, a more sprightly younger brown-and-white dog lay on his back, legs up in the air, sunning himself, not far from 'his' graves. Pepsi imagined a big smile on the dog's face, and smiled with it. Shiny black ravens strutted about here and there, pecking at the grass or flying away suddenly as if called out on an emergency. Somewhere a cat mewed, but couldn't be seen.

He must have fallen asleep talking to his mother, cap in hand, head resting on the infant-sized chunk of rough mountain rock that sat uncomfortably on the grave. Painted on the face of the rock, in red and white and blue, was a crude-looking cross, graffiti-style. His own artwork.

Two pairs of strong hands seized him by his arms, shook him

awake and jerked him up to a standing position, 'You're coming with us, boy,' said one grinning face above one pair of hands. The other grinning face above the other pair of hands simply nodded in triumphal gloating.

Pepsi was only glad that he did not have the gun in his pocket, where it would have been easily noticed and taken from him, but in a plastic bag and rolled up inside Maria's old clothes. The men didn't even bother to look inside the bag nor try to take it from him as they forced him to walk between them, one holding on to his left arm and left ear, the other, his right arm and right ear.

## A regret, a deduction, a surprise, two questions

Pepsi cursed himself for not telling Maria to go and look for Marcos Pollini if he didn't come back. What would happen to her now if he couldn't keep his promise . . . ?

But he would! He was more determined than ever that he would.

However, now was not the time to try anything. Now was the time to go with it, see what happens. Take it as it comes.

At least he would get a free ride to where he wanted to go anyway.

He tried to figure out what could have happened. Putting two and two together he nearly made four. It must be Caddy, he thought! He would have alerted Romano. Told him *the kid* had a gun, might come gunning for him. Get him before he gets you. That way Caddy would get him too, *and* get his gun. Pepsi was surprised. Somehow he hadn't thought Caddy had the brains to work that out.

But if that was so, why then did the men not try to search him for a gun, ask him about it?

How did they know he'd be here?

And why were they Tania's brothers and not Romano's lackeys?

Romano wouldn't ask them for a piece of candy, much less a big favour like hunting out his would-be-killer son. Nor would they have obliged if he had asked. There was no love lost between him and his wife's brothers, all seven of them.

## A misunderstanding and some good food

'So where is it?' said Tania in her fiery red, then in her mousy brown. 'Would you like a glass of milk and chocolate crispies?' knowing this to be Andrés's a.k.a. Pepsi's ultimate favourite breakfast, even though it was nearer high noon.

Tania was receiving Pepsi in her own private parlour-cum-kitchen where she liked to relax and cook for herself what she liked, how she liked and generally do more or less what she liked. On Saturdays, without meddlesome cook or obnoxious husband around. Especially if she could pack away the two brats too, along with their possible father, to visit their poison-sweet grandma. Poison-sweet to her grandchildren. Simply poison to all else.

Of late she had absolutely refused to be a part of the visit on grounds of health. The 'filthy' air of the place gave her asthma. She could pant for breath better than the best – especially during Sunday Mass – and even Señor Romano wouldn't assert his authority to the detriment of the church's solemn quietude, or to the disadvantage of his wife's mousy brown health – he hated paying doctors' bills. He had done enough for the medical profession during his attempts to attain fatherhood.

Pepsi hadn't had milk and chocolate crispies for breakfast now for an entire century, or so he would have said, if asked. But it was the first question that got him. Mistaking the 'it' of her *where is it*? for the gun, he concluded that they – at least she – knew about the gun!

He swallowed his saliva, studiously avoided looking at the plastic bag thrown carelessly by his feet, and ignoring as best as he could the fourteen strong masculine eyes boring holes in his skin – belonging to the seven sturdy brothers of Tania, each bigger and more honed than the other, more proud. Fourteen bulging biceps, glistening with sweaty health in the midday heat, formed a semi-circle behind his back.

'Yes, please,' he said to Tania, after he'd made up his mind what to say, and then turning to one of the seven, 'Could you get me a glass of water, please, Uncle?'

'I'll uncle you, you little . . .' hissed the young man with streaky blond hair, standing up menacingly and glowering at Pepsi, but Tania gave him a look of her own and he sat back again, reluctantly, saying, 'Go get your own bloody water.'

'But you told me not to move, Uncle,' Pepsi looked at him with wide innocent eyes.

Tania gave another shut-up look to the brother as he opened his mouth, went to the mini-house-sized fridge, took out a carton of orange juice, poured it out in a large glass and took it to Pepsi.

'Here. I know you like orange juice. This one has real orangey bits in it. Just the way you like them. But first,' she said, quickly moving her hand away as Pepsi, forgetting his poise, greedily reached for it, 'first you have to tell me where it is!'

He should have known it wasn't going to be that simple.

'Where is what?' he said with genuine testiness. Why in Christ's name should she be so interested in Caddy's gun!

'The . . . Oh Lord give me patience with this child! The . . . the proof, or whatever you have, from the hospital or wherever!' And when Pepsi looked wonderfully innocent and confused, this time quite genuinely, she sighed and said, 'All right. I have no time for games. I'll be straight with you. You be straight with me. I can make life easier for you. Here, just to prove to you that I really know.

'I don't *have* to, but I will. Just to be nice to you.'

As she spoke, she brought out a tiny audio-cassette from somewhere on her person, inserted it into a pocket-sized radio/cassette player and turned it on.

It was last night's telephone conversation between Caddy and Romano.

Tania recorded every call that Romano received. Most of them she half-listened to and then put away safely for future reference, if required. But this one, this one needed attention. And action.

She wanted that proof more than Romano. What she would do with it she hadn't exactly decided yet. Whether to deny the boy his rights or to hold it over Romano, whatever; she wanted to get hold of it before *he* did!

She had promptly called her seven brothers to her aid. In a strange sort of a way she had befriended the boy when he was here, and had learnt about most of his haunts, and those of other street kids. She sent each of five brothers to five different places where she thought Pepsi might be hanging around, going by what he had told her; and two to his mother's grave, going by her gut instinct. Her gut was right on.

While Tania put a smug winner's look on her face as the tape played on, Pepsi had difficulty in restraining his surprise, *and* relief. *From where did Caddy come up with all that shit!* True, Pepsi *had* threatened to get some proof, one day, of his paternity, but that was just an idle, boyish, boast. Wishful thinking at most.

He had to try hard not to burst out laughing. And phew! They didn't know about the gun after all. He wiped imaginary droplets of sweat from his forehead with an imaginary hand.

'OK,' he said after a pause, 'OK, you got me. You know. But I haven't got it on me. I don't even know exactly what it is,' he thought to bring that up quickly before she started asking him for details. 'Just some bit of paper with scrawls on it. Probably nothing. I can't even read it.'

'But *where* is it? That's what we want to know, you little . . .' started one of the brothers, the one with the darkest hair and blackest of eyes.

'Shut up, José,' said Tania and shut him up. Then, turning to Pepsi, 'He is right, you know, Andrés. It is to your advantage that *I* have it rather than Romano. If he gets hold of you he will make mincemeat out of you before you can say mincemeat. Even if what you have is nothing. A fake. That won't stop him going after you. He feels guilty. And guilty men are afraid of shadows. He is afraid. And Romano afraid is not what you want, whether what you have is true or not.

'And if it *is* true, he will destroy it, whatever it is. I will keep it, safe. You may not believe it, but I have your interests at heart, certainly more than he has. And I will give you something for it. Something you could use to get away from here, live somewhere you are safe, from him and the streets; maybe go to a school or something . . .' she knew he loved school, '*He* will give you the police and the prison cell, that is if you are lucky. Or a bit of the earth next to your mother.'

Pepsi was getting interested. Very interested. She could give him what he wanted most at this time. Help him get away. Take Maria to her Heaven.

If only Caddy realised what a favour he had done him!

But he had to play it carefully. If they thought he was bluffing, any one of the seven surrounding him could swallow him whole without even bothering to mince him up.

Before he could come up with anything Tania handed him the orange juice, 'Here, have this first, I would have given it you anyway. And I'll get you . . . the rest as well.'

She watched the boy gulp down the juice, then put a bowl of milk and a packet of chocolate crispies on the dining table and pointed to a chair.

'Have something to eat, and then I'll sort something out for you to . . .'

She got up, disappeared for a while and returned with a wad of notes in her hand. 'Half now, and half after we get what you have,' she said.

## A plan, a confession

It was all going so well, and then suddenly . . .

' . . . No, you! He gets nothing till he produces the paper . . .' one brother.

' . . . We will take whatever you want with us and go with you and wait in the car. You get what you have to get . . . Doesn't matter *how* long it takes . . . Doesn't matter *where* Nico One is or where Costa hides out or when Ballsy gets into sewers. We'll wait. Wait for as long as it takes . . .', brother number two, naturally reddish hair turned blondish by the bottle.

'No, Tania, for once listen to us! We are your brothers. We have always supported you, done what you asked. For once, listen to *us*. You give half now to this kid, that half is more than he has ever seen in his whole fuc . . . blooming life! He won't come back! I tell you, he WON'T come back. He gets the full, everything, *after* WE get what he says he has.' Another brother.

'I, for one, don't believe a word of it. I don't think he has a fuc . . . an effing hang-all with him. He has managed to bluff that fool of a Caddy. A feeble-minded chicken could do that. That Caddy hasn't enough brains in him to outsmart a retarded cow. I think this kid here has nothing to give us except his fuc . . . hot air, from his behind. OK, OK, his mouth. Words. Words is all he has. But even IF he does have something, give him *anything* now and let him go, you will never see hair nor hide of him again. Take my word for it . . .' yet another brother . . . and so on and so on and so it went.

The brothers won this round. Tania saw they had a point. There was nothing to lose and probably a lot to save, especially her face, by playing it the way they wanted.

They would take him in the car, and whatever he wanted with him . . . and wait for him! Wherever he said. For however long.

Once he had brought what they wanted, he could . . . etc. etc. etc.

It was not going to work out the way Pepsi had hoped.

He would have to think of something else. Buy time. He didn't need to break into the house, he'd now have to plan a break-out!

And it would have to be during the night.

'It can't be today, then,' he said as boldly as he could. 'It will have to be tomorrow. About eight in the morning.' That would give him the night.

'Nothing doing! We have already wasted our Friday night looking for you, most of it. Tonight is Saturday night, I want to get this over with today and party the night away. I have to see . . .' one brother.

'And I have to . . .' another brother went on to explain what he had to do.

'I am absolutely dead beat. No way am I waking up at seven tomorrow to . . .' yet another brother.

All the brothers came up with their objections.

Actually, Pepsi could have given a later time, but now that he had said eight, he wanted to stick to it, otherwise it would appear he was just making things up as he went along.

'That's when we boys, and girls, gather to plan our day. That's the only time I can see all of them to know who has it. We pass things round, safest way to keep something . . . safe. I have to have them all together to . . . to be sure I get it back.' He crossed his arms firmly over his chest.

It was Tania's turn to assert her authority again, 'Now now, boys. You did say whenever.'

Pepsi could breathe free again. He would collect whatever he could during the night, and vanish.

But he couldn't find anything. Everywhere were locks, guards, dogs, snakes . . .

He got nothing. Nothing.

But then he remembered his mother.

So what if he got nothing.

He was nothing. He got nothing. It was OK.

*I am nothing. I am nothing. I am nothing.* He began to repeat to himself. She was right. There was great comfort in those words. If you are nothing, nothing can hurt you; nothing can touch you. Nothing matters.

He felt light as air. As light as nothing. As happy as nothing.

You didn't need a Heaven to be happy. Heaven was nothing.

He wanted to go out into the garden and dance and sing: *I am nothing, I am nothing, I am nothing.* Tania had told him not to go out as she didn't want him to be seen by anybody in the house. But he didn't care. Out he ran, singing and dancing, floating in the air, *I am nothing, I am nothing, I am nothing.*

The mountains around him echoed back, *I am nothing, I am nothing, I am nothing.*

Soon the trees joined in, and the grass, the flowers and the birds and the butterflies. All joined in the chorus, *I am nothing, I am nothing, I am nothing, I am nothing, I am noth . . .*

'Wake up, Andrés,' Tania poked him in the ribs, but gently. 'It's dark outside. If you have to sleep, go up to the . . . the children's bedroom. They are with their papa at their grandma's. Come, I'll take you.

'D'you want something to eat first?' she said, looking at his thin, drawn face.

'Yes, please, Tania,' he said almost without thinking.

Tania disappeared for a while, came back with a bowl of hot soup, some bread and an omelette.

She looked at him as he ate, then went out again, and returned with a brown envelope in her hand.

'Here, take it. This is extra to whatever else you need. Don't tell the boys about it. All right. Not a word.'

As Pepsi extended his hand, he remembered his bag, with the gun.

'Where is my bag?' he almost squealed.

'Don't worry, I put it upstairs. It was under our feet here.'

He had this great urge to ask if she had looked into it, but kept his mouth shut. If she had, she would be talking about it. It would only arouse her suspicions to say any more, but he was uneasy about it being somewhere other than by his side.

He opened the envelope she had given him. It had money in it. More money than he had ever imagined, in his hands. She reached forward and touched his hair, softly, and there was kindness in her eyes.

With the food Tania had brought for him still in front of him, the money she gave him in his hands, the dream of his mother fresh in his mind, and the kindness in Tania's eyes before his eyes, all his bravado crumbled. A solitary ghost from his mother's grave rose and came up to him and softened his rough edges away. He lowered his head and whispered, 'You can keep the money.' He extended his hand with the envelope. 'I haven't got it.'

'Haven't got what?'

'The proof. Nothing. I haven't got anything. Nothing. Nothing is what I have. Nothing. Like my mother. Nothing. Nothing. Nothing. So you can keep your money and your food and your pretend caring and let me go. I just want to go. Just let me go. Please . . .'

Tania froze, looked at the boy for a long moment that seemed to stretch out to eternity, as if trying to size him up, get to the core of him. Then, suddenly, coming to a decision, motioned with her hand for Pepsi to hide the money on him, turned away from him, and yelled, 'Mario . . . Mario!'

Mario was the youngest, the best-looking – and wanted to think of himself as the hardest, though in his heart he knew he was no match for José, whom he openly resented and secretly admired.

Pepsi didn't even want to think what Tania had in mind for Mario, or him.

He just felt empty. Emptied out. Like a bag of nothing. He put the envelope with the money in a pocket he had sewn on to his vest, almost without thinking, and looked at the wall across the room with empty eyes.

He could deal with Caddy's hate or his father's fears or the indifference of the streets; he didn't know how to cope with kindness.

Mario arrived and looked enquiringly at Tania, 'Is he giving grief?' he asked, giving Pepsi an unpleasant look which helped to make him feel more like himself again.

'No, he isn't. I just want you to do me a favour. Yes, another one. Take Andrés back to where you picked him up. Or wherever he says.

'DON'T, just don't ask questions. Just take him back. Go, go get the car to the door and I'll get him ready.'

'Get him ready,' sneered Mario. 'Is he going out to dine with the Queen of England?'

But he complied, and went out to get the car.

Why Mario, thought Pepsi. Why not Pablo, or Frederico. Even the Fox or Coyote!

Tania read the look in his eyes, 'They are all out. It is either Mario or José! They were the only two who volunteered to go with you tomorrow and stayed back. But I'll warn him. He'll take good care of you. Don't be afraid, OK!'

She sat down on the nearest chair and told him to go and get his bag from upstairs. He knew where the room was.

## Saturday night adventure

Mario had driven in silence for about half an hour till they came to a bend of the road overlooked by the barren side of the mountain, a steep fall down the other side.

'Get out!' he said to the boy, 'Just get out before I roll you down into the valley.'

Pepsi hurriedly got out and the car screeched ahead, but then stopped. Pepsi believed Mario was going to leave him there, turn around, and go back. He did turn around, but instead of driving on homewards, he stopped the car next to Pepsi and got out.

'Give it here,' he extended his hand with a swagger of his hips, and waited.

When Pepsi didn't respond, he moved further forward, 'Come on. Give it here. Whatever it is that you have conned out of my sister. I am sure she has given you something. Money, if I am not mistaken. I am also sure I know how to make better use of it than you do. Any night, especially on a Saturday! So hand it over.'

As Pepsi remained motionless, Mario made a lunge towards him. 'Will you give it to me easy or do I have to strip you naked and pull it out of wherever you have stuffed it.'

'OK, OK, Uncle; don't go mad, Uncle,' Pepsi was back in his stride, and more. He was going to deal with this one. Deal as he had never dealt with anything before. He had the money, a chance for a new life. For himself, for Maria; for his mother, somehow, dead and cold though she lay beneath the dead and cold earth in the dead and cold, castaway graveyard where the castaways of the living were cast away to rot among the castaways of the dead. 'It's in my bag. Just give me a minute.'

Mario relaxed and moved back.

The money safely in his pocket, Pepsi reached into his bag and pulled out the gun.

'One more step and I'll shoot your balls off, Uncle,' he said, pointing to Mario's crotch.

Completely unnerved, Mario tried to recover his cool. 'You think you can scare me with that toy, you mother-fucking son of a bitch you . . .'

The 'mother-fucking' did what he just might not have been able to do otherwise. He pulled the trigger. 'Don't you dare say a word about my mother, you son of a . . .' and fired again.

Both bullets whizzed past Mario's thighs, hit a rock-face projecting behind him and ricocheted eerily in the night. He went on his hands and knees, scrambled into his car and drove away as if followed by the big cats of Namibia, shouting, 'I'll come back for you, we all will, and then . . .' his words were lost in the wind, but not their impact.

Pepsi looked up at the night sky, dull and starless. It stared back at him with no reproach, no approval, nothing.

But he didn't care. He was free now. As free as he could be, with Caddy and his mates, Romano and his men, and Mario and his brothers, all out hunting for him!

He looked at the gun in his hand, and without any warning, as if seized and shaken by a posse of devils, he began to quiver and tremble and collapsed on the hook of the road in a fit of shakes that had little to with the increasingly cold night air.

For quite some time he lay there, bent double and unable to take control of himself or his body, breathing erratically. But gradually, becoming quieter and calmer, he rolled himself into a ball and nearly fell asleep when the piercing lights of an oncoming car forced him to jump up and get to one side.

The gun was still in his clenched hand. He loosened his grip over it, looked at it for a split second, then hurled it down the valley.

Following the gun, he began to clamber down the hillside. It would be much quicker getting back to town this way than along the road. Also, if Mario brought José and a couple of rifles along to look for him, he would be following the road. He didn't want to be on it, if he did.

He felt much lighter, and more at peace with himself, now that the gun was gone.

## Going back home

When Pepsi was coming down the stairs after getting his bag with
the gun from Ricardo and Reinaldo's room, he felt the banister
with his fingers, then the palm of his hands. He used to slide
down it, once. Suddenly, he didn't want to leave. He belonged
here. Here belonged to him . . . And then Mario had come up,
grabbed him by the scruff of his neck and dragged him down the
stairs and out of the house. He felt he was being thrown out of his
own home.

Now, half-walking half-running half-scaling down the hillside
in the murky polluted night air rising from the sprawling city, he
felt more as if he had escaped from prison than been banished
from home. That was not his home. His home was the squashed
little smoke-blackened room where his mother burnt her lungs
out with cigarettes and crucified her soul on penises.

That, too, was no more.

Now home was the street. The never-ending street that ran
through the guts of the city, and from city to city, above ground or
under, up the world and down the world and round the world and
back.

It had different rules and same rules, different gangs and same
gangs, different smells and same smells, different fears and hopes
and same fears and hopes; but it was always home, though never
a home.

It was there Pepsi had to go now. Seek the comfort of brothers
and sisters, their warmth; yet not stay long enough to taste their
rivalries and aggression. Just rest for a while, have some fun, talk
over old times and imagine new ones, enthuse himself, infuse
some hope into Maria – decide on the best route to Heaven.

Once he was down at the very bottom of the hill, on the verge of one of the turning twisting streets that would take him to *his* streets, he stopped to get his breath back.

He laid himself down on the grassy slope of the hill and stared up at the sharply glittering stars in the utter black of the night, free from the dirt and grime of the world below. It was all so peaceful. Hard to believe he had been through what he had just been through, hard to believe he had done what he had just done.

He was about to fall asleep when he realised that he must get going if he was to make it back before dawn. He turned over, and was getting on his hands and knees before standing up when his fingers touched something cold and metallic. The unexpectedness of it made him jump as if bitten by a snake. Something gleamed in the night light, almost under his feet now.

It was the gun.

He had clambered down almost exactly to the spot where the gun had landed as it rolled down.

## Parlour games

El Cuervo was showing off his tightrope skills by walking along the railing of a bridge over a stream running through a deep canyon below – his arrow-straight long black hair, long as his arms, blowing wildly in the wind, his wild black eyes sparkling in the dazzling light of the sun as it danced in the waters below. Close by, next to a dumping lot for industrial waste, El Botas was throwing a knife high up in the air and catching it by its handle as it came down. The lot was wire-fenced all round, but there were big holes in it, and in spite of its reputation as a death trap, it was used by kids and petty thieves to hide when in utter desperation. The long arm of the law was loath to stretch its hand inside its polluted grounds.

Risking life was one excitement in a seemingly pointless exis-tence. There weren't usually many people around that site. But the bridge was a connecting link to the city and a caravan of trucks and cars, including police cars, was always on the move, both ways. As such, the big risk was not hurtling down into the fast and furious stone-riddled currents of the stream fifty metres below, or getting a knife in the throat from above, or getting choked by poisonous fumes, but being visible. More so for Pepsi and Maria than most. But sometimes the most obvious was the most likely to be overlooked. At least so Pepsi hoped. None the less, he had asked Maria to keep well away from him here, and to stay with Giuseppe and his flock of cousins, mostly girls. There was less chance of her being spotted among them than on her own, or with him or other boys.

Pelon had found the body of a cat somewhere, probably knocked dead by a passing car, and was throwing it around at the other kids, some of them catching it and throwing it back, others trying to avoid being hit by it, one or two just running around screaming, either in fear or delight. Pepsi watched for a while, then made a sudden jump in the air, caught the cat, gave it a kiss on its forehead and laid it deep inside a thickly growing acacia bush, crossing himself. He wanted to speak with El Cuervo, but dared not attract his attention while he was in the middle of his across-the-canyon-walk on a surface no broader than the palm of his hand.

Twice EC fell on to the bridge walk but jumped back up on the railing so fast Pepsi had no time to raise an arm and wave. Any verbal signal would have been much too foolish.

The light of the day was beginning gradually to disappear and the Giuseppe clan was getting nervous. One of theirs had nearly got it in the neck only a week before and they wanted to go underground, leaving Maria with Pepsi. Sometimes, one of the Death Police saw you during the day but left you alone, only to return gunning after dark.

Suddenly EC's foot seemed to slip, he wavered in the air and then fell towards the river; but then, catching hold of the railing with his right hand, raised his head above it, let out a loud happy laugh and shouted, 'Fooled you all! Tee hee hee hee . . . .'

More fool you, thought Pepsi, but waited till EC yanked himself up again and then down on to the bridge walk. Certain that he was going to stay there this time, Pepsi yelled, 'Hey, EC, crow man, get here, I need to talk to you.'

'Oy, Pepsi kid. Where have you been? Thought you were meat for the birds. Good to see your two feet still on the ground, but no longer shoeless. And why that cap? What's been going with you!'

## Of friends and snakes

El Cuervo began hearing out Pepsi, eyes getting wider or tighter or squintier at different parts of the story, throwing an occasional expletive between long puffs at his self-rolled cigarettes.

'You fucking with me, no! *Really*,' EC the Crow Boy threw his half-smoked cigarette on the floor and stamped his heel on it when Pepsi came to the part about Tania giving him a wad of notes. Picking up the squashed cigarette, he rounded it back up as much as possible and lit it again, but with a more thoughtful and serious look than he had had up until then. His cool went completely at the point where Pepsi fired at Mario. Jumping three feet in the air he began an imitation war dance round the tree they were sitting under, waving his arms about and whooping like mad. Pepsi joined in. Maria, hiding in a bush close by, could barely suppress her giggles, even though *she* was not supposed to make any noise.

When the boys had calmed down, and Pepsi came to the end of his story, EC said, 'This calls for a meeting. Tomorrow night. In the burnt-out patch of the forest of the spirits. The spirits will protect us there, if we can get there safely. I will go tell the kids now, those who are here, and they can spread the word. Even Bato the Boot and his boys will come, I am sure, out of curiosity if nothing else.

'I will announce that you are being hunted by the police, by your father, and your uncles. That you need to save your life and take Maria to her junk yard family. And that you need all the support you can get. Any sweater, a long coat, a couple of blankets, all the money they can come up with, food . . .'

'Wait wait *wait* . . .' Pepsi interrupted, shocked and bewildered, not believing his ears, 'Just wait. I have all this money and you are going to ask those poor kids to . . . Are you mad. I was going to give them, and you, some of this . . .'

'No mate. *You* wait. If you are in trouble, they will rally round you and do the best they can. They find out you have all this money, and things can get dirty. Take my word for it. You might end up with a knife in your back. And not just from Bato. Money can turn buddies to snakes that crawl in the dark and hiss and strike. I have seen it happen before, for something much, much less than what you . . .'

'Then why have a meeting at all! Why tell anyone, I can just leave . . .'

'Because, thick-head, they come from all over the place to this city. Some even from nearby countries, like Maria. They will be able to tell you the best ways to get where you want to go. Places to stop over, caves to hide in, mountains to avoid, deserts to cross, rivers to swim, who knows what; names of people, relatives, friends you could stay with along the way, get help from.

'Only don't mention the money. And DON'T, don't even tell *me* how much it is. I don't want to be the one to snuff you out.

'A joke. A bad joke, maybe, but I really don't want you telling me how much. *You never know what money can do to a body dicing with its soul to see the next day in* – that's One-Wing Crow, my grand-uncle, speaking! But leave me some cash. I will make it up to those who lose out helping you. And more. I swear on my crow hair that falls straight down my back, and one day will reach down to kiss the earth, our mother. According to what you want or think is fair. I promise you that.

'We are blood-brothers, in spirit, you and I – even if your hair curls, even if your mother's mind was always in the white man's church no matter where her body was, and even if that bald coot of a father of yours behaves like he is one of the conquistadors – you and I, we are true brothers in spirit. I will not let you down or trick . . .'

'I know, I know. You don't have to say it. That's why the first chance I get I come to you.

'Listen. Here is what I would like.

'You know Gerardo, the one with the fever. I want you to take him to . . .'

EC looked away and cast his head down. 'Why, what's the matter?' Pepsi asked.

'We . . . we put him in the stream last night. He drifted away into the peace of the . . .'

'He died?'

'No. No, no. Well, he's dead now. For sure, I hope, but . . .'

'You mean you drowned him, ALIVE! How could you . . .'

'You don't understand. He was all burning up. Crying and couldn't breathe and his lungs were hurting like hell. Like Nico Two. You remember. At least Nico Two was strong. Poor Gerardo was just a baby. And he was suffering so. We sang for him and held him to our hearts and laid his burning body in the cool, cool stream. He smiled. For the first time in days, he smiled. We made a bed of branches for him. He floated away, peacefully. To join his ancestors in the Happy Land.'

'Who else?' asked Pepsi in a resigned voice.

'No one. All are fine. Except Miguel. He blew part of his nose away sniffing who knows what. But Placko, Placido, you know? He's back. We thought he'd been hit, but he's OK. We had a real dance when we saw him. Alma put her arms round him and cried till she laughed. It was great. You should have been here to see it.'

Pepsi saw it, in his mind, and was happy to see it.

'And Sarita found her mother's ring she thought she'd lost. It wasn't even proper silver but she was so . . .'

'Yeah, I know. She was looking through every sewer, every drain, sifting through all the dirt she could lay her hands on. Where did she find it?'

'It was in Pedro's shoe all the time. He thought it was a bit of a stone and was so used to it hurting he didn't bother to take it out. One morning he pulled it off as it was getting up his nose – always slept with his shoes on in case he needed to run – and Leon kicked at it, like a ball, and that loosened the ring out. It was stuck in a hole in the heel. Can you believe it! But that Imelda, she's in trouble. Real trouble.'

'Another baby on the way?' said Pepsi.

'Yes, but worse. She went and told the father, Juarez, the one with the shop by the . . .'

'Yeah, yeah, I know. Carry on.'

'Well, she went and told him she was expecting. He threw her out of the house and started to hit her and hit her, saying he would beat the kid out of her belly. She fell on a corner of the street where a big rock was lying. She picked it up and landed it on his skull so hard half his brains flew out. Now she's in real trouble. Someone even saw her running away from his house.'

'She *killed* him! He *died?*' said Pepsi, voice rising and falling questioningly, still trying to take it in.

'Well of course he died, numb-head. He lived with no heart, but even he couldn't with half his brain licking the street! She didn't know what she was doing. Just trying to save herself and the kid inside of her. And oh, Domingo broke his leg. Again. The same one. He *will not* stop kicking at walls! And sometimes, somehow, they kick back. Last time a brick fell off one of the walls he was kicking and nearly broke his kneecap. We've put a stick on his leg and tied it up, but he's in bad pain. And Magdalena can't stop coughing. Can't hide anywhere because of her. Her cough is like a come-on signal to anyone looking out for us. Poor girl, she feels so bad about it.'

## The meeting

What EC called the forest of spirits was a village-sized gathering of trees either side of a disused railway track. You could still hear the ghosts of old freight trains and elegant passenger carriers whistling their way through it. It was always dark and cool in there, even during hot summer days, as if the place created its own climate and generated its own light.

The meeting was well attended and went well.

Pepsi got more suggestions and names – of people and places – than he knew what to do with. Some way out of his way. But he wrote them all down on the insides of packets of cigarettes handed over to him from all around; wrote them down meticulously, in block capitals, with little maps drawn in some cases, and put them in his pocket for reference, as and when.

And there was no end to the things offered. From a radio and a tea kettle to safety pins and toothpicks – who knows what could come in handy in a time of need! Pepsi was spoilt for choice.

El Gato, the Cat, had a rucksack no one knew about, but he said he would give it only if he came along too. His cousin lived somewhere along the way and he wanted to try his luck with her rather than end his days in the gutter here.

El Mudo, the Silent One, who could not or would not speak but had hearing sharper than a bat, produced a stove and a gas canister, but made signs to show that he too would like to go with them. He was one of El Bato's boys and sick of being bossed around by him. He did not say so, but everybody knew.

El Ciegito, the Blind One, who could not see what everybody else saw but saw what no one could see, had nothing to offer; but he too wanted to go with Pepsi, for very much the same reason as El Mudo. Bato took the weaker and helpless ones and used them for his purposes.

EC said it was a great idea to be more than two. Two, he said, was the most stupid number to be when you are being pursued. More than two, you can cover for each other, play tricks on whoever is behind you, give people the runaround. One, you have only yourself to look after, and that is fine; no responsibility to take for another. But two, especially if one a girl – everyone remembers a pair. Tells whoever asks where they went, what they did, what they ate: everything.

That's how Dalton and Alvarez got done. Always together, just because they liked diving into each other's assholes. They could have made it one by one, or with others. But together, always together, they were as easy to spot as Bonnie and Clyde. Only it was more a case of Claude and Clyde. May their spirits find the spirits of their ancestors without too much wandering in the darkness of death's domain.

Pepsi asked if Imelda wanted to come along since the police could be after her soon for Juarez's murder, but she said no. Not if Vicente wasn't going. She was stuck on Vicente even though he treated her like a pair of shit-loaded knickers and had pimped for her since she was eleven. Vicente wasn't going anywhere. Not anywhere out of the big city to anywhere where there was 'no business'. So Imelda wasn't moving, come what may.

EC said he would have loved to come, but he had his 'children' to take care of here, and he couldn't desert them.

Pepsi had to get something out of his system, 'How can you take care of them if you are risking your ass every day, showing off, walking across canyons for no good reason other than . . . other than . . . well, no good reason at all,' he concluded lamely.

'That's why they listen to me, all who are here tonight, and whenever I want them, wherever. Because I can walk across canyons. And fly over rivers and mountains. I am The Crow, remember!'

'A crow has to prove nothing,' said Pepsi. 'He crosses over canyons and flies over rivers and mountains when he has to, not to show off to others.'

El Cuervo was rattled. He wasn't often rattled, but he was rattled now. 'Well, well, well. Look here, Mister Mastermind. Just because you can read better than anyone here and are the only one I know in the history of the universe who steals newspapers from kiosks doesn't make you an expert on crow nature or man nature or nature. So you keep your face to yourself and shoot off your mouth only when there are no ears about.'

'I just want you to be here when I get back, that's all,' said Pepsi, humbled; adding, '*If* I get back.'

'I will be here,' EC softened his voice, 'I will be. I will be, I will be . . . maybe . . . surely . . .

'Tell you what! We are blood-brothers in spirit. Let's today become blood-brothers in the flesh too. And then I'll make my promise to you as a blood-brother, I'll be here when you get back. And you promise to get back.

'Do you hear me. I'll be here only if you get back. If you don't, if you die on me, I will know. Believe you me, I will know. The spirit of a crow will come and let me know. And then I will have to die too, to be with my blood-brother. So you want me to live, you will have to live too.'

And with that he borrowed Bato's knife and cut across the side of his wrist, and Pepsi stretched out his forearm and EC cut a similar slash through his wrist, and they joined their blood and became true blood-brothers in the eye of the night sky and all that lived beneath its shelter and all that lived above its blue; from those that crawled to those that walked on legs – two or four – to those that swam or flew; from those that needed air to breathe, and moved and ate and drank, to those that needed neither air nor food nor movement; from those that could be seen and heard to those that could only be heard or only be seen or be neither seen nor heard; from those that existed in the single illusory world of the real to those in the many real worlds of illusion.

Crow remembered this chant, and a few others, which he also sang out loud and clear in a language nobody there understood as he danced within an imaginary circle, sprinkling his blood on the grass and the trees and in the air, signalling Pepsi to do the same; his head jerking back and forth, going round and round, his arm-long, arrow-straight, crow-black hair circling the air above him in a delirium of violent ecstasy, his feet thumping away, pounding the earth like there was no tonight.

And then, suddenly, he was stone. One arm hanging down, hand touching the thigh; the other arm raised above his head, elbow bent, hand suspended in mid-air above the shoulder, fingers spread out. One leg up in the air with knee bent and toes pointing down, the other leg stiff as a tree trunk. Neck twisted at an odd, almost impossible angle, one ear listening to the earth, the other ear open to the sky; eyes shut, mouth wide open.

After a moment's petrifaction, he slowly eased his limbs to a normal standing position, raised his fingers to his lips to silence any possible talk and hissed through clenched teeth, almost like a serpent given speech, 'They are here. Climb up trees, no more than two in one tree. Don't move, don't speak; until I give the word. No matter how long it seems. Stay silent, stay still; until I say so.'

Pepsi was still trying to take it all in when he felt a flutter above his head. He ducked involuntarily and saw something move, like a pair of wings; and then it was gone.

Before he could figure out what it was, the Crow Boy spread his arms out to his sides and, shaping his hands like claws, only palms up, he shot them up towards the trees with violent sudden-ness; and everybody – frozen until then, including Bato – came to life and started clambering up trunks of trees and going high into branches.

Pepsi found himself being pulled to his left and more or less carried up a tree. When he opened his mouth to ask something, EC shushed him up.

When they were in the safety of a thick clump of branches, EC produced two leaves of a strangely absorbent yet sticky surface. Wrapped one over the cut on his wrist, and gave the other to Pepsi to do the same. Then, pulling out some vine that crawled up the tree, he wound it tightly round a few times on Pepsi's wrist, and then his own.

After a long silence, EC spoke, 'You saw it, too. Didn't you?' said the Crow Boy.

'Saw what?'

'I saw you see it. You jerked your head and looked up.'

'It . . . it was nothing. I thought I heard wings, a flutter. It was nothing.'

'It was Death. It hungers for you. Don't go. Don't go to where it leads you. It is waiting for you there.'

'How do you know?'

'It was in my vision. When I was home, when my family wasn't burnt out, I went to a sweat lodge. With my father. I was very lucky. I was chosen by my ancestors. Very few are. I had a vision. I didn't understand it then. I do now. Now that I have more visions.'

'You didn't even know me then. How do you know it was about me?'

'I know.'

'If what you say is true, all the more reason I should go.'

'Why?'

'I must take Maria to her family, her Heaven. I want her to live, even if my sister didn't, even if I have to die; especially if I have to die.'

Why?'

'Call it *my* vision.'

'Then remember two things. One, that Death is a friend. Do not be afraid of it. It is a true friend. And two, fight it. Fight it to the last. It is a friend that likes a good fight, an honest fight. The more you fight it and the longer you keep it waiting, the better it receives you when you get to its door.'

'Where did you get that? Another vision?'

'My grandfather taught me that, and a lot more, when I was in my mother's belly. I had forgotten it all, but it comes back to me now. In different ways. Sometimes when I least expect it. Like when walking the canyon.

'I believe you can do it. Give a good fight to Death. You have it in you. I have seen it in your eyes, even though you've told me you are nothing. Give Death a good fight, and it might even let you live!'

## Caddy's first stand

Time went by. Nothing happened. No one appeared.

Pepsi was beginning to think EC had led them up trees for no reason when there was crunching of leaves under boots, voices.

One man in ordinary clothes and two policemen came out into the clearing, all three had guns drawn. Although there wasn't much light Pepsi was sure neither of the policemen was Caddy, though he could smell him. Cannot be far behind, he thought. Or maybe he was imagining it, obsessed by him, as *he* was with him.

The men were whispering, talking softly.

Finally one of them said in a normal voice, 'There is nobody here. We are just wasting our time.'

'I tell you they are!' said another.

Pepsi nearly fell off the tree. It was Caddy's voice. He was the one not in uniform!

'I heard something too, I am sure. Like singing or something,' said a third voice.

'It was the wind whistling through the tree. Tell me, why on earth would they gather here to sing. They are not stupid. They may be many things, but stupid they are not,' the first voice again.

'Who knows what they are or what they do and why,' Caddy again, 'But I know they are here, somewhere. I can smell that . . . that . . .' He looked up at trees, and began shouting, 'I know you are there, somewhere. You son of a bottle. A broken bottle!' He fired randomly up a few trees.

Pepsi's blood chilled inside him. He only hoped no one got hit, and nearly moved, but EC restrained him with an iron grip on his arm.

'I will get you. One day I will. And I will get my . . .' Caddy began then stopped abruptly. He nearly said *get my gun back.* But the other officers were not supposed to know that. He had told them that Pepsi had tried to snatch his boy away from Anna when she was out shopping with him. That he had threatened to kidnap Juan and make him like one of 'them'. That was the reason and the fear he had stated to enlist their support. The two with him were part of the Death Police anyway, but they did not discriminate and did not like going for specific targets. Just got whoever was available when they happened to be out for the kill. But this time, the safety of a colleague's child had made them join in for a particular head-hunt.

Caddy continued shouting, walking back and forth and all around in as much space as the clearing permitted, his voice ringing out clear and near one moment, distant and echoey at another.

'I will get you. I have taken leave from police work, first time in years, simply to be free to follow you, I know where you'll go, with that little . . . I am not a fool . . .

'Mario may forget you, Romano may call Julio off; but I am not going to rest till I have you. And that . . .'

'Leave off, Caddy, there is nobody here. You may not be a fool . . . but you are making a fool of yourself. Making us look . . . fools! Come on. Let's go. And keep to the train track. Even if the mother-fucker is here, I am not getting lost in this jungle for his ass.'

The next night, before they set out, Pepsi gave some of Tania's money to EC. *Cough medicines for Magdalena, a proper plaster for Domingo's leg, a doctor to check if Imelda's baby is all right inside her . . . but not the regular doctors, they will report you. Go to the social worker down by the other side of the river, or maybe to Marcos in the blue house on the second corner . . .* And of course shoes for this one and a coat for that one and sweets and cigarettes and necessities of that sort . . . etc. etc. etc. . . .

And so it was that, accompanied by El Gato, the Cat; El Ciegito, the Blind One; El Mudo, the Silent One, and of course Pepsi, Maria started her journey back to her Heaven.

## The tiers of Heaven

Heaven spread across the surface of an uneven rocky plateau close to the border in the north-west of the region, edging its way down along the southern side of the terraced mountain, almost to the banks of the nervously meandering river in the pit of the valley below.

It was the largest dumping ground of garbage and waste, not only from the capital, only thirty kilometres away, but also from other parts of the country. It had its own landscape, its own atmosphere, its own climate. Little hills and vales and platforms of rubbish undulated or spread their way all across the mesa and down along the mountainside, changing their shape and appearance and locale daily, even hourly, like sand dunes in a windy desert, depending on new truckloads of deposits and the eager onslaught of those who lived around and upon it, picking its riches to make a living out of life. It was harsh with metal and soft with mud and slushy with rain, turning itself into life-giving compost or death-inviting poison, depending on what lay within its self-generating soul. It festered and smelt and let out fumes and cut your feet with metallic fangs or sucked you into itself with its many slimy mouths; but it was home and bread and meat to many thousands who had nowhere else to go and no other way to survive or support themselves and their ever-increasing families.

It had been called the Scroungers' Heaven and the hell of decent citizens. But since decent citizens were rarely seen near it, except occasionally to take photographs or comment on the filth-ridden life of its 'residents' – sympathetically or otherwise, depending on their political affiliations, moral inclinations and election time – it got stuck with the nickname preferred by the community of so-called scroungers and their ilk: Heaven . . .

There was a delicate balance of solidarity against outsiders and cracks within its layers in the community. Those that lived upon the mesa itself, on the top tier, in crudely constructed brick houses, got the first pick of the best that the decent citizens had ejected from their lives and homes and dinner tables. Those a few metres lower down, often in tin shacks and magnified wood and cardboard boxes, got the second choice. While those existing way down below, always in fear of the river exploding its banks, with their shacks and boxes seated on stilts, were left with the leftover rubbish from the rubbish.

This social order was strictly observed. Anyone found transgressing was dealt with according to the self-inflicted laws and mores of Heaven, often more unjust and harsh than the laws and traditions of the motherland that had reduced them to the state they were in, and about which the leaders of the community complained with severe regularity at every possible opportunity, with genuine fellow-feeling.

The tension that developed from this common, uniting bond of deprivation, and the all too common divisiveness of self-interest, in a strange surreal sort of a way kept the community vibrantly together, regardless of the ingenuous mindlessness of its own people and the calculated heartlessness of society at large.

Maria's family lived in the bottom tier of this hierarchy. But Luis Zapata was a strong and energetic man who did some labouring work in the city, as well as helping his family in sorting out the garbage and, so, by the standards of Heaven, managed to provide a good enough life for his wife, four children, two brothers – one older and semi-disabled, the other only sixteen – his mother and father-in-law. Maria, six, was the youngest of the three girls; Cristiano, four, was the only son.

Pumpkin the puppy, 'a girl-dog', was the latest addition to the family, just four months old and with them practically since birth. Maria had found her clawing and whimpering in a black rubbish bag, barely alive, and taken her in against all protestations of Luis.

She 'borrowed' a now empty bottle of perfume her mother had once found and which she had kept even after it was all used up because of its 'beautiful shape', and a child's old-fashioned milk-feeder teat to feed her all hours of day and night, slept with her and took her with her wherever she went.

They lived a fairly commonplace, fairly contented life; but even such non-lives can hold surprises, and the Zapata family were about to be surprised.

Luis found – not in Heaven, but in an alley near the building site he was working on – what could have been a diamond bracelet. Unless it was paste.

That was about two years ago.

## Diamonds are for never

There was something different about Luis when he got home that night. Even his dilapidated pick-up van rattled differently as it came to a stop outside their stilts – at the very bottom of the mountain, not many metres away from the ever-moving bank of the river.

He didn't take Bernardette in his arms that night and pull the blanket over their heads to be able to kiss her without being seen by the others in the room. Just turned towards the wall and went to sleep. Or pretended to. Bernardette always slept on the open side of the mattress in case she had to get up if the youngest cried, or the others needed anything.

Nolsen, the semi-invalid brother, always shouted for water at night, no matter how much Bernardette made sure he had a glass by his mattress, and even though he was quite capable of getting it for himself from the jar in the adjoining room that served as a kitchen-diner and living room. But he was her husband's older brother and she had to respect him and tolerate his temper and whimsicalities, and his general attitude which was of a grudge against the world that all associated with him were supposed to share, like it or not. After all, it was Luis who had to suffer the most, not only because of him, but also her father, who was getting more and more senile by the day and forgetful of the simplest of things.

Luis was afraid to tell his wife about the bracelet. Her life could be in danger; all their lives could be in danger if word got round – and it always did in Heaven, if anyone found anything special. Normally it was no more than a matter of some talk and a little envy, maybe a little thievery or attempted thievery; but a diamond bracelet! He couldn't even imagine what the reaction might be. Even if the bracelet was fake, rumours would say it wasn't. More-

91

over, it would be alleged that he must have rummaged secretly at the upper level to have found something like that. They wouldn't accept the building site story, even if they believed it.

But first he had to know if it was real . . . Then, suddenly, out of the blue, it came to him! How simple! *It would cut glass*, if it was real. Why didn't he think of it earlier. He had been so absorbed thinking about it that he really did not think about it.

He jumped over his wife in the middle of the night to get to his shaving mirror. It was cracked right across its face and he had been meaning to get a new one anyway.

He tried his test.

Nothing.

Not even a scratch!

Ah well! It was too much to expect. Probably a furious girl-friend or wife, finding out her lover's gift was a fake, had chucked it away in disgust, thrown it in his face . . . something like that.

'What have you there?' Nolsen tapped him on the shoulder from behind.

Luis jumped guiltily, dropping the bracelet on the floor.

Nolsen bent over and picked it up with a speed Luis had never seen him exhibit, not even when going for his food – even though he loved his food and was always 'starving'.

Nolsen's eyes popped, he took a deep breath, his crutch slipped from under his armpit but he didn't fall over as he usually did without it. 'A diamond bracelet,' he whispered under his breath with such awe as if he was in the presence of the Good Lord Himself. And then repeated himself, this time with full gusto, 'A diamond bracelet!!!'

'Hush, hush,' said Luis softly, 'I don't want the world waking up. And it is NOT diamond. Just paste. See,' he held up the mirror, 'not even a scratch!'

'Oh yeah!' sneered Nolsen, 'And what is that?' he pointed to the crack in the mirror.

'That's a crack. It's broken. Has been for ages. I have been wanting to buy . . .'

'Crack! I've never seen a crack in it before.'

'Because you've never looked in the mirror before. This, or any other. How long since you last shaved? Or washed?'

'Don't give me that crap. You think I'm an idiot just because . . .' Suddenly remembering he was meant to be an invalid, he sort of staggered and collapsed, gracefully sliding against the wall, bracelet still in hand.

## Developments and consequences

Word spread. Within a matter of days.

Nolsen swore he had nothing to do with it; but Nolsen would swear he didn't have a nose on his face if it suited him, or just for the heck of it.

Luis thought the best thing to do would be to involve the community elders. He would speak to three of them, bring them home with him, show them the bracelet, tell them where, when and how he found it; and, if necessary, give it to them to decide what to do with it. Even a fake was worth a fortune compared to what they usually found in the rubbish, but it was not worth risking one's life.

But by the time he could get them all together and they got to his house, the bracelet could not be found.

'Where is Nolsen?' said Luis after a while, nervous and short of breath under the glare of the elders, a glare which openly said *how convenient for the bracelet to have gone missing just when we arrived* . . .

'He went for a walk, with Maria,' Bernardette replied in response to Luis's question.

Nolsen often did, taking Maria with him. Not just because he always wanted someone around him to fetch and carry and order about; he was genuinely fond of Maria, enjoyed talking to her and almost never laughed except when she was with him.

Maybe he knew where the bracelet was; maybe Maria hid it somewhere.

Best wait for them.

So they waited.

And waited.

The elders went away after a time.

Luis and Bernardette had by now stopped worrying about the bracelet and were worried about Maria and Nolsen.

They were often away for long walks by the river. Nolsen would sit on a rock or a fallen tree, while Maria threw stones across the water surface, picked pebbles, gathered flowers and herbs, or just played around. Sometimes she sat next to him and he made up stories for her, or she for him. In recent weeks, Pumpkin had added even greater interest and variety, certainly more activity, to their ramblings; and they had started staying out even longer.

But not this long.

Luis went to look for them there. No sight nor sign.

Soon Bernardette, Carlos, the young brother of Luis, Angelina and Sara, the two older daughters were all out searching. Along with many of the neighbours, originally sceptical, thinking that the whole thing was a ruse to distract attention from the bracelet.

No one saw Nolsen or Maria again. Nor the bracelet.

They did find Pumpkin, semi-conscious, bleeding and in obvious distress, her head beaten in with a piece of rock next to where she lay. She recovered physically, but clearly sickened for Maria, looking for her in all her old haunts, inside the house and outside, but nothing. Luis, who had never been too fond of the dog, now became devoted to her, in remembrance of his daughter, and with this burning hope in his heart that if anyone could find Maria, it would be her little girl-dog.

Some rough, ready and shady characters of Heaven who spent more time away from than in the community diagnosed that Nolsen must have had the bracelet with him and got killed for it, real or not, and Maria taken across the border to be sold. There were many childless couples, especially from rich countries, willing to pay huge sums of money for a child. And someone as pretty as Maria, with large brown eyes and rich auburn hair that shone in the sun like red gold, could fetch a fortune.

The police agreed with them, and that was the extent of their help.

Luis and Bernardette were devastated, but there was little they could do. Luis scoured the city and wherever he could go. Asked every stranger in the street, begged the clever ones to write to the papers, but they didn't much care. The disappearance of a child, even from worthier households, was not such a unique thing after all. And Nolsen was a misery-guts and a malingerer. No loss to the community or to the world, though there were those in Heaven who grieved for Luis and Bernardette, longed for Maria to return, and even missed Nolsen's misery and malingering: they knew what pain, real or imagined, sometimes the imagined more than the real, can do to the soul of a being. They continued to remember them for many months in their Sunday Service, crossed themselves each time their names were mentioned, calling on Mother Mary to look after them and shield them with her love, wherever they were, in whichever world.

Pumpkin sat in Maria's little corner, ears pricking up at the slightest noise, day or night; and wildly sniffing and running about when the family was out collecting. All Bernardette could do was hope and pray that their little Maria was safe and well, leading a life of luxury with some wealthy parents in California or some such exotic place.

And she could have been.

Except that she managed to run off and get lost in the crowd while the 'adoptive' couple were looking for a taxi to take them to the airport.

## The journey begins

The rucksack turned out to be an old army reject with so many holes it could hardly keep anything in but blankets. But since blankets – three of them – were virtually all Pepsi had taken, it was fine.

It would have been much easier to keep each blanket separate in a plastic carrier bag than all together in the rucksack: heavy enough on its own, with the blankets it weighed more than El Gato himself. Yet he insisted on carrying it on his back.

It was the one big thing he had really owned in his entire life and he wouldn't part with it. And the more it had in it, the heavier it was, the lighter he felt. In his heart.

*But his body is bound to give in, sooner or later,* thought Pepsi, and then a more fair distribution of weight could be sorted out.

'Why are we going north, when we have to go south?' said the Blind One after they had walked for about an hour.

Pepsi wondered how he knew which direction they were going, but did not ask. 'Because Caddy knows I will go south, to Maria's country. I have to try and lose him; at least confuse him.'

The Silent One grinned to himself. He knew that already.

But Maria was not interested either way. She was getting tired and sleepy. Pepsi decided to look for a safe spot for the night.

Tomorrow they would jump a freight train, together; or catch a bus going further north, in two groups – Maria, El Mudo and El Ciegito in one bus, Pepsi and El Gato in another – and meet up at the other end.

One of Pelon's cousins lived in Rosa Tula. He drove cross-country trucks for a living. He might give them a lift down south, if he was there. Pelon had sounded sad . . . *but he is a greedy man. Does nothing without money. Won't save his own grandma for free. So I doubt if he . . .*

But Pelon didn't know he *had* money.

Neither did Caddy! Otherwise he would have blurted it out when he was ranting beneath the trees the other night.

So they had more routes open to them than some would think.

## Nature intervenes

It started off as a light rain, no more than a spitty drizzle – and a slight wind.

Then nothing. No rain. No wind.

All went still. Silent.

Absolute silence. Absolute stillness. Not a bird twittered. Not a leaf rustled.

All of a sudden a roar of clapping thunder and a lightning that lit up the night sky like an upside-down sports arena large as the universe.

El Ciegito let out a scream. El Mudo jumped two feet in the air. El Gato froze. Pepsi had to think, do something, find a shelter before the storm broke.

But there was nothing around them except the rocky terrain. And some scattered trees; but he knew better than to look for hollows in trees during thunder and lightning.

El Gato the Cat, suddenly unfreezing, caterwauled like a frenzied tom chasing a mate or challenging a rival, ran to the tallest tree in the vicinity and soared up it like a flame before Pepsi could stop him. When at the very top of the tree, he waited for what Pepsi feared for him – another clap of thunder, another flash of lightning.

They came, and with a vengeance. Another clap of thunder, another flash of lightning. The Blind One screamed again for he could see before his dead eyes the rivers of hell let loose, their waters, boiling with the fires of hell, rushing towards him with insane fury, devouring land and rivers, town and country, turning all and everything into a muddy lifeless slush; the Silent One jumped again for he could hear the world splitting asunder, ready to swallow him and all he loved within itself. El Gato used the white light that swept across the skies to scan the earth spread naked before his yellowy-green eyes. He caterwauled again, this time with a triumphant note of conquest running through it. As speedily, easily and stealthily as he had climbed up the tree, he clambered down, screaming in a mixture of human and cat-speak, 'There, there, miaoow, miaoow.'

Jumping on to the ground and shaking Pepsi by the shoulder he pointed to his left with a long-nailed finger, 'There, there's a massive big cliff sticking out of that mountainside there. We can hide under it. Maybe there's even a hollow down below it!' And he caterwauled again, beating his chest like Tarzan, his yellowy-green eyes glowing in the dark with excitement.

There *was* a hollow underneath the cliff projection. But the foot-distance to it was much greater than the eye-distance, and their progress was made all the more slow as they had to half-carry, half-drag El Mudo and El Ciegito. None the less, they managed to get inside the shelter of what turned out to be a warm and generous cave, before the heavens broke. And how!

'It is raining tigers and wolves, it is raining tigers and wolves, it is raining tigers and wolves,' screamed El Gato, walking around on all fours trying to make a purring sound before curling up in a corner and dropping off to sleep in no time at all.

'We'll rest a while and then find something to eat. You must be really hungry,' Pepsi whispered close to Maria's ear, but he wasn't sure whether she heard him or had gone to sleep. It was either too dark for him to see, or he was blinded by flashes of lightning.

El Mudo – Alex – and El Ciegito – Jaime – wrapped their arms around each other and let their minds wander to happier days, as they often did. They were first cousins, born within days of each other in their grandma's house, almost fourteen years ago. They were older than both Pepsi and the Cat Boy, but half their size, and looked about nine: undernourished, abused by life and the living as they had been for most of their lives. Since the one who did talk didn't say much about anything except what was immediately necessary, and the other didn't talk at all, nobody knew much about them and assumed them to be about nine. Most street kids had learnt not to pry into each other's histories and accepted anyone who came along at face value. Some talked and talked about themselves, others said little or nothing. Either way, it was OK.

Jaime and Alex used to live only a short distance apart, in small brick-built houses in the little town of Calviro about thirty miles west of the Big City in the mountain's cradle. Their mothers spent most of their time together, sometimes just cooking and weaving and gossiping, sometimes going to the street market, buying a few things they needed and could afford, looking longingly at those they didn't particularly need, or couldn't afford even if they did – like a cooking stove you could work by pumping gas into it. Jaime's dad had hung up a couple of hammocks under a tree at the back of Alex's house, and sometimes, whenever there was an hour or two free on a lazy, hazy afternoon, their men out working the fields, they would lie in their hammocks, gently rocking themselves, and telling each other stories like little girls, their children playing around them, their screams of laughter and joy somehow adding to the silence, like singing cicadas.

One spring day Jaime and his family – his little sister, two older brothers, mother and father – went for a little picnic lunch under a tree in the Alzavero Park behind the big bus station. They often went on Sundays, after church, usually both families, sometimes along with a few other neighbours. It was unusual for Jaime's family to be on their own. Jaime was five at the time, and it was at his insistence that they had gone that day. Alfredo, Alex's dad, had wanted them to wait till next Sunday for he had some little tasks to attend to at home – mend the broken leg of a bed and something else to do with a cracking wall – and he needed his wife to stay back and cook him something special as he worked. He had wanted Jaime's mother to stay back and keep his wife company, but she said, 'Oh Alfonso! Jaime has so set his mind on going, and he will be so disappointed.' *More you than him!*

thought Alfonso to himself, who had never much liked the woman his brother had married. *Always leading his poor wife to the town market to gaze at things they were never meant to have, sowing needless desires in his wife's innocent and contented heart.*

A sudden thunderstorm hit the town that day, lightning struck the tree under which Jaime and his family were sheltering, killing all, and blinding Jaime.

Jaime was taken in by Alfonso, but he never forgave him for being responsible for the death of his dear brother and the other children, especially Sara, the little girl of whom he was very fond, not having any girls of his own. He was even sorry for his sister-in-law's death. *Always wanting to be better than she was, but faithful to his brother, and a good worker in the house.* Somehow, all his anger, his grief, seemed to direct itself against the surviving boy. That he could no longer see was God's curse on him. Confirmed by the fact that doctors said there was nothing really wrong with his eyes, and that he could see 'if he wanted to'. *When the shock wears off . . .*

His grandma used to pray to the ancestors every day and every night to come down from their home in the skies and help the poor orphaned boy regain his sight. And it seemed to be working! He was beginning to discern some light and shade, even shapes, when came another unexpected storm, violent as the gods . . . with far more serious consequences for the entire town and many others in the neighbouring areas.

Torrential rains brought rivers of mudslides coming down the side of the mountain, burying most houses and killing half the people. The only ones to escape from the Alfonso family were Alfonso himself, and the two boys, Jaime and Alex. Everyone else was lost: his mother, his wife, his three sons, cousins, uncles . . . And Alex lost his speech. The doctors didn't help much, some people said some mud must have gone down his throat, would clear out, wash out . . . in time . . . he should be able to speak. Maybe . . .

Alfonso had always thought there was something evil about that boy, Jaime. At least, he *now* believed that he had always thought there was something evil about Jaime, whether he had or not.

Renata, an old aunt of Alfonso, came over regularly to help him look after the children and the house. Look after him, actually. He had gone into decline, lying about the house, unshaven, unwashed, not eating unless fed. Although he had lost faith in the Blessed Virgin and the ancestors, he still kept hoping that one night *She*, or *They*, might come, kiss Alex's lips, and make him speak; even caress Jaime's eyes to bring them back to life.

But neither the Blessed Virgin nor the Blessed Ancestors ever came. Instead, one bleak and black, soulless and starless night, when strange and unspeakable stirrings rise up from within cracks of broken hearts, the evil ones rose from their hellish abode in the bowels of the earth and grabbed hold of Alfonso's soul. At their instructions, he rose from his bed, put on his trousers, his jacket and his boots, tore up an old shirt of his, stuffed a rag in Jaime's mouth, tied his kicking legs together with one sleeve, his hands with the other, wrapped him up in a blanket, picked up the sleeping blind boy in his arms, carried him out, God alone knows how many miles to the north, and left him at the foot of the mountains for coyotes or pumas or wild dogs to put an end to his miserable life and return some peace and happiness to his home, lifting the curse the boy had brought with him.

It was almost dawn when he got back. Just on an impulse he went to have a look at the sleeping Alex, but he wasn't in his bed.

At first he thought Alex must have wet the bed as he had started doing, woken up, felt guilty, and hid somewhere when he heard him coming. He called out his name. First angrily. Then gently, saying he wouldn't be angry, not this time, even if he had wet his bed. Jaime and Alex used to share a bed, but recently, not having any other children left, or grown-ups for that matter, Alfonso had started putting Jaime in one of the many spare beds. Whether it was for his good, or whether it was in the back of his

mind to carry him out one night without disturbing Alex . . . ?
Even he wouldn't have been able to answer that question with any
degree of certainty.

*He must have gone to Jaime's bed, looking for him,* thought
Alfonso. In order not to let Jaime's curse rub off on Alex, he had
put Jaime's bed on the other side of the house; but one often
sneaked in with the other. A sense of anxiety got hold of him.
What if Alex had gone to Jaime's bed and found it empty? What
would he have done!

He ran to Jaime's bed. No one there. He ran about all over the
house, and outside, shouting and calling, but Alex was nowhere.
He ran back out to where he had left Jaime. But nothing there. *No
one.* Not even Jaime!

It continued to rain tigers and wolves. And continued and
continued and continued. Water started to creep into the cave; not
from the room-wide opening through which they had entered, but
from somewhere behind them, from what appeared to be the solid
body of the mountain.

## Of suspicious women – one

Mrs Cadez tilted her head, bird-like, squinted knowingly at her son fidgeting uncomfortably in a chair next to her, and lisped through the gaps in her teeth, 'Sounds dogshit funny to me!'

Caddy recoiled, as if stung, 'There's nothing funny about dog . . . about that,' he mumbled under his breath, flexing his fingers towards his palm and rubbing his nails together erratically.

'You are right!' said the plump-faced, lump-bodied woman, resolutely crossing her plump arms over her lumpy bosom, taking a deep breath and raising the said bosom to a gravity-defying scale before letting it drop to its usual level of liquid levitation. Her scaly brown scalp peered accusingly at Caddy through thinning, snowy white hair as it nodded emphatically to underscore her crisp, trisyllabic response.

The lack of colour and thickness of hair and other ravages of time apart, her face was as much a replica of her son, as her son's was that of his son. In fact, in his late teens, Caddy was often teased by friends that he wouldn't grow a moustache because he wanted to look like his mother.

Anna opened her mouth as if in a bid to defend her husband but thought better of it. It was best not to interfere when mother and son were at it. Besides, in this case she happened to agree with the mother, even though she hated to admit it. *Why on earth would Caddy suddenly want to go back to his village to 'look for his roots' and to visit his father's grave!* And for what *could be* a period of four days to four weeks! Why so vague about the time? So very vague . . . It did sound dogshit funny, whatever the old woman meant by it.

Caddy straightened his fingers, brought the palms of his hands together, looked at his mother then looked hastily away as she looked straight back at him, cleared his throat with a prolonged throat-clearing-noise and said, 'I thought you'd be pleased. After all, I haven't been to papa's grave for years an . . .'

'You're right!' interrupted Constantina with another nod of her formidable head.

She pursed her lips and became meaningfully silent, staring at the wall behind Caddy's head in such a way that he couldn't be sure whether she was staring at him or the wall, then leaned forward and spoke in a hushed voice, 'Since when this longing to, to . . . *visit papa's grave?*' she mimicked Caddy perfectly. 'The only reason you'd go to his grave – God rest his soul, though I doubt it – would be to make sure he was still in it. And there can be no doubt about *that* now. Not even in your . . . *special* . . . mind.'

Caddy went red. Anna felt sorry for him. Constantina could be so cruel to her son. It was not always so much what she said, but the way she said it, the way she looked at him, or did not look at him!

Poor Caddy! He had such a *simple* mind. A child's mind. To call it *special*, and in that special tone of voice was . . . was . . . just not right! His father had treated him badly because he believed he was not clever enough, *simple*. His mother was making it sound worse by her heavy-handed irony. It was not fair. Not fair at all. At least he hated his father. It was easier to accept rejection from those you hate. But he loved his mother. He deserved better from her. She was just taking out her resentment against his father and brothers on him. The father who humiliated her all his life by his flagrant affairs. And the brothers who did not share with her the success they had made of *their* life.

It wasn't right. Not right at all. After all, it was *he* who was keeping her. Both his brothers, of whom both she and their father had been so proud, always had some excuse not to have her – at least not for longer that a few days at a time. And they had big houses, lots of money, servants . . . But their *friends were coming over*, friends *she* would find irritating; or *important guests* who would require all their attention; or loud parties *she* would hate, or they were away on holidays . . . something or the other. Poor Caddy was always there to serve her hand and foot.

'Mama . . .' Anna began in protest, but Constantina silenced her with a flick of her wrist. She knew things, things that woman of his did not know, and it was best that she didn't.

Her mind went back to that winter's night, all those winters ago. Caddy was ten, Rico twelve, Rigo nine. All three boys had a nature project to finish for school, given to them some three weeks before and to be handed in the next day.

Rico had worked on butterflies. He had collected and fixed butterflies of twelve different species on his work-book, looked up books in the small village library and written a page on each butterfly, painstakingly, in his best handwriting.

Rigo was working on frogs. He had gone from house to house and asked if anybody had any magazine with pictures of frogs and which they didn't need any more. There weren't many nature lovers or magazine readers in the village! The poor boy wore himself out trudging from street to street and door to door. But he did manage to get a few good pictures that he meticulously cut out and pasted on plain foolscap sheets, and even cut out words to paste.

Caddy said he would write about fishing. His father took him out fishing, not so much as a favour to Caddy, but because *he* liked to go fishing. Perhaps Caddy had wanted to write about fishing only to please his father, to spend some time with him. Whatever, nobody saw any work produced by him. But the night before the work was to be handed in, Constantina heard some furtive foot-steps in the boys' room. Their father wasn't in. He wasn't in most nights, and she was past caring where he was or who he was with. But she was worried about the safety of the boys, so she quickly wrapped a shawl around her shoulders and ran to see what was going on. She caught sight of Caddy soft-footing his way out of the house, through the window! Now, more curious than worried, she silently went over to the partially open window and looked out. A chilly wind was blowing in and she was half-tempted to shut it, but she didn't want any noise to warn off the boy.

There was always something cagey and secretive about the boy, just like his father. It was a pity they didn't get along well together.

Probably because they were too much alike, in the heart of their being, in spite of obvious differences: Caddy was shy and tongue-tied, unsure of himself and lacking in confidence; his father bombastically loquacious, certain of everything, no matter how wrong he was, and went about the world in a buoyant wave of self-assurance. She had gradually come to know what the father was carrying on with in most of his many secret lives; here was an opportunity to see what the boy was up to in the middle of this freezing, windy night.

He walked up to the shelter of the big chestnut tree to the left of the house, threw something on the ground, then, pulling up his nightshirt, squatted. Constantina was aghast. Had he gone out in that weather simply to . . . *to shit!*

Could it be that the boy was just being *considerate*. The toilet was just above her and Rico senior's bedroom – if he was there – and, when flushed, it made a hugely rattling noise followed by the sound of a cascading waterfall. Many a time it had woken her up, but usually it was by Rico senior's nightly excursions, more and more frequent as he grew older. She had begged him to have it sorted out, but his response was the same as to anything else she wanted: soothing placating noises, promises, and nothing!

Was Caddy trying *not* to be like his father! Trying to be kind to her. Maybe that was why he went through the window, for going out the door would have meant going through her room, and he knew she was a light sleeper. She wished he had gone somewhere further away from the house. Perhaps it was too cold . . . Even so, he would have ended up with a frozen ass.

Whatever, she decided to move quickly away the window and get back to her room. But she must have been lost in thought for longer than she realised, as Caddy came up to the window while she was just halfway through the door. However, each pretended not to be aware of the other and went to their respective beds.

*Did she come up to the window and look out!* said Caddy to himself as he rolled over in his bed.

*Did he have any toilet paper or something?* she wondered as she fell back to sleep.

It was only in the morning that the truth revealed itself. The screams of the three boys cut through the house, unafraid of waking their father who had come in not too long ago and was fast asleep.

'What in the Lord's name . . .' said Constantina, meeting the boys half-way as they were coming running to her.

'Our work . . .' 'My work . . .' 'All our hard work . . .' all three boys were crying and talking at the same time, tear-stained faces flushed with emotion.

It didn't take long for Constantina to discover the cause of all their distress. The neighbour's dog had ruined all their school projects by doing poo all over them! *He must have sneaked in some time, as he sometimes does, got locked in – because of the cold all the windows were shut – and somehow . . . etc. etc. . . . .* Caddy was doing the explaining. *I did my best to clean it up as much as I could before Rico and Rigo could see it. I didn't want them to . . . considering all the work they had put in . . . etc. etc. . . .*

Constantina eyed him with an incredulous, shocked expression. And although she averted her gaze soon enough, he could tell that she knew, and she could tell that he could tell that she knew . . . And she was sure that his project work would have been no more than a couple of pages scribbled with rubbish. But she never said anything.

Some unexplained things around the house now began to make more sense. She could even believe the erstwhile friend she had broken off with and not spoken to in the last few months. She had accused Caddy of sitting on her three-year-old daughter when she left her with him only to get some orange juice for him.

'You haven't got a woman hidden somewhere now? Like your dear old papa?' Constantina's scalp peered at her son once again, and Anna shivered within herself to hear her own fears so openly expressed. Fears that she had been trying her best not to acknowledge.

Later, alone with Caddy, little Juan in her lap, she managed to get the truth out of him. She always did. No matter how hard he tried, and there were times when he did try hard indeed, in the end, she got the truth out of him. Always.

He was taking time off to go looking for that boy, Pepsi. He had learnt he had run away down south, to where that girl came from, Maria, the girl he was always with. He wanted to get to him before anyone else in the police got him. In a foolish moment of anger he had told his colleagues that the boy had done something bad, really bad, attacked an old lady or two, tried to rob and kill them, something like that. He was truly sorry about it now, but then he was so mad at being duped out of his gun he didn't know what he was saying . . . If they got to him first, God alone knew what they might do to him. Probably shoot him on sight, he wouldn't be surprised, or at the very least beat him up bad. He wanted to get to him before that, to make sure he did not come to any harm. He knew how fond Anna was of such kids, and he – sometimes against his better judgement – wanted to help them out, if he could. He had spoken to Jeremy, a man from England who ran a shelter for street kids, and he had agreed to take Pepsi and the girl in for rehabilitation. But he had to find them first. He had four weeks' leave coming to him. Hopefully he would get the boy within a week and he would take Anna and Juan for a long break to the beach resort of Xalico. One of his officer friends had a little place there, which he had agreed to let them have for free. He was trying to keep this a secret from her, to surprise her, but now that he was being pressed for it, he could hide it no longer.

He begged her to not to tell his mother about it, but Anna was so thrilled by it all that she did. If only to show to her how wrong she could be about her son. Though she was careful only to talk about the holiday, not Pepsi and the gun.

Constantina began to sneeze when she heard about it. She could always bring on an attack of sneezing when she did not want to talk about something, like admitting she was wrong.

## Of suspicious officers and gentlemen

'We are going out tomorrow night. *Street cleaning!*' said officer Raffo, with an elbow nudge to officer Domingo and a wink to Caddy. 'See you at the usual place for some beers before we start.'

'I . . . I may not . . . be here tomorrow,' Caddy stuttered, both tempted and disappointed, twitching his thumbs, 'Can't we go tonight? It is only six . . .'

'We can't. I have promised my wife . . .' began officer Domingo, then stopped and looked suspiciously at Caddy, 'What's with you? You are looking all nervy.'

'It's that garbage rat and his itch bitch. They must have split by now, I am sure of it. I . . . I . . . think I know where he is headed, and I will be going after him. I should really have gone today, but was getting some grief from the family, so had to . . . If I leave it another day, he will have too much of a head start.'

'What *is* with you!' sneered Raffo, 'We are out to sweep dogshit off our city streets. Wherever and whatever. Why are you so stuck on one particular turd somewhere out there, when we can get bucketloads down here!'

Caddy flinched at that reference to dogshit cropping up again. 'You *know* why. He threatened my . . .'

'Oh come on! Be sensible. It must have been a spur of the moment thing. And it's over. You can't seriously believe that that bloody little cur can have the guts . . .'

'Or the means,' Raffo butted in.

' . . . to try and kidnap a police officer's child. Have you *ever* heard of anything like that *ever* happen. Ever! Calm down and think rationally. Tomorrow is the one day in a long time we are all free, AND that snooty, self-righteous bastard Calino is out of the office and not sniffing around to smell who is up to what.'

'And, AND,' Raffo again, 'if you think that sewer rat is headed out of here, how can he be a threat to your child here? He can't have it both ways, and neither can you! So make up your mind. Are you with us, or not?'

'Yeah. It'll be fun to have you, but if not . . .'

Caddy had nothing left to say. The hunt for Pepsi and Maria would have to wait for yet another day.

## The haunted cave

Water was creeping in through cracks. Drip dropping from corners. Seeping in. Infiltrating. Slishing and sloshing. Quivering all over. Irregular ripples advancing and retreating, bubbling and tumbling, dancing to the tune of the winds howling in and out of the cave with a primeval force all their own.

Pepsi was wrenched out of a nightmarish sleep in which gargoyles of even more than usual hideous and distorted shapes and faces – worse than those his father had got round the front and back walls of his house and which Miriam, his father's mother, hated with all her heart and soul and which never seemed to belong to that house for the obvious reason that they didn't – were making hideous and distorted gurgling noises and spouting foul-smelling, poisonous water out of their ugly and distorted mouths. Just in time. Another few minutes and the invading water would have got to them. He jumped to a squatting position, the real fear of the real water replacing the dream dread of the dream water, and with eyes still sleep-drenched, but by now used to the black of the cave, he looked around for a means of escape or a place of safety, and saw a niche to their left that was at a higher level than the rest of the cave floor. He shook and shouted the others awake and started herding them towards that alcove, and within seconds the still half-asleep Maria, El Mudo and El Ciegito were huddled together inside it. El Gato, fully awake and alert in the swish of a tail, found a smooth curve in the rocky wall and leant against it with his back, knees pulled up to his chest. Pepsi cradled Maria to himself. El Ciegito was staring fixedly into the darkness around him, a fatigued, resigned-to-death look in his scared and scary, sightless eyes; El Mudo was more or less holding him in his arms. Both boys were wondering, simultaneously, in their Siamese twins' sort of way, if being abused by El Bato and chased by the coppers might have been a better option than being stranded here in a flooding cave. Both decided against it. They were more frightened of the power of man than the power of nature, having seen enough of both in their short lives. At least nature was impersonal. Or did that make it all the more dangerous? But their young minds, however aged by suffering, were not sophisticated enough to raise that question, much less reflect on it or answer it.

As time went by, the water began to rise, and it became clear that sooner or later it would get to them here as well. Something had to be done.

Another flash of lightning, this time brightening up the entire cave with an almost cool, bluish light in which they saw that behind the elevation they were on, a ledge extended upwards at about a seventy-degree angle – an uneven craggy slope, almost like a naturally carved, erratic stairway.

Pepsi said he would go up first, to see if it was safe. On all fours, and as carefully as he could in the now back-to-blackness cave, he managed to reach the top end of the slope, which to his joy opened out into another hollow in the mountain: a cave upon a cave, dry, and feeling quite fresh, as if there was a good supply of air up there.

He could hardly contain himself and almost hollered to the others to follow him, but thought better of it. An exuberant scramble up could be dangerous. In spite of its cragginess, the slope was quite slippery in some places. At one point a sharp flint had scratched his ankle – there were bound to be more. Caution and responsibility had been so ingrained in him, after months of looking after Maria, that, toning down his boyish glee, he came half-way down again, almost tripping up and cursing, stretched out his hand and asked Maria to crawl up, carefully and slowly. As soon as she was within reach, he caught hold of her by the shoulders and helped her up, carefully and slowly. Once she was safely on top, Pepsi shouted for the Cat Boy to assist Mudo up, but the Silent One clambered up on hands and knees like an ape, without any help from either of the older boys. More astonishingly, the Blind One followed, with such ease and alacrity it was as if he could see every nook and cranny, every segment, every curve, any rise or fall, of the rock incline. The Cat Boy was the last, and happiest: miaowing and purring and laughing and beating his chest, emitting Tarzan-calls, making his hands into paw-like fists and licking them. Pepsi had long ceased to be either amazed or amused by El Gato playing both Tarzan and the lion, but Maria still found it funny and fell into a fit of uncontrollable giggles.

The kids were making so much noise of their own that at first they failed to hear some other sounds coming from deep inside the upper cave. But gradually, as they quietened down, they thought they could hear sounds, sounds like moaning and groaning, hissing or sighing.

El Gato was the first to speak, 'Did you hear that?'

'Hear what?' said Pepsi, although he had heard.

'People! There are people in the cave!' whispered El Ciegito.

'Ghosts! I hope they are not ghosts,' Maria began to feel cold fear travelling up and down her spine.

'It is just the wind,' said Pepsi, 'Wind rushing through cracks and crevices of the rocks.'

'We've got a torch,' said El Gato, 'somewhere . . . I'll find it . . .' He began rummaging in his rucksack.

'Well, if you have the torch why didn't you get it out in the first place, it would have made it so much easier . . .' Pepsi began but the Cat Boy interrupted him.

'You knew about it as much as I did. Why didn't you . . . In fact you were the one to . . .'

Just then a big choking noise was followed by some abrasive, scratching sounds.

Maria gasped. El Mudo put his arms around El Ciegito. El Gato froze. Pepsi didn't know what to do or think. But he would have to make a decision soon. After all, this trip was his idea, and they were all his responsibility.

'Let's just wait. Listen. Don't do anything stupid. Don't do anything at all. Most likely it is the wind. Or an animal trapped. If it's the wind, as I think it is, then nothing to worry about. If it is an animal, flashing a torch will only scare it, make things worse. If nothing actually . . . well . . . happens . . . If it is just, well, noises, well . . . let's go to sleep. In the morning . . .'

'What if somebody gets us in the night?' said El Gato.

'Ghosts,' said Maria.

'There is no somebody!' said Pepsi, ignoring Maria and still looking at the Cat Boy, but not half as sure of himself as he tried to sound. 'Why wouldn't they talk normal if they were, instead of pretending to be like the wind? Tell me why?'

'Maybe they don't want to be found.'

'Then why make any noise at all? See, there is no sense in what you are saying.'

'It's ghosts, I know it,' Maria forced herself as close to Pepsi as she could.

'Oh, shut it, Maria,' blurted Pepsi, 'you can be such a baby at times.' Pepsi regretted saying it almost as soon as he had said it, but he had to assert himself a little if he was to have some sort of authority.

Maria moved away from Pepsi and began to sob. Pepsi ran his fingers through her hair and drew her closer, saying he was sorry; El Gato began rummaging through his rucksack again and hissed and spat because he couldn't find the torch. Soon an uncomfortable silence fell upon the scene, and it was a while before Pepsi heard it. The silence!

It had gone quiet, still. No more groans or scratching.

'See, it was the wind. What did I tell you? It must have died down. What did I tell you . . . !'

By this time all were too tired to argue. A sudden weight of exhaustion fell upon them like a landslide, and they rolled into a deep, deep sleep. Even the resumption of groans and moans and choking and scratching noises did not disturb any of them, nor bring on a nightmare for Pepsi.

## Of suspicious women – two

'Whatever is the matter with you? Looks like you've got a goat stuck in your throat,' said the woman who had spent most of her life repenting having given birth to Augusto Romano. And yet, in a strange sort of a way, she was proud of him too. He was born into poverty and nothingness, he had worked his way to wealth and fame; his name was known throughout the land. Not many beyond the street they lived in knew *her* Romano's name, Miguel, the boy's father. But those who did loved and respected him. He was a gentle man, as kind to a street dog as to a cousin. There wasn't a neighbour alive he hadn't done something for, be it as pleasurable as taking Renata's little orphan boy out to some game every weekend, or as hard as rebuilding poor Mr Giuseppe's storm-damaged house. She couldn't think of anyone who really liked Augusto. *She* certainly didn't like him, no matter how hard she tried.

But perhaps he was right to be the way he was. After all, where did all his father's love and goodness get him! Killed at the age of thirty-four, fighting off some hoodlums who had come to rob old Roberto next door. She had never forgiven him for dying, nor the world for killing him. And it was only a month after Augusto was born. Thirty-three days, to be exact. She had known in her heart that that boy would bring nothing but bad luck. Known it since the moment the boy had aimed his little willie and pissed straight at her only wedding photograph that she always kept by her bedside.

'You'd better swallow it, or spit it out,' Miriam continued with her *goat in the throat* metaphor, 'or else you'll choke on it before the day is out.'

Tania enjoyed the thought of Romano choking on a goat in his throat, but she kept her face bland and expressionless and mousy

117

brown. Miriam was right, though. He did look most uncomfortable. Had done so ever since Caddy had called him again to let him know that 'the boy' had disappeared, and God alone knew what he was going to do next.

Tania wondered what Romano would do next. There was something distinctly fishy in the way he had been acting lately. Of course there was something distinctly fishy in the way he acted any time of the day or year; but there was something more to it that usual this time. But what bothered her more was the way in which her brothers were behaving. Especially Mario. Ever since she had sent him to take Pepsi back to the city, he had had that weird look on his face. He had just finished high school and had been all excited about going to college or university, preferably in the USA. He seemed to have forgotten all about it and looked edgy and angry all the time. And she had caught him whispering to José, and even the other boys, all of whom shut up on seeing her. That was not how things should be. She was very close to them, and they shared all their secrets with her.

Worst of all, she had seen Mario and José going into Romano's room, *and staying there for over an hour*. They hated the sight of him, and he of them. What was going on that they were willing to share with him, and not her? In a way she knew. It was bound to be something to do with Pepsi. But why would they speak to Romano, and not her? Perhaps she knew the answer to that too. Because she had been kind to the boy, and they did not like that. So they had teamed up with Romano. But what exactly were they planning? The trouble was, they knew she taped all Romano's telephone calls, so they would not discuss anything with him over the phone. What if they told him she was taping his calls! If the boys went over to his side, life would become difficult for her. To say the least. And all for that bastard boy of Romano. She felt sorry for him, but he was certainly not worth all this. But how was she to regain the confidence of her brothers? Find out what they were plotting, with or without Romano's help. Up until now she always felt she had the upper hand in whatever went on in the Romano household. Suddenly she was not too sure. And it worried her.

She would have to sweet-talk Frederico, or Pablo. They may not know everything, but enough to give her some idea, enough to take away the feeling that she was treading on flimsy glass all the time.

## Ancestors

Alex was the first to get up. He woke up Jaime, and together they set out to explore this cave upon a cave. It seemed to stretch out in all directions. They had just turned round a bend when Alex saw them. The ancestors!!!

The rain had stopped. So had the wind. The sun was up and its sharp, knife-edged rays of heat and light sliced their way through cracks and holes in the south-eastern walls of the rocks – cracks and holes which could have been the work of erosion through water and winds over the centuries, or man-made, by people who may have once used these caves to dwell in.

A dusty yet radiant mixture of floating, cogitating particles of silver and gold light, as if transmitted from a cinema projector, hovered hesitantly above the faces and bodies of the ancestors as they sat or lay in a craggy, uneven, arc-shaped heap against the craggy, uneven rock-wall at the farthest end of the bend, about twenty feet away from the boys.

Alex saw, with unbelieving eyes, the pale, blanched faces of the dead, now back among the living, glimmering and glowing in the shimmering, divergent rays of the late morning sun penetrating the murky darkness of the cave upon cave.

Two females, one with shoulder-length hair of spun gold, the other with a straw-brown shock of locks sitting on her head like an inverted bird's nest. One of the men had not much hair to speak of, though he had a young face, another man was blond like the girl, and the third with dark brown, wavy hair.

Alex focused on the hair, as it was on the heads of the ancestors that the brightness of the sun was more directly pouring itself, like a silent yet turbulent brook of light – like a dissimulation of halos stretching out joyously to intermingle and greet each other.

*Ancestors!* He thought to himself. And just as he thought the word 'ancestors', so he uttered the word: A*ncestors!*

The first word he had spoken, since his house and mother and brothers and most of those he had loved and that which he had known perished in the storms and the mudslides that followed, brought upon the heads and homes of men by the gods of wrath.

And as soon as the Blind One heard the Silent One speak the word 'ancestors', his eyes lit up, and *saw* the ancestors!

Just as Grandma had said, just as Aunt Renata used to say, the ancestors would come and save us, they always do, only sometimes the evil spirits get to them first, hold them captive in the bowels of the earth, behind trees or mountains, or wherever. But somehow, at some time, they manage to free themselves, get to those who need them: for good always wins over evil, always!

Only this time *they* had got to the ancestors before they could get to them.

Just then the Cat Boy came past them, eyes wide open, virtually falling out of their sockets, elbows bent, hands stretched out like claws, silently and stealthily moving towards the five that lay tied and gagged – the torch that he had last night been looking for in the rucksack sticking out of his trouser pocket.

The Blind One could see every move the Cat Boy made, the Silent One began to mutter and mumble almost incoherently anything and everything that came into his head. The ancestors began to make choking noises with their throats, and scratching sounds with their fingers and nails upon the walls and floor of the cave, just as they had done the previous night.

By now Pepsi and Maria were there too. Pepsi was holding on tight to the little girl, but she tore herself away from the protective arms of the open-mouthed boy and rushed towards the group of five and began to ungag and untie the men and women. She might have been exhausted by the walk and overwhelmed by the storm last night, nervous of the dark and the cave, insecure about ghosts

– but she was not going to stand about gaping idly at people who so needed help.

After a second's hesitation, Pepsi ran over to help; and the Cat Boy, becoming human again, also joined in.

Jaime and Alex looked on as living stones.

The mouth of the cave smiled broadly but said nothing, as ever.

## Yet another find for Luis Zapata

Vivecca liked looking at the television. It was a brand new tele-vision, 33 inches of wide-screen beauty complete with stand, still in its box when Luis found it. It was in a house he was 'going through' after its occupants had gone. Was it left by mistake when they were moving out? Not likely, unless they had moved not just out of the city but out of the country, or were somehow unable to get back for it. More likely some thief, seeing an empty house, was storing it there till it was safe to sell. In which case there might be something else around. He searched all over the house, the court-yard, the balcony, the rooftop, but nothing. Nothing new or elec-tronic or particularly worth having. Just junk, some rotting kitchen cabinets and old cupboards already vandalised. Which meant the TV couldn't have been there for long or it would have gone by now. He thought he had better hurry out before someone, or more than one, bigger or younger than him came to claim it.

He put the set in his van and made straight back for home even though he still had a job or two arranged in the city for that day. He already had an old but serviceable aerial somewhere among the scrap lying about in the little piece of land beneath his house, and he proudly fixed it high on top of the roof – the house being on tall stilts made the antenna visible from quite a distance.

He had put on the aerial once before, soon after he found it, years ago, thinking his neighbours would think he had a TV; which they did. They even came to see it, but finding nothing giggled all the way back to their homes. Luis was humiliated beyond belief, especially as Bernardette had pleaded with him not to do something 'so obviously stupid' and likely to be found out. But since no one had come to visit them for ages – partly because they were all a bit wary of Nolsen, and partly because the old man, Bernardette's father, said and did peculiar and sometimes unpleasant things on a more or less regular basis, like coming out in a torrent of abuse or taking off all his clothes and waving himself about – he did not expect anybody turning up on their doorstep.

But now he could show them. Let them come, one and all. Not only did he have a TV, but a smacking new one with a 33-inch wide screen, a streamlined black surround and a matching black stand. Quite a few things had to be moved to make a place for it, and it looked grand where it stood, dominating the room, making the shabby rolled-up beds along the wall opposite look even shabbier.

It didn't matter if they had no electricity and it couldn't be turned on. Those living on top of the mesa and facing electricity pylons managed to steal power for their use, sometimes at the risk of their lives. Two were known to have died in a few of the earlier attempts, but people had learnt to be more careful. A little friendly consideration towards the local constabulary kept the law out of the equation. Down here, at the lowest level of both topography and hierarchy, there were no such possibilities. But it still did not matter to Luis. You could see the television, even if you couldn't watch it.

And Vivecca, Luis's mother, loved to see it. Sit in front of it and stare at it. Especially as, on top of the set, in pride of place, just below the gold-leaf-framed painting of the Madonna and Child hanging on the wall, was a gold-leaf-framed picture of Maria, taken when she was three, five years ago, three years before she disappeared. With her failing eyes she could barely make out the set much less the features of Maria; but they were imprinted on her memory and she didn't need eyes to see her favourite grand-daughter's face. Whether or not she was her favourite when she was around, even she couldn't say; but for now, there was no doubt in her mind that she was her favourite. Any recollections of showing a preferential partiality towards the little boy had gone for ever. Instead, she now went out of her way to ignore him, which he had come to accept, gradually; but which had seriously upset and disturbed him all that long, long time ago. Long, long time, for the now six-year-old Cristiano; but it seemed just like yesterday to Bernardette. And she still thought putting up the aerial, even with the television, was a stupid idea.

'What good is it? This big, blank, dull screen staring back at you, mocking our stupidity. What good is it? To you or anyone. Why not sell it and get a pair of good shoes. Some clothes for your children? For yourself, even if you are not interested in anything decent for my old body any more.'

'I will sell it. I will, I will. I promise you I will. Just give me a few days. Can't you see how mama loves it. Let her have some joy, in her dying days. But I will sell it. You are right, of course. As always. What use is it? This big, blank, dull screen . . .' imitating her voice good-naturedly, and with a wink and a smile, 'I know, I know. Just give me some time. I have to be careful, you know. The cops are on the lookout these days for stolen goods. Who knows where this came from! You don't want me getting into any trouble? Do you now? Let some time pass. When it is safe.

'And I will buy you the most beautiful silk dress you ever saw in your life. Red as your lips, smooth as your ass. Your body is not old. It is still young and beautiful, more beautiful than the first day I ever saw you . . .' And he took Bernardette in his arms and gave her a strong manly kiss, after which he knew she would forgive him anything, no matter how stupid. For stupid was the worst he ever was. He had never done anything really bad in his entire life. Not the way he looked at life. And she knew it, and she loved him for it – and for more . . .

## Of the street, in the streets; and off the wall

It was a very humid, very hot day. You could have poached an egg on the pavement.

The Alianza market was busy and colourful as usual, swarming with locals and tourists, vendors and buyers, dogs and the odd cat, a crowd of crows and other less boisterous birds, all making their contribution to life, business and atmosphere.

Pelon was having a smoke with Margarita in one corner of the square. Margarita, thirteen, heavily pregnant, gave her two-year-old son the glue jar hidden in a brown paper bag to have a sniff at so he would stop snivelling about being hungry. He became quiet and peaceable soon enough. She passed the bag on to Pelon, but he waved it away, cocking his head towards her belly and giving her a look – a look he held for a couple of seconds, hoping she would get his meaning. She gave him a look back, shrugged her shoulders, took a long, deep drag at the butt end of the cigarette stuck in her mouth until the little red ring of fire at its base nearly burnt her lips, then, tonguing out whatever little was left of the papery tobacco, blew perfect smoke rings that hung about lazily in the air before dispersing in the hazy heat of the afternoon – staggeringly still, despite the hustle and bustle of the market.

Pelon, trying to imitate Margarita, had a cough attack. The cigarette end stuck to his lower lip and he nearly scorched his fingers trying to tear it away – and no smoke rings, more like crooked fingers of smoke. Margarita's face opened out with a huge, superior grin, and she began to giggle in a hiccuppy manner while hiding her yellowy-grey teeth and angry red gums with her brown glue bag. Pelon let out a hollow yell of a laugh of his own to cover his embarrassment and was about to say something simply to say something when, from the edge of his eyes, he saw Omar, sitting cross-legged, yogi style, at the far end of the street. This gave

Pelon an excellent excuse to get away from Margarita and the situation. With a wink and a flick of his fingers to indicate he'd be back, he ran straight up to Omar – just escaping being run over by the first of a set of three stretch limousines, white – and stood in front of him, his small figure towering over the even smaller boy, feet wide apart, hands on hips.

Omar jerked, as if electrified. He was a four-foot-something seven-year-old, with spider-leg legs, spider-leg arms, a huge bumble-bee head and moose eyes. His first impulse was to up and run, but then, gritting his teeth, he looked up at the nearly-five-foot, ten-year-old, matchstick-legged, toothpick-armed, thimble-chested Pelon with a defiant air, mouth clamped tightly, hands covering some candy and stuff in his lap which he had stolen and was now trying to sell.

'You've been told to keep out of here,' hissed Pelon, with less authority in his voice than he would like to have had.

'Your friend, the fat one with funny ears and a bad stink, he told me to keep out of Rivas. You can't keep me out of everywhere. Your lot don't own the streets!' Omar sounded big for his size.

'We do!' Pelon found his voice getting stronger. 'We live on the streets. The streets belong to us, we belong to the streets. Your kind just come out here to make a few bucks and then go back, to your *homes*!' He dragged the word 'homes' out as long as he could, and as sarcastically as possible, unaware of the envy that crept into it, 'To your *mamas* and *papas* . . . The streets are *our* home, and we don't want outsiders barging in and taking what's ours.' He and his mates had been kicked out of places often enough by others; it felt good to have the power to do it to someone else.

The relationship between the children *of* the streets and the children *in* the streets was never an easy one. Violent at worst, wary at best.

Those *in* the streets came to work, during the day or night, depending on the nature of their work. They came to beg. Or sell: cigarettes or water – or themselves or whatever. To shine shoes.

To sing and dance; put hugely blown-up balloons on their bums and chests, and thick coats of make-up on their faces to look grotesque and amuse and entertain. Or just steal. They had some sort of a home to return to when they finished, when they had earned a loaf of bread or a bag of glue. And even if they did not have anyone to look after them, there was someone they had to look after – siblings, a parent; even two parents.

Those *of* the streets also begged or sold or were sold or did some or most of the things that those *in* the street did, but they had nowhere to go back to when their day, or night, was done. Nowhere except the pavement or a shop front, an abandoned factory, a burnt-out house or an underground sewer or a friendly tree or a protective bush. And no one to go back to, except each other.

Before Omar could reply to Pelon, Pelon suddenly leant over and catching hold of Omar by the shoulders whispered close to his ears, softly, conspiratorially, 'Stand up, stand up. Quickly.' Then added, 'Have you any money on you?'

'You'll have to kill me first . . .' Omar stood up, shakily. Out of his lap dropped a bar of chocolate, some throat lozenges, three packets of chewing gum and a packet of cigarettes. He was near to tears and going the colour of old rust, 'You are not taking . . . my Pop will kill me if . . .' Pelon shut him up by putting a hand on his mouth.

'Listen, stupid! See that pig? Out there,' Pelon pointed with his free hand to a policeman standing on the other end of the street. 'He will come to you in a sec and ask if you have made any money? If you say yes, he will take it. If you say no, he'll beat you up. Or take you to jail. Make up your mind what you want. Or get lost for a while. And hide that stuff.'

Pelon was tempted by the bar of chocolate and nearly stooped to pick it up; but then he saw the hunger and pain in the frightened eyes of the scrawny little kid in front of him, trying hard to be a man. It reminded him so of another little boy – himself. He didn't like the new man his mother had brought into their room.

He used to beat him up, made him eat dirt when he was hungry, and once cut his head open with a knife. When he went crying to his mother, blood dripping, she said, *If you don't like him, you will have to leave home.* And so he did, an open wound in his head. The wound got infected and he lost most of his hair soon after. That was how he became known as El Pelon, the Bald One, and was still called Pelon, Baldy, even though that was three years ago and he had grown his hair back, except for a narrow, meandering scar from the top of his left ear to the centre of his scalp, like a dried-up river bed running roguishly through the forest of his roughish dark hair.

Pelon looked again at the bar of chocolate, lustily, but looked away. Let the bony boy one keep his chocolate. *He* had had quite a few recently. The Crow Boy had 'earned' some rich guy's wallet, or had great luck at the shops, and got all of them loads of sweets, and many other things besides. Big, *important* things! Pelon couldn't even bring himself to wear the beautiful new jumper he had got, even though he always felt a bit cold, even when it was warm.

He was about to move away when Omar, gathering up his stolen merchandise and stuffing it inside his shirt, grabbed him by the sleeve and said, 'Is he one of the bad cops my Mom . . . ?'

'No,' interrupted Pelon, 'he is one of the better ones. The bad ones come at night. And if *they* get you, you'll have nothing and no one to worry about.' And with that he disappeared round the corner leaving Omar to make of it what he liked.

After a moment's petrifaction, Omar leapt back to life and with the nose of an anxious little puppy soon sniffed out Pelon among the crowd and was by his side tugging at his shirt. 'Can I stay with you?' He raised his sad moose eyes and looked deep into Pelon's wary-boy eyes with a pleadingly questioning, worriedly hopeful look. 'Just for a while. As long as that . . . that cop is here. I won't be any bother, I swear, on my mother . . .'

Pelon opened his mouth, shut it again, sighed, shrugged his shoulders and carried on walking, Omar tagging alongside. They had hardly gone a few yards when each boy felt a strong hand, descending with a sudden and decisive swish from somewhere behind them and landing on their necks. The hand didn't hurt; and they could have run out from under it but were too taken aback even to try.

## A strange stranger

*Resisting arrest* was something Pelon had done before and would do again, regardless of consequences, but somehow there was a different feel to this situation. Before he could even think of how to react, a forceful and resonant, yet somehow unthreatening, almost comforting, voice said, 'Would you boys like to eat something?' A tall man, thin-faced, greying hair, dressed in a light blue suit, white shirt and a red tie, insinuated himself between the two, releasing their necks and putting an arm around each, loosely, but with the promise of a tightening hold, if necessary.

'Yes, please,' Omar was the first to speak.

'Then come with me.' His arms still around them, he gently but firmly steered the children towards a café that sprawled out on to the pavement, yet was contained within a decorative fencing of lattice-work, blue-painted, about eighteen inches high.

The man let go of the children, pushed open a small, symbolic, lattice-work door, entered the open-spaced eating area, and motioned to the children to follow him. A smartly dressed waiter immediately stepped forward and, with a verbal and gestural apology to the man, turned towards the children, face metamorphosing from sycophantically smiling and ingratiatingly pleasant to ugly harsh, and began to shoo them away with both hands.

'If they don't come in, I don't,' said the man, making an austere courtesy to the waiter.

There was a momentary flicker of uncertainty in the white-and-green-clad waiter's dark brown, puppy eyes – he looked eighteen but could have been younger. Lowering his eyelashes and shrugging his shoulders and turning his hands palm-side up, he relented. Had the man been a local, he might have put his foot down, but this man was so obviously a tourist, and so obviously of the well-heeled variety, that he had to concede. The man pressed a ten-dollar bill, American, in one of the waiter's innocently upturned palms, and ignoring the look of absolutely astonished surprise on the boy-waiter's face, disregarding the curious eyes of the assorted variety of clientele already within the latticed enclosure, guided the street boys towards a set of four comfortable-looking white-painted straw chairs to the left, next to the pedestrian walkway with all its vibrant busyness.

The man picked up the menus and, keeping one for himself, handed another to the boys, 'Choose anything you like, anything!' he said in his quiet, hypnotic voice, as his eyes began to peruse the menu to make his own selections.

Omar looked at Pelon who pretended to be absorbed in the menu while thinking of Pepsi. *He* would have been able to read *all* of it, he had no doubt. The shuffling of their collective feet and the shifting of their eyes made the man realise they couldn't read. He should have known.

'I am sorry, I'll tell you what is here, and you can . . .'

'Please, please, sir,' Pelon felt he had to hold his heart in both his hands lest it fluttered itself to death, 'Please. My . . . my sister is round the corner. Can I bring her over, too. She is very hungry. She . . . she has a baby to feed,' he turned ghostly pale as he said this last. Perhaps the man did not like babies, or would decide it was taking too much advantage of his generosity – whatever his motives, Pelon was not naive enough not to think the man might have some reasons of his own. But for the time it didn't matter. All that mattered was food. For himself. And more so for Margarita. She didn't hang around with them normally and so the Crow Boy hadn't seen her recently to have got anything for her, or fed her even. Jesus only knew when she last ate, properly. It wasn't easy stealing with one baby tagging along, another in the belly. Helped to beg, sometimes, if the coppers didn't interfere or take what you made. Not that all did. Some looked the other way; one even put a penny in your bowl. But you never knew what to expect. Sometimes you up and ran from a kind one, at others you

132

sat around and got done by the other kind. Of course, after a while, you came to know many of them; but never all. Besides, duty rosters changed, new ones came along . . .

'I am sorry,' the man leaned forward, looked into Pelon's eyes, and smiled, 'I should have asked. Sure. You can bring them along. In the mean time, I'll order. If you let me know what you like . . . she likes. The food could be here by the time you get back. Go. Bring her along.'

'Anything. Any food,' said Pelon as he stood up to go. Omar tried to get up and follow him but Pelon pushed him down. The man might go away, if left on his own; change his mind. 'Stay here. I'll be back in the shake of a tail.'

The man beckoned to the waiter, 'Let the boy back in, please. He's gone to fetch his sister. She's hungry!' He gave a nod and a wink which the waiter didn't know how to interpret, and didn't try.

Pelon wasn't too surprised when Margarita didn't seem terribly excited over the prospect of a free meal. He snatched the glue bag from her hands and threw it away. One young man in trendy black gear, buoyantly walking on the balls of his feet, swinging his hips and whistling a Ricky Martin tune, gave them a look back; but a number of other people pushed past them in both directions without paying any attention. Though they were in one of the back alleys of the market where it was relatively quieter, the human traffic was still heavy, either going into or returning from the main square.

He had to more or less lift her up from the pavement and make her walk, carrying the little boy in his arms.

This time the poor waiter nearly had an apoplectic fit: Margarita's hair were matted with dirt, her clothes no more than tattered rags, the little boy was naked with dried-up snot all over his face and hands. He held up his trembling hands and looked pleadingly at the man, 'Please, sir . . . I can't . . . My boss . . . my job . . . ! *Please*, sir . . .'

The man thought for a moment, walked up to the waiter and put a twenty-dollar bill in his hand. 'Lay a table for us outside this trellis. Away from your customers. And here is another twenty dollars. Give it to that girl,' pointing to a waitress, 'if she would take this girl to the ladies' room and clean her and the child up a bit. And get her and the child something to wear from one of the stalls. Bill me for it, whatever.'

Twenty American dollars was far more than either of their salaries. He agreed, as did the waitress.

Had she not been as much out of the world as she was, Margarita might have resisted, strongly, any attempt at being cleaned and washed by a stranger in a strange place. As it was, she went along in quite a docile manner, and came back looking quite 'acceptable': head covered in a scarf, her big belly hidden behind a nearly new, billowy, flowered dress reaching down to her ankles. The boy had clean baggy shorts on, a couple of sizes too large for him, held up by a ribbon of sorts. After the makeover, food! Fairy-tale food! For the first time in her young (if with a nearing-its-end-look about it) life, Margarita was beginning to feel almost human.

Once the meal was over, complete with desserts and coffee and milk-shakes and a cigar for the man, he asked if they would like to go anywhere, anywhere 'I could drop you off'; then after a pause and a drag at his cigar, 'Have you got a home to go to?'

'I have!' chirped Omar. His words seem to catch the man a bit off guard, but he regained his poise and asked the boy exactly where he lived.

'But I can't go home, not just yet,' said Omar, remembering his 'goods for sale' and fishing them out of his shirt front, 'I have still not sold . . . My Mom . . . Pop . . .' he fumbled for words as he felt the chocolate bar had half melted and gone all soggy. He felt like crying. If he had not had *the* most wonderful meal of his entire life, of *anybody's* entire life, so far as he knew – he *would* have cried. Pelon too eyed the chocolate. He might as well have eaten it. He could still eat it, even though his stomach was stuffed full up to his throat.

'Do not worry,' said the man, 'I'll buy these off you. How much did you want for them?' and without waiting for a reply took out a wad of notes from his wallet, this time in the local currency, and handed a few out to Omar while taking the sweets etc. from his hands and laying them down on a plate on the table.

'As for you,' said the man, looking in turn at Pelon and Margarita, 'if you do not have a home to go, I can take you to a place I think you will like. And if you do, you can invite some of your other friends there too!' So saying, he fished out a mobile phone from the inside pocket of his jacket and spoke softly into it. Moments later, a stretch limousine, white, arrived and parked itself on the road beside them. A liveried chauffeur stepped out of it and waited by the pavement, trying not to have a look of reverential curiosity on his withered, leathery brown, heavily moustached face.

## Angels

'Angels! God's little angels!' said the woman with the crow's nest on her head, being the first to be set free.

That seemed to be the general sentiment among the five when all were released. They all spoke with a strange accent which the children had to concentrate to understand, and they spoke to each other in a strange language which Pepsi believed was French.

Once the initial excitement of release (for the captives), and the shock of discovering them (for the children), was past its peak, there was a flurry of conversation: comments, questions by the group amongst themselves and to the children, alternating between two languages while shaking their legs, jumping up and down, bringing their legs back to life, massaging their own and each other's shoulders, rubbing the palms of their hands together, opening and shutting their mouths, licking their lips, spreading their arms out to the sides and back down again, bending over and touching their toes, feeling the skin of their faces, taking long deep breaths, shaking their heads and turning their necks round and round . . . not to mention hugging and kissing Maria and Pepsi and Alex and Jaime and the Cat Boy.

'*Oh, you wonderful, wonderful angels . . .*'

'Let's hurry out of here before they get back . . .'

'They haven't been for two days . . .'

'*Where are you from? How did you . . . ?*'

'I don't think they are coming back.'

'You can never tell . . .'

'*Did someone send you here?*'

'Oh, don't be silly. How can any one *send* them here . . . !'

'I think they just left us to die . . .'

'What use are we to them dead? They have to be back!'

'What if they've been caught! Then they . . .'

'*Are you all right, children? You look . . .*'

'Had they been caught someone would have come to save us . . .'

'Only if they opened their mouths to *tell* where we were.'

'They *did* tell! And the powers that be sent us the kids! I'm telling you . . .'

'O yeah! Be serious . . .'

'*Are you hungry, kids? We are. Have you any food . . . ?*'

'For God's sake! Are you now going to take food from the . . .'

'Let's first get out of here . . .'

'I have to go somewhere first . . .'

'So have I.'

'I need some water, NOW!'

'I am dying of hunger.'

'I am just dying.'

'I never felt better in my life. I am happier than I have ever been . . .'

'Let's first get out of here! Pleeeaaase!'

'*Oh, my little angels! Come here, my little . . .*'

'Yeah! I agree. You can be as happy as you like and we are very happy for you to be happy; but let us just get out of here now.'

'I think I'm going to be sick.'

'Wait till we get out of here.'

'I can't . . .'

And so on and so on . . .

With all the hugs and kisses that the children got, and the love that seemed to flow out of the five adults despite their condition – their fear, their hunger, their exhaustion – Pepsi began to feel he was already in Heaven. Not Maria's Heaven, but the real thing! And perhaps, after all, he *was* something, somebody; not just nothing, not really!

## Another day in Heaven

'Look what I found!' shouted Cristiano, chubby face glowing like a bronzed apple, chubby little right arm raised, chubby little thumb and chubby little forefinger holding up something round, red and insignificant, tousled auburn hair very nearly on fire in the radiant heat of the midday sun.

Angelina took a quick sharp look at the object in Cristiano's hand in case he had really found something better than her. In good times there was always an unspoken competition going on between those two. During bad days they were only too happy to get what they got. Sara didn't seem to care much either way. She went about her business with her hands and feet in trash and her mind and heart in a world only she inhabited. No one could tell what she was thinking, not even Bernardette, who knew her family, including her in-laws, better than they knew themselves.

These were good times. The best since Maria went missing. They even had the sparkling new wide-screen television sitting on its sparkling new steel stand where once the old dresser stood on its crippled legs.

'It's only a button,' scoffed Angelina, now well past her tenth birthday and veteran among the children of the young families in their tier of the neighbourhood. Most here were either the quite young, or old ones whose children had grown up and left, or just left.

'But it is a *red* button,' said Cristiano, peering at it in the half-light of the pre-dawn sky, a sulky righteousness creeping into his triumph, 'like the one Mama lost from her red dress. She'll need it . . .'

'No, she won't!' said Angelina, 'Papa is going to buy her a new dress, a new red dress. Of pure silk. Once he has sold our TV.'

'I don't want our TV sold,' moaned Cristiano, vaguely aware that that might mean denying his mother a new red dress, of pure silk; and feeling uncomfortable – without quite making the connection between the two undercurrents of thought running through his mind.

'Why not? It's only sitting there, doing nothing.'

'It's not! It's not!' screamed Cristiano, 'Nana watches it, all the time.'

Angelina made a face at him, at which he rushed angrily towards her, hands made out into claws, dropping the red button in the process.

He was upon her before she could step aside and by the sheer force of surprise impact threw his elder and stronger sister on the sea of garbage, face down. The raggedy bag hanging from her left shoulder came off, spilling out Angelina's harvest: a few empty cans of assorted soft drink cans; a rather scary-looking, half-bald Barbie doll, the remaining half of its straw-like blonde hair sticking out at all odd angles and covered in some gooey stuff; and a table leg. Not much, but the day had just begun. The sun would be up soon, the light would be brighter, and booty would be easier to find. But the kids had learnt to feel things by touch so well they could fill a bag blindfolded. They quite enjoyed this early morning 'run' before washing up for school.

Sara didn't seem to care. She went about her business with her hands and feet in trash, her mind and heart in a world only she inhabited.

From her perch on the terrace-on-stilts that surrounded the wooden shack of the Zapata family, Vivecca saw the sun fooling around with Cristiano's unruly auburn hair as he and the girls were making their way back home. From this distance the boy could have been Maria. A vein in Vivecca's neck began to throb, sending pulsating shots of pain through the right side of her head. The presence of the boy often did this to her, and she tried to keep him away, or keep away from him; which was the same thing, but not quite.

Cristiano and Maria were the only two who had inherited her hair. The hair of her youth. Strangely, when Maria was around, she gave most of her attention and affection to the boy. But since the girl had . . . gone . . . a change had come over her, a change she could not explain to herself. The sight of the boy upset her. It broke his heart, and hers too, but there was nothing she could do about it.

If only she could talk about it to someone.

If only Ronaldo was here. Her husband.

She had married him for better or for worse. But it had only been better and better, day after day. Till the day he died. It was then that the worse began. With the hurricane that took him. The hurricane, the rain and the mud. The rivers of mud. The sea of mud. Devoured him. And their house, with everything they owned or cherished and loved. And her little girl. Alma. So very much like Maria. When she was around she found it hard to deal with her. Now she could think of no one else but her. She wasn't always sure whether she meant Maria, or Alma. Alma, the best beloved of her father. Died clinging to him. She could still see them both, in their last moments, when Luis pulled her away to safety. Nolsen got hurt and was never the same again, in mind, body or heart. And now he was gone too. Carlos was just a baby then. If she hadn't been holding on to him, she could have held on to Ronaldo. Perished with him, like Alma. They could have spent an eternity in each other's arms, drenched with happiness, soaking with joy, blessed by the Lord. She had never forgiven herself for not being with him to the last. Nor Carlos for clinging on to her when she could have held on to her husband, her lover, her friend. Nor Luis for taking her away from him.

Still, Luis had been good to her. And his brothers. Took care of them, unwed and wed. And Bernardette had looked after her like she was her own mother. She had a great deal to be thankful for to the Lord. A great deal. And yet, and yet, it wasn't always easy.

# More of ancestors and angels

It turned out three of the group in the cave were from Médecins Sans Frontières – not that *that* meant anything to the children; but they did understand that they were doctors, from another country. France. Pepsi knew about it. He had always wanted to see the Eiffel Tower and to dance and sing on its very top with all of Paris looking up at him from down below. He would sure be something then!

The doctors were here in a neighbouring country to look after the people still living in makeshift refugee camps since last year's hurricane; diarrhoea, cholera and other diseases were spreading widely all over the place. The other two, the blonde young woman and the balding young man, were from the French Embassy. They were taking the doctors for a drive through the country when, on a lonely sandy stretch of road, their vehicle was held up by two jeeps blocking their path. Three men carrying rifles, wearing black baseball caps, faces hidden behind bandanas, stepped out of one of the jeeps and ordered them out . . .

They were blindfolded, their hands tied behind their backs, and ordered into the second jeep. They were taken to a bungalow about three hours' drive away where they were untied, their blindfolds removed and they were made to make a couple of phone calls and write two letters. At first they were kept in reasonable comfort in a pleasant enough room. But then, about two weeks later, something happened to change their captors' attitude. Either a disagreement among themselves, or some threat or disappointment from outside. They were heard arguing and shouting at each other for almost an entire day. Some time during the night they came into their room, blindfolded and tied them once again, got them into what felt and sounded like a dilapidated old pick-up and drove around for what must have been hundreds of miles, most likely crossing a border or two. They were brought to this cave and tied to a free-standing pillar-like projection, and gagged; though their blindfolds were taken away. That was about a week ago. For the first four or five days the kidnappers came round once every day with a supply of some food and water. They hadn't for the last two days.

The children shared some food they had with the doctors and their friends – packets of crisps and sweets, bread, cheese – which they devoured while making their way down and out of the cave as quickly as possible in case their kidnappers came.

Once outside, they had no idea where they were or which way to go. The dirt road Pepsi and the children had been on last night seemed to have vanished without a trace. Pepsi knew that they were no more than a day's walk away from the capital. But in which direction? He had no idea. He was a city boy and had never gone much beyond his father's house, which was in the opposite direction anyway. They had taken a bus to the little village of Potosi, famous for its flower market, and then walked north. He had simply followed directions based on topographical landmarks given to him by the Crow Boy: a red mound with its head on one shoulder, a crooked tree bowing to the rising sun, a criss-crossing ditch . . . Eventually they were to come to the small town of Puebla, from where they could board a train or take a bus.

The sketch which Pepsi had made of the 'road map', if it could be called that, had got wet last night and faded away to nothingness. He could recall most of the landmarks, but not necessarily in the right order; and besides, he had to get to one of those first before trying to work his way forward or backwards. He began to experience, with claustrophobic gloom, what he had feared from the start: his skills as a survival guide through unfamiliar and quite possibly hostile territory were not up to scratch. The Crow Boy had warned him as much.

They were in a spectacularly stunning landscape of eerily dazzling wilderness. To the west, in the distance, rose spectres of rows and rows of sky-kissing mountains surrounded by a hazy, lazy, bluish mist; earthy brown hills littered with glimmering, sunlit patches of verdurous vegetation just behind them. In front, an endless spread of desert flowers of all colours and hues and shapes and sizes; prickly pears, boojum trees, barrel cacti and saguaro and the giant cereus, all springing out of a golden sea of sand breaking with waves of scattered rocks. Pepsi tried to look for the tall tree El Gato had climbed last night, but could see no sign of it, or any other tree of similar stature. Whichever way they looked they met with the same undifferentiated splendour, the same unmitigated beauty.

The balding young man was trying to figure out his north from his south, but since the sun was almost at zenith point he was having difficulty telling his east from his west.

Just then, somewhere a long way away, blew a long, hoarse whistle, followed by a chug chugging chug chugging chug chugging . . . drawing ever closer, and closer . . .

For a longish instant it almost went unnoticed.

'A train!' Pepsi was the first to shout as he jumped in the air.

'If there is a rail track here it shouldn't be too difficult to find,' exclaimed the woman doctor with such excitement that the bird's nest on her head shook ever so violently and Pepsi feared it might drop off, exposing an unnaturally pink skull to match her unnaturally pink skin.

'We can follow the track,' said the blonde young woman, equally excited, 'It is bound to lead us . . .'

'We need follow it nowhere. Probably die of exhaustion and dehydration before we get to some habitation,' said the blond doctor. 'We should just sit by the track, wait for the next train, and when it is approaching, stand in front of it, all of us . . .'

'It will mow us down, silly boy,' said the thatch-headed, bird-nested one.

'This is not going to be one of your high-speed French trains,' said the balding young man, 'Probably a run-down freight train or a tired old overloaded passenger carrier with a half-asleep driver bored out of his mind who will only be too glad for some excite-

143

ment. I am sure it will stop. Especially with ten of us blocking its way.'

'*Five!*' the wavy-haired one raised his palm in the air and spread out his fingers, 'I doubt if they'll take any notice of poor little local kids.'

'On their own, perhaps not,' said the balding young man, 'but alongside us, it will add to the overall impact.'

The wavy-haired one shrugged his shoulders, the rest nodded agreement.

The children didn't understand the language of the doctors and their friends, but they had got the general idea even before the balding young man tried his Spanish on them.

The ten of them began hurrying towards the direction of the sound.

## Night of the bad cops

La Casita was a derelict building, once housing a cinema that hadn't seen a movie in years. Now it was an illegal garbage dump; and behind all the filth and rubbish, it housed cardboard boxes that housed some of the city's homeless and, among them, an itinerant community of street kids.

It was to La Casita – about twenty miles from the city centre beyond a now abandoned housing development which never quite took off, due to shortage of money or fraud or political incompetence or a combination of all three – that officer Raffo, officer Domingo and Caddy were now heading, boisterously, pumped up with drink and jokes and righteousness, occasionally patting their guns with affectionate pride.

It was to be their big night out!

'You should've seen the limo!' Pelon said for the umpteenth time, shaking his head from side to side, as if disbelieving the memory of his own eyes, mistrustful of his own experience.

Sitting in the desolation of what once might have been the auditorium of the cinema in La Casita, he was telling his excited audience the story of his day.

After dropping off Omar as close to his home as possible – there was no navigable road beyond that point – the man in the red tie and the blue suit had leaned forward and whispered something to his chauffeur, and they began a long drive through picturesque country roads until they came to a walled enclosure. Margarita, who had started to show signs of discomfort for some time, turned deathly pale and held on to Pelon as the man suggested that Margarita and Pelon go with him into a rambling old house inside the enclosure.

Margarita been there before, and wasn't sure she wanted to again.

It was a non-religiously run home for abandoned or abused children.

Surprisingly, after a grumpy and rebellious bout, Margarita agreed to 'give it another try', but only after she was assured that her previous running out would not be held against her, nor would she be rebuked for getting pregnant again. Last time round she had stolen quite a few things from there, including some boxes of condoms – but only to sell when she 'escaped'.

Pelon opted out of the offer of the home, and went back to join the gang. The Crow Boy was sharing out the goodies bought by the money left by Pepsi. Most of them had never had it so good, and it was a good time for a laugh all round.

During the babble of conversation – questions, answers, remarks, ejaculations and exclamations of wonder and disbelief and envy and joy that followed Pelon's highly coloured account of what happened – the Crow Boy was strangely overtaken by a peculiar feeling of isolation, of not belonging. Without a word he walked away, and seating himself on an overturned cardboard box, back resting against a stony wall, began taking in deep breaths of fresh air. But it was difficult. Despite the cool night and the open air, it was as if he was in a hot airless place. As if all the oxygen in the atmosphere was being consumed by some fire, fire that was burning the place up, making it hot, and hotter by the second. Or as if he was in a sweat lodge, naked, a thick woollen blanket wrapped around his body. The blanket, with a pattern of bright yellow stars and a full moon – the night sun – in its centre, had been lovingly and painstakingly woven by his grandmother over many months, especially for this occasion, and later for him to be buried in, when the time came. The heat from the red-hot stones, glowing in the heart of the narrow cave-like space, reached out to him with the ferocity of a jealous lover; and when his relatives, both dead and alive, came to pour water over the burning rocks, the fuming steam ascended in drunkenly wayward vapours and enveloped him, making him light-headed. A curious indescribable wave of panic rose from the back of his neck and started to shoot up and down his spine. To calm himself he stretched out an uncertain hand to pick up one of the steaming rocks and light a smoking pipe, *the* pipe: the pipe carved and smoothed out of the mystical red stone; the pipe belonging to his great, great ancestors; the pipe that his grandfather had carefully cleaned and polished and left by his side . . .

He was brought back from this world that no longer was to the here and now by the phlegmy cough of an old man reclining against a box not far from him. The transition somehow added to his light-headedness and a claustrophobic feeling of dread squeezed at the muscles of his heart. With a helplessness he could neither explain nor understand, he watched the old man pull a box of matches out of a pocket of his tattered trousers, strike a match alight, and fumble for a cigarette in his shirt pocket. He was clearly drunk, his hands unsteady. His attempt to put the cigarette between his lips failed and it rolled down on to the cracked floor below. The man tried to bend over to pick it up with one hand, still holding on to the lit match between the thumb and forefinger of his other hand. Suddenly, with a squeaky yell, he flung out his arm and threw the burning match to his right as far as it would go.

Whether it fell on some liquor from a bottle broken by a kid or a parent or the man himself, or on some solvent lying about, a thin line of pulsating fire suddenly came alive and careered across the broken floor, followed by the bursting open of a gigantic flower of flame; its petals, stretching out like tongues of some satanic lizards, reached out to some tinder-dry boxes . . .

By the time officer Raffo, officer Domingo and Caddy drove up close to La Casita, an angry fire was violently busy, hungrily devouring the ramshackle remains of the building; its many and multifarious red and gold wings seemed to flutter out to the skies and beyond, setting the blackness of the night alight with their fierce glory, the stars fading away to give way to the quirky, dis-embodied sparks of flame that crackled and bristled wildly and randomly in the atmosphere. The greyish black smoke, floating and flying in and around, infused the whole scene with a myste-rious, mythical, mystical aura. It was an awesomely beautiful sight, so majestic in its splendour that even the aesthetically untuned threesome gawped at it, open-mouthed, almost running the car into a lamp-post by the pavement. Not that they would have realised it was beauty they were admiring.

Stopping at a safe distance, all three got out of the car, their guns all ready and cocked, even in the circumstances. They could hear screams and shouts, saw people fleeing in all directions, some groggy with sleep, others with drink or drugs, not entirely sure what was happening.

'Our work is being done by the Lord!' Domingo lifted his arms up to the skies, 'Burning up all this dross in the hell they deserve . . .'

'I think we had better get back,' said Caddy, nervously edging backwards from the heat of the fire.

'Fuck, no,' shouted Raffo, 'not before we've had some fun with this lot!' So saying, he aimed his gun at no one in particular and began to fire randomly in the general direction of anyone he could see.

He scored a hit as the fire highlighted one person going down with a scream. This encouraged the other two, and they too began to shoot at whoever was in the range of their vision, howling glee-fully at every hit, cursing the misses.

'Fire into the fire, send them from the hell of this life to the hell of afterlife,' Domingo screamed a laugh and looked at Raffo and Caddy for approval, believing he had come up with a witti-cism that was both earthy and holy.

It was only the sound of wailing sirens that made them stop and hurriedly put their guns away in their belts.

Soon there was a fire engine, a couple of police cars and any number of TV crew on the scene.

Raffo recognised one of the policemen who came out of one of the police cars. He walked up to him and spoke, 'We tried our best to help these poor people here, Marisol,' he waved his arms in a circular motion in the air, 'but there was nothing much we could do.'

'You must be in shock, sir,' said the policeman, looking first at Raffo, and then at the other two who had come up to stand beside him – and indeed they did look quite peculiar – 'just get back in your car and try to relax. We'll do what we can.' And so saying he and another policeman joined a couple of firemen who were trying to get some hobo types away from falling chunks of burning concrete. Marisol, a modest man by nature, felt a bit guilty over feeling glad that he had this opportunity to show his superior officers that he was willing to risk his own life to save the lives of a few wretched, desperate sods.

## On screen and off


Caddy should have left for his Pepsi-hunt that day, but last night had been quite exhausting, more so than he had realised at the time, and he couldn't even bring himself to get out of his bed in the morning, much less out of the city. His wife and mother had decided to take advantage of the situation and treat themselves to the rare pleasure of leaving Caddy to look after Juan junior and going out on their own, 'looking at shops, streets and people', even buying something they could afford. There were times when both the older and the younger woman wished Caddy would bring home some more money, like many of the other officers did: 'taking care' of shops and businesses, doing 'favours' to people and accepting 'gifts' in return. But Caddy was 'too good' a man for that, according to Anna; 'gutless', according to the mother.

Caddy relaxed back in his favourite sofa, a light blanket thrown over himself; Juan, open-mouthed and breathing some-what heavily, slept by his side, head tucked into the bend in his father's waist.

With one hand gently ruffling the boy's hair, with the other gently masturbating himself, Caddy was watching some home improvement/DIY programme on their rather ancient telly. Last night's tiredness had still not entirely left his limbs or his eyes, and he dozed off for a while only to be woken up by a louder, more strident and persistent voice droning into his ears. The midday TV news. Not his favourite. He was about to get up and switch to another channel – the remote control had broken down and he had not got round to replacing it yet – when he saw a few uniformed police officers on the screen in a familiar setting. He sprawled back once more. Always good to see what the force was up to, even though the uniforms of this lot were somewhat different from his.

It was about some kidnapping. Not too unusual in some parts, but still, always interesting to hear about. Some French people this time. If most of that lot stayed where they belonged, there would be less of all this, he thought, and was about to elaborate this point to himself when he was hit by high-voltage electricity. Or it felt like it. He sat bolt upright, eyes popping out of his sockets, staring at the screen with hypnotic intensity.

The scene had shifted from a studio set-up and the chief of police with some of his henchmen answering the questions of assembled journalists to the forecourt of the French Embassy where the ex-abductees were being debriefed. And there, standing alongside some foreign-looking men and women, there, there was *that* kid on the screen. *And* his wretched girl. Along with a couple of others of that losers' lot. All talking to some news guys, *outside the French Embassy across the border* . . . It was Pepsi doing most of the gabbing, with that size fourteen mouth of his!

Caddy could hardly believe his eyes, or his ears. The bloody lot were being treated as some sort of heroes!

It was only after he had had a few beers and walked the length of the room more times than he had pubic hairs that it occurred to him. What a stroke of wonderful luck . . . God was on his side after all.

He now knew *where* the boy was. Thanks be to God. He could get there in just a few hours! He would never have gone that way. He would have gone south, the reverse of the route taken by those coming up here from their filthy shit-ridden slums. Yes, thanks be to God for leading him to the right path. All his tiredness went, like yesterday's sweat, evaporated into thin air like it never was.

If only Anna or his mother was home, he would have left there and then. But it would be hours before they got back. He knew their routine well. They would not come back till . . . till . . . till all the shops were shut and the streets left to dogs and sewer rats – or something like that. He cursed like he had never cursed before, certainly never in front of his boy who was awake now and making hungry noises. But he felt too tense and boiled

151

up inside to attend to him. Waving his clenched fist wildly about in the room he began pacing back and forth all over again, back and forth, back and forth, back and forth . . .

And he began to think of the downside of his good luck. He had planned on contacting the police of every town or village he passed through, describing Pepsi and the girl as dangerous kids, making up some stories of them attacking, *viciously attacking*, maybe even killing some old ladies or whatever – he couldn't tell them he had bungled up his kill *and* let him steal his gun – and so make sure they'd help him catch the little lout and his baby moll. But now he and his gang had been seen as *rescuing* people: foreign people at that, who were always considered more important than local ones. He might have difficulty in trying to convince . . . .

He stopped pacing and slouched back into his sofa, sweating more than just the exercise and the weather warranted.


'Come on, you guys,' said a friendly French voice, ' you're on TV.'

Pepsi and the kids brought their milk-shakes and burgers over to the lounge of the 'safe house' where the group from Médecins Sans Frontières were temporarily staying, not far from the residence of the French ambassador. On the TV screen was a somewhat differently edited version of what Caddy had seen in his house.

'You kids are famous now. This will have been shown all over the world before the evening is out. You should be real proud . . .'

But Pepsi had stopped listening. It took him far less time to realise that Caddy would in all probability now know where they were than it had taken Caddy to get the same fact. Yes, Caddy would know . . .


The TV news was on as Romano tried on a new wig he had ordered from the USA through a trusted friend. It certainly looked much better, more attractive, *more natural*, than his regular one. But, and that was a big but, people would notice his head looked different. Would they attribute it to a different hairstyle? Or a different wig? Would it convince them he had his natural hair all along, the change of style proving it? After all, people with real hair did change styles! Or would it do the opposite and expose him as a serial wig wearer, a toupée shifter?

He wasn't paying much attention to the news, when, from a corner of his eyes, he saw a familiar face, heard a familiar voice. It was Pepsi . . .

His heart sank. Had the boy gone public? Did he really have some proof that he could take to the press and TV, denounce him as a deserter father! Would do his career no good. No good at all. These thoughts and fears passed through his mind within a fraction of a second, only to be replaced by the awareness of what it was really all about.

An unexpected surge of pride began to swell within his breast. He was a good boy, he was. So beautiful to look at: those sad, large eyes, just like his mother's. And that handsome head of thick, curly hair. Nothing like the mousy brown of Tania's mousy brown boys. And so well-spoken, such a refined voice, good vocabulary; nothing like the street kids one heard and saw littering the streets of our good city. His heart ached for him. One day he would have to take the boy to himself. One day. When his position in the country was secure, secure enough to be forgiven the mistakes of his early life. Yes, one day he would proudly display his beautiful boy to the world. One day. One day.

Why not now!

Now that the boy was being hailed as a hero. There were others, too; but all the cameras were on him, he was answering all the questions. What better time to acknowledge him than now!

He would ask Julio to go and get the boy.

Of course, he wouldn't do anything rash, anything hasty, anything stupid. But before he decided on anything, he would like to get hold of the boy, know him, as it were, again; make sure that in his wilderness years he had not been up to something . . . dire, disreputable, desperate . . . something to bring shame upon him, his name, his position . . .

He picked up the phone and rang Julio's mobile.

Anna and his mother were soon back. It had started to thunder and rain, and Constantina didn't like being out in such weather. In fact, she didn't like being anywhere when it thundered – but home was the safest if it couldn't be helped.

Anna could immediately tell that Caddy was in a state of agitation, though whether it was good agitation or bad agitation she couldn't be sure.

'Whatever is the matter, Cad.' She sometimes called him that when she tried to mother him, especially in front of his mother when she was embarrassed to call him names she did in private, even avoiding 'darling' and 'honey'. 'Was Juan a lot of trouble?'

'Oh, no. Not at all. He was diamond good!' *Diamond* was his acceptable variation on 'damned', which he thought was diamond clever of him. Actually he had picked it up from some kid at school years ago, he couldn't even remember who it was any more, and had genuinely begun to believe he had invented the term himself. It was just a word, but it gave him immense pleasure, though he would often forget to use it when it could have been used, and later remember and curse himself for forgetting.

'It is just that . . . I . . . have to go, *now*, you know, go, like I said . . .' He didn't want to say much, but he looked at Anna meaningfully and moved his chin up meaningfully, '. . . you know!'

Constantina looked at both of them even more meaningfully, but it was a jaded meaningfulness rather than a curious one. She got up and started walking out of the room, 'I am going up to change out of my wet clothes,' she said. There were times when she couldn't be bothered with the follies of her son. Anna was welcome to them, and him. After a promising start, it had turned out to be a disappointing day. She wanted a period of quiet and rest, all to herself.

'Why on earth do you want to go *now*,' began Anna, as soon as the mother had gone, 'at least wait until . . .'

Caddy squeezed himself between Anna and the boy as she was taking some sweets and a packet of crisps out of her handbag to give to the hungry Juan, and told her what he had seen on the TV, about Pepsi.

'See! I always told you he was a good lad,' she clapped her hands with delight, dropping some sweets in her lap, 'So, so, what makes you look so . . . . so strange. You should be happy. You have found him, that's what you wanted, isn't it? Isn't it?' she looked into his eyes with a piercing gaze. That was her way of making him tell the truth, which she believed she could always make him do.

'Yes, but . . .'

'But what! And why the hurry in going? You can take it easy now. Call the police there, tell them who you are, and ask them to hold the boy . . . keep an eye on him, till you get there. Simple.'

'Yes, I know *that*. But . . . but, well, what do I tell them? Can't really say he has taken my gun, now, can I? I'd look a real ass then, won't I?'

Anna thought this over for a moment, frowned to herself, then the frown disappeared and her face lit up, 'Why, tell them the truth. The rest of the truth. Tell them you recognise the boy. A runaway. That you know his father, that he is a respectable man, an important man, and would very much like to find his son. So tell them not to let him get lost again till you get there. So there. Romano *is* trying to find him, isn't he? So everything you say will be true. And it will make them keep Pepsi under observation or whatever you call it till you get there. Won't it?'

Caddy couldn't believe what a clever woman he had married. And so good. In bed, and out of it. Then a cloud hit the air. 'But then, they might say *they* will contact the father. But I want to get to him first. If they know his father is an important man, a politician, a future president even, they'll think it'll be worth getting on to his good side, you know how they can be . . .'

'Don't tell them who he is. You can't do that anyway, Romano will fry you for breakfast if you do. Just say he is a very private man. Doesn't want everyone to know about him. Not until he has sorted the matter out with his son. Say you are a family friend . . . which you are . . . and he has asked you to find him, which is right, isn't it . . . see, easy! Don't you worry, I promise, just tell it as it is, and they'll keep the boy for you.'

'And the girl,' he muttered to himself, sneering at the sofa arm, 'mustn't forget the girl . . .'

Just as Pepsi's mind was running round in circles thinking of ways to make a run for it, another item on the TV news caught his attention.

It was a fire.

In a building Pepsi knew well. He had spent many happy nights there, along with many of his best mates. And if that wasn't shocking enough, he saw the face of Caddy behind two officers being interviewed outside it. 'This place is notorious for drug users and sellers . . .' Were *they* there looking for them? And if so did they . . . ?

Pepsi's heart missed a beat. Inside the sky-tall flames, he could swear he saw a crow, a beautiful, shiny crow, a larger-than-life crow, its wings on fire, struggling to fly out . . . It was a trick of the light, the black of the night behind the soaring flames somehow assuming the shape of a fluttering bird for a fleeting moment, but it left him numb and shaking with a fear he could not quite comprehend.

## Choices and decisions

'Will Gato be coming with us?' Maria asked, looking at Pepsi.

'That is for Gato to say,' said Pepsi, looking at El Gato.

'Of course I'll go with you,' Gato almost screamed out his words, 'I don't want to be here. I don't even want to find my cousin any more. I like this life on the road, man, like any red-blooded tomcat!'

The children were on their own on the back terrace while the grown-ups were busy talking in the study across the hall. Pepsi was planning his getaway. But before he could do that, he had to decide: a) who would come with him and b) where to head for, or how, without upsetting or appearing impolite to their hosts who were being so good to them.

They had promised they would find good homes for them, some good people to look after them, love them, take care of them. They were especially fond of little Maria, and the blonde young woman was keen to adopt her for herself. Her term at the embassy was coming to a close, and she wanted to make arrangements to take her back with her to France. But Maria, although she liked the girl very much, wasn't sure about it. Her one experience of being 'adopted and taken to another country' had proved a terrible and terrifying ordeal. And though this was a completely different situation, she could not help associating the one with the other. But most of all, she wanted to go back to her old Heaven, her mother, her father – her home!

'These guys will help you get to Heaven, if you tell them about it. Ask them. Far quicker and safer than I would. And surer!' said Pepsi, his heart breaking within him at the thought of losing Maria, but it was true, and had to be said.

Maria thought it over for a moment. Then, 'I want to go with you, please.'

Pepsi was the only family she had known in the last many months. She wanted to have the best of both worlds. She wanted to get back to her old family, but she did not want to lose her 'new' family – Pepsi – in the process.

Pepsi didn't argue the point, 'All right,' said he, feeling guilty, but relieved, happy. Losing Maria, he would have lost heart. It was the desire, the need, to look after her that drove him on, through the best and the worst.

Alex and Jaime had retreated back to their old selves, El Mudo going silent, and El Ciegito not seeing, though he didn't want to move away from the television. The French doctors said that they needed time and treatment, security and love, which they were willing and able to provide. Pepsi talked it over with the boys, and they chose to stay back. They had not enjoyed their journey so far, and were not too keen on carrying on anyway.

That left El Gato. And to him, adventure and excitement were a great deal more tempting than security and comfort.

'Let's go in and watch some TV,' said Maria. TV was the best thing she liked, and it almost made her want to stay back. But then, they had a TV back home, and with a bigger screen than the one over here!

## In the black of the night

It was a black night. The sky was black. The stars were black. The normally radiant hammock of the quarter night-sun was black. The wind was black. The crow was black.

The black of the crow was lost in all that black; and yet, to Pepsi, it was clear as black in the white of the day-sun.

It hung motionless in the black air, its wings spread out in suspended animation, framed within the open window of the bedroom, as if frozen while trying to fly into the room. But for no more than a second before disappearing into all that black – black that ceased to be black once it disappeared. The stars shone again with their twinkly-eyed brilliance, the quarter moon was resplendent in its pale light, the wind was clear.

Pepsi rubbed his eyes, half-awake now, yet his dream clear in his mind. He looked again at the night outside the window to make sure it was like any ordinary night.

It was. And no sign of a crow. But how come it was open! The window. Pepsi was sure it had been shut. The air-conditioner was still humming away. It wasn't anything new to him. He had it in his father's house, but the others found it fascinating, and given the choice between fresh air and that had opted for it enthusiastically.

On wobbly feet he got up and more or less sleepwalked to the window to shut it. It was only when he was lifting up the frame and a gust of cool wind caught his face that full consciousness returned. *He* himself had opened the window!

To jump out on to the balcony, from there to the patio roof, and then away! With Maria and the Cat Boy. The time had come to go.

An official-looking man, tall with a stoop, a large crop of ginger hair forming a sort of hedge around a bald patch in the centre, greyish-blue eyes and articulate hands, had knocked on their door late that evening. He was met by a local man working for the French Embassy. Within seconds and after a few words exchanged, both were casting quick, interested glances towards Pepsi. The man was soon taken to another room where he remained for about half an hour. On his way out there were more looks for Pepsi. At a wink from Pepsi, the Cat Boy stealthily followed them out, unseen in the dark. Unfortunately, he couldn't understand what they were saying, but he did hear Pepsi's name mentioned a couple of times.

When the local man came back into the house, he looked smilingly at Pepsi, ruffled his hair and gave him a near hug. They were quite used to this affectionate treatment from the French, but it was definitely something new from any of the local men, at least away from French eyes. It was weird. Unsettling. If the visit from the tall, stooping man, and the references to him had engendered mistrust, dislike . . . apprehension, he would have understood it better, been able to cope with it better. But this almost unnatural show of affection was eerily unnerving. He cringed deep within his soul.

Yes. It was time to go. Just go. There was no other way. Nothing he could say to his hosts, whether he told the truth or prevaricated, would make things any easier. Quite the opposite, in fact. They would never allow them just to return to the streets. Even if that man had not turned up. Whoever he was, and whatever he had to say. So it was best just to go. Leave a note of thanks, and go.

That note he put on the table and opened the window, but when he turned to Maria she was fast asleep, cuddled up inside her silky duvet. As was the Cat Boy. Pepsi didn't have the heart to shake them awake and, after a while, plopped into bed next to El Gato – Alex and Jaime were sharing another bed – and fell into a deep sleep himself . . . until woken up by the black dream of the black crow in the black air of the black night. Maria was on a divan by the Turkish carpeted wall. The blonde girl had been wanting to take her to her room to sleep beside her, but Maria had insisted on remaining with the boys. The blonde felt defeated, sad; but understood. *That's how these poor kids on the street manage to survive. By sticking with each other, huddling close to each other. Looking after each other. Even, perhaps, by just looking at each other! To know that they were still there . . .*

More important, in this case, as far as Pepsi was concerned, it would have been difficult to smuggle Maria out if she was in a different part of the house, with another person in the room with her.

But now that zero hour was here, a curious dread began to crawl over his skin. The dream of the black crow framed in the black night in the black air of the window, still floating in the black of his mind, brought a black terror into his heart, a terror so black he could only escape from it by escaping into the light of the night.

He would have to wake up Maria and El Gato, and take it from there . . .

## Strong-arm tactics

On to the balcony, on the patio roof, and on the ground. A brief pause for all to be together and to breathe in the fresh air of the cool night; then forward to the gate, out of the gate, and straight into two pairs of strong, waiting arms. One pair grasping Pepsi, the other Maria.

No amount of shin-kicking and wrist-biting was of any help.

The Cat Boy speedily melted away into the night, unnoticed, rucksack on his back, picking up a small bag Pepsi managed to throw his way.

The two pairs of strong arms belonged to Mario and José, the prime thugs among Tania's seven brothers.

The small bag contained an envelope full of money, and a big, ugly gun!

Hidden among the thick branches of a tall, unnatural-looking tree, imported, one of many lining the avenue, El Gato cater-wauled so loudly and lustily that half the cats in the neighbourhood turned to jelly with an unnamed emotion cruising through their veins . . .

# A cat strike

In the fragile light of the four-day-old moon, from his high point in the tree, the Cat Boy watched the two muscle-jocks as they lifted Maria and Pepsi off the road. José had one arm wrapped round Pepsi's shoulders, pinning his arms, hand over his mouth to stop him from screaming or biting; his other arm was round Pepsi's waist, in a bold, tight hold, allowing his feet to dangle helplessly, just inches above the road. Maria was held in a similar manner by Mario.

Gato was waiting to see which way the men went, so he could clamber down and pussyfoot behind them. Trail them to where they took Maria and Pepsi, and plan a way to get them away. It was a newly built suburb, miles out of the city, with straight, unbending roads, set in a grid pattern. They could only go north or south, until they got to the east–west intersections and, unlike in and around the town centre, could not disappear into the higgledy-piggledy lanes and streets that crisscrossed all over the place, twisting and turning crazily, springing out surprisingly and unexpectedly from the main artery of the city, the Avenida Francisco. The Frenchies, as Gato called them affectionately, had taken them around the town centre, as well as the local neighbourhood, so they knew. Like most street kids, they were good at learning the layout of a place quite quickly. Gato especially.

They started walking towards Gato's direction of the road and stopped below *his* tree . . . It worried him. Did they know he was up there? If they did, the game was up. But how could they! He was just thinking about what to do with the bag containing the money and the gun, in case they had cottoned on to him, when he saw them head towards a car, parked beneath him, just slightly to the left of the branch he was on. He could hardly believe his luck! Sudden change of plans without wasting any time on details . . .

With silent stealth, he got on to the branch directly above the car – there was enough wind about to account for the slight leafy rustle that the drag of his rucksack created – and waited for his moment.

Just as Mario was wiggling about trying to unlock the car while keeping a firm grasp on Maria, Gato dropped the rucksack directly on to his bent back. Simultaneously, with a snarl and a hiss enough to frighten a regiment of cats away, he jumped down upon José's head.

As the utterly and truly stunned brothers cursed and reeled – Mario forwards, José backwards – Pepsi and Maria fell out of their grasp and ran. Gato made a move to reach for his rucksack lying to the right of Mario, but Pepsi turned round and dragged him back by the collar, shouting, 'Run, stupid, run. Forget the stupid . . .'

The brothers, dazed and confused, not sure what had actually happened, stood about with hands raised, open palms saying, 'Whaa the bloo . . . Whaaa the fu . . .', shuffling their feet, feeling their backs and their necks; but soon had the good sense not to throw away precious moments wondering, and began to chase after the children, even though they were out of sight by now. And the night had turned darker, the faint light of the moon disappearing behind a concoction of floating clouds.

## The downside of wearing shorts

They found a cluster of bushes outside the gate of a rambling villa and hid behind them. Although it had gone a bit dark now, Pepsi knew it would soon start getting brighter. He had left it too late to get out of the house, and dawn was not far off. It would be safer to stay hidden, less likely to attract attention, than to keep running.

'We'll stay here until it's safe . . . well, for a while at least,' whispered Pepsi, 'then we'll get out, one by one, and meet at the red garage, you know the one. You go first,' he turned towards Gato, 'after about ten minutes, Maria. I will follow close behind her. We'll hang around in the garage, and when the first bus comes, whenever, we'll hop on it.' The safest place to hide was among the town crowds and the host of street kids that were sure to be there. At least until they made their next move.

The red garage was a large ramshackle structure, quite out of keeping with the tone of the rest of the area. It was at the back of a huge three-storeyed house with overgrown gardens, not far from the embassy house they were in, but in an erratic, angular direction. Almost directly behind the red garage was a bus stop. Anatole, a chauffeur from the embassy, had pointed it out to them while out on a drive to show them around. 'You can catch a bus from here straight to Avenida Francisco,' he had said with a nudge and a wink, 'if ever you want to have a naughty night out in the town.'

Although Pepsi wanted to wait a bit longer, just to make sure, Gato was itching to go, so he said, 'Oh, all right then. But watch out! Wait for us there. For at least an hour. Don't go looking around. Just stay put. If we are longer than an hour, save yourself. Take the bus to town. Maybe meet you there, where other kids hang out.'

Pepsi's instincts had been right. They should have waited some more. Even Gato's catlike movement was enough to create enough stir in the stillness of the night for José to notice some shifting in the bushes as he happened to be walking along that way. He froze. Not wanting to make his presence known, if indeed there was someone behind those bushes.

Walking on tiptoe, his big frame floating like a gigantic ghost through the night, he moved with a silent smoothness hard to believe in one so rough, rugged – and huge. Once by the edge of the bush he had seen move, he could just about see Maria's auburn hair reflecting the moon, now stripped of clouds. He made a sudden but sure lunge forward and managed to grab hold of Maria by the shoulders as she sat crouched on the coarse grass behind it. He lifted her up as easily and lightly as if she were made of cotton wool. Totally unprepared for this situation, Pepsi, who had been crouching beside Maria, jerked his head up with a shock, and all he could see were the flapping legs of the loose, summery shorts that José was wearing. Without thinking what he was doing, he shot his hand up José's leg closest to him, up his shorts, through his boxers, seized his naked testicles and squeezed with all his strength, at the same time grabbing his calf by the other hand and sinking his teeth in.

José let out a sharp squeal and let go of Maria, kicking his leg to get it away from Pepsi's bite while getting his hands down to his crotch to free his balls.

'Run,' Pepsi shouted to Maria, taking his teeth out of José's legs but continuing to crush his nuts even harder, 'you know where.'

As José doubled up, yelling with pain, Pepsi let go, abruptly, and ran.

José was still doubled up by the time Mario found him by following his yells. Some windows had also lit up on hearing the shrieks, but no one dared come out to investigate.

## Of an old rucksack

Pepsi made it to the red garage, sure that he wasn't followed. He was relieved to see Maria waiting for him. He had been worried she might have got lost, or if Mario had heard his brother shouting and come across Maria on his way to look for him. But she was safe, and here. No sign of El Gato, though!

'He should've been here hours ago,' Pepsi flung his arms in the air with a look of tense exasperation. That was an exaggeration, of course, but he was right in principle. Gato had left well before Maria, and he was quick on his feet, more than anyone Pepsi knew.

If he gets caught he'll be in real trouble, he thought, especially as he had the money and the gun. Not only the brothers, but anyone catching hold of him would have questions to ask, to say the least.

Fortunately, just as Pepsi was beginning to wonder whether to go and look for him – against his own advice he'd given to Gato – Gato turned up.

Before Pepsi could ask him where he'd been and what happened to him, Gato began blabbering loudly, 'It's gone. No sign of it. I bet it's those goons . . .'

'What *are* you on about?' hissed Pepsi, 'Here we are worrying our heads off and . . .'

'My rucksack. What else d'you think. I went back . . .'

'You mean, you risked your skin, *and* ours, just for that stupid . . .'

'What do *you* mean! *Just* for . . . It was my best thing. My best thing in ALL my life. I've had it for two years now. Kept it safe from all . . .'

'I'll get you another one. I have enough money . . .'

167

'Money! Oh, yes. Money, you have. You sneaky old . . . merchant! You!!! Here we were, all starving, and you had all that loot. And the gun! I always thought you were the . . . the gentle one . . . the softie. And you have been out robbing and gunning . . .'

'I have *not* been out robbing and gun . . . That money is my . . . Tania gave it to me. My father's wife. Look, we haven't time to go into all that now. And I left a lot of it behind, to more than make up for what I took. Ask El Cuervo if you don't . . .' And suddenly, at the mention of the Crow Boy, a strange sadness rose from the deep recesses of his heart and took hold of his whole being, like fire. He could feel, and see, voracious tongues of flickering flame licking his eyeballs, and uncalled-for tears rolled out of his eyes to quench those flames.

Gato didn't even notice that Pepsi had stopped in mid-sentence. His attention was distracted by the sound of a vehicle coming their way. Pulling his ears back, which he had the weird ability to do, he stretched out his neck and sniffed the air.

'Not their car,' he said, and relaxed back as a mini-van passed by the road behind them.

'But not our bus either,' said Maria.

'That won't be for a while,' said Pepsi, now back in the real world, 'it is too early for that.'

'Here,' said Gato, throwing the bag with the money and the gun towards Pepsi, 'you keep this lot. Us cats want none of it. Money or guns.' He raised his nose up in the air, adding, '*And* I don't want any old rucksack you buy me. I want my old one. The one I earned for myself . . .'

'There's the bus now. There's the bus! Let's . . .' shouted Maria.

'It *can't* be, I'm *telling* you,' interrupted Pepsi, irritably. Gato's cracks had left him feeling vaguely angry, and hurt; on top of the fiery sorrow that the thought of the Crow Boy had aroused in him in a way he could not understand. 'It's much too . . .'

But it was the bus. A special service for some shift workers of a factory some ten miles to the west.

The people in the bus would surely remember the three kids who got on the bus that time of the night, or morning . . . Especially as one of the boys picked out a shiny new bank note of high value to pay the fare. But it couldn't be helped. This was the quickest way to get out of there and into the town. Pepsi was willing to take the risk.

## Caddy on the loose

First flashing his police identity card, and then producing a photograph of Pepsi taken from Romano, Caddy leaned forward towards the vendor at the market stall in the popular square behind Avenida Francisco and repeated what he had been asking at other stalls and stores: *Have you seen this boy pass this way, alone, or with a little auburn-haired girl . . . ?*

He was cursing himself for taking Anna's advice and not rushing over immediately to *acquire* Pepsi. The bugger had absconded from the embassy house. The people there seemed as concerned as Caddy, but for very different reasons. They deeply regretted not having put a guard on the kids, but didn't think there was any need of it, didn't dream they would run off like that in the middle of the night.

But perhaps he needn't be too hard on himself. Mario and José *had* taken the initiative, and they made a mess of it. They were evasive about details, but admitted the kid had managed to give them the slip, mainly because *he knew the area better than we did*, which was not entirely untrue.

The local police had established that the kids boarded a dawn bus from near the embassy house and got off at Avenida Francisco. No trace after that.

But it was early days, only two days, in fact, since they disappeared; and with the home bobbies, the French guys, Mario and José all out looking for them, someone was sure to get the boy. And once *anyone* did, he'd find a way to take it from there . . .

But even if all others failed, he, Caddy, would not. He'd get Pepsi. If it was the last thing he did. It would certainly be the last thing to happen to *that* mangy cur!

It was then it struck him – what should have been obvious from the start. Where best to hide a bale of hay? In a barn full of hay . . . Where would a mangy cur be invisible? Among a host of other mangy curs!

He would go and look among the town's walking waste to find his bit of walking waste!

## Caddy on the prowl

He could hardly wait until the dark. But he waited.

He had checked out the underbelly of the town during the day, where the sick generation roamed the night streets, selling and buying and stealing – selling what they had to sell; buying what they wanted to buy, could afford to buy; stealing anything they could lay their hands on.

He parked by the kerb in a recess, where he could keep an eye on his car from both ends of the street when he got out. At first he remained inside the car, assessing the situation. To his disappointment, he could not see anyone. Of course, there were many hidden nooks and corners in this rundown part of the town, a couple of unlived-in houses, and the kids could be hidden anywhere. Recent publicity re death squads gunning down visible street urchins during the night had made them more vigilant, driven them into sewers in some cases.

There were a couple of other cars in the neighbourhood. One man came out of one of them. He stopped to light a cigarette. No sooner had he done that, a couple of kids appeared from nowhere and approached the man. So that was it. They waited for the men to show their hand first before making an appearance.

A few minutes later, Caddy came out of his car, sauntered lazily along the pavement, then stopped and began to whistle softly to himself. He didn't smoke, and couldn't think of anything else to do. He didn't have to wait long.

A scrawny, scruffy-looking boy of about twelve or thirteen sidled up to him, almost as if he had been just behind him all along.

'I am Carlitos,' the boy smiled, showing crooked brown teeth, his breath making Caddy reel a step back, 'So, what you looking for? We've got a right cracker of a new girl.'

Caddy was going to ask about Pepsi, but the mention of a new girl made him think of Maria, 'About eight, pretty, auburn hair?'

The boy thought that over. The hair was a problem. Not many kids with auburn hair around on the street. Grown-up girls, yes. The colour, care of the bottle. But kids . . . No eight-year-old either. Though a couple of eleven-, twelve-year-olds, half-starved and glue-thinned, could pass for eight.

'I have just the girl,' said the boy, brightening up. 'Just hang on a breath!'

Caddy waited, unsure of the situation. The boy turned up with a scrawny girl with jet-black hair shuffling behind him.

'Here,' said the boy, cheerily, 'Jo. Eight next week. Beautiful auburn hair, only she dyed it black, just yesterday. Pity that. But natural auburn, I swear on my mother's life, even though she's dead. Can't say what happened to her. Not my mother. She had malaria. I mean Alma. Such lovely auburn hair . . . Alma, I said, why on earth . . . But you know how eight-year-olds are. Want to look like all the others.'

Caddy, who had been trying to interrupt the boy without success for some time, finally lost his patience, and shook the boy silent.

'Forget the girl,' he hissed through clenched teeth, 'What about a boy, about twelve, this boy,' he fished Pepsi's picture out of his pocket and waved it in front of both of them.

Carlitos's cheery composure was suddenly dented, and for the first time he edged a little away from Caddy. He gave the picture a quick look, then, swallowing, he paused, as if for thought, then, as if coming to a conclusion, stuttered, 'Not him . . . but . . . but . . . what about . . . me! I don't usually . . .' he dragged the *usually* a long time, 'but . . . Don't you dare tell anyone . . .' he managed a giggle. 'I have a reputation, you know. Tough as nails . . . It will cost you . . .'

Caddy had an idea what was going on, but admitted it to himself for the first time. Losing all control, he again grabbed the boy by the shoulders, this time with all his strength, and with a curse was about to hit him with a raised fist when a huge shadow emerged from the background assuming the shape of a large, tough-looking man.

'So what's going on here!' It sounded more like an order than a question, as he caught hold of Caddy's elbows and pushed him away from the boy.

Carlitos shook himself free. 'This man first asks for an eight-year-old girl. I bring him Alma. Then he . . . he . . . wants a boy, twelve. I say I'll, well, go; not that that's what I like doing, you know, don't you! And he starts pushing me around. For no reason! I was doing him a favour, I mean. An eight-year-old chick, and a boy. Real pervert, and a bully . . .' He was talking in short breathless sentences, as if more trying to explain himself than expose Caddy, as if more afraid of the man than Caddy.

'He's got it all wrong, I was only . . .' Caddy began, but the man put a finger on his lips. 'Hush, hush, hush,' he said, 'we don't like losing our cool here, now do we?' He raised a thick eyebrow, smiled, strong white teeth contrasting with Carlitos who had also put on a smile to imitate the gestures and expressions of the man.

'Let's get it straight. You asked for a girl, an eight-year-old girl; did you or did you not?' he cocked an eyebrow again at Caddy.

'Yes, but I was . . .'

'No buts. So you asked for a girl. An eight-year-old girl. That's sorted. Now. Did you ask for a boy, a twelve-year-old boy?'

'Yes, again; but you are not listening . . .'

'No. *You* are not listening.

'Now listen. You asked for a girl. An eight-year-old girl. You got her. You asked for a boy. Twelve. You got him. Now. Listen again. You pay up. You got what you asked. Now payment time.' He stretched out his right hand and held it in front of Caddy, palm-side up.

Caddy had been averting his eyes up until then, but something in the man's manner finally made him look up at him. There was authority there, not just gangland talking. He opened his mouth, changed his mind and reached for his wallet. The man reached forward and grabbed it from him, held it in his hand for a tanta-lisingly long moment, watching Caddy's reaction; then grinned broadly, the grin fading when he saw the money – just a few small-denomination notes. Caddy never carried much money on him. The man took all the notes, then gingerly replaced one back and returned the wallet to Caddy, 'I am a fair man, take no more than what is due. This,' he held up the notes, 'for an hour,' his grin made another appearance. 'Call again, and bring your friends.'

Fair, thought Caddy, fair . . . ha, ha and ha! Even with that small amount of money you could buy a whole colony of this refuse of mankind for all time, much less two lousy specimens for just an hour. That's what Caddy thought.

But he said, 'Fair! How can that be fair,' with the hurt voice of a truculent schoolboy confronted with the housemaster, 'I haven't done anything *to* pay for,' yet gratefully pocketing the wallet; grateful too, that he hadn't been asked to hand over whatever else was in his pockets. Beside credit cards, which he kept separate from the wallet, his identity card was there, and he would have hated to be caught out as a policeman. Of course he would have come up with a story to explain, but rather not . . .

'Quite right, you haven't *done* anything. Yet. But the night is young. You have a car, I'm sure?'

Caddy nodded.

'OK. Take the kids with you, and *do* "anything", anything you want. As I said, I am a fair man. One hour!' He held up the index finger of his right hand; then, as Caddy turned to go, he looked at the kids, winked, pointed to Caddy and made a thumb gesture towards his pockets.

Caddy saw more than he was meant to and nearly made a run for it without the kids, but then, why not . . . They were just a couple of half-starved, half-out-of-their-head kids. He could handle them.

He started walking towards his car, motioning to the kids to follow him. They did.

## An adventure in the dark

'I know a place, just round the corner,' said Carlitos, almost excit-
edly – it wasn't often he got to ride in a car – 'An old shop. Junk
shop. Old chairs and stuff like that. No one there. I can get in
through the window and unlock it. Do it often and no bother.
What d'you say, eh?' he looked anxiously up at Caddy's face from
the passenger seat next to him. Alma was sprawled in the back
seat looking half-asleep; certainly not all there.

Caddy kept driving. Carlitos didn't say anything, but was
clearly anxious. After a short while he tugged at Caddy's shirt-
sleeve, 'Where are we going? You live nearby? Don't go too far. If
we are late, the boss will kill us. You don't know him like we do.
Please. You will drive us back, if we are far from here? You will,
won't you? Can't leave the boss waiting. If you had more money,
he would have let you have us for the night. But with what you
had, an hour is the limit. Please . . .'

All Carlitos's smart-alec behaviour had gone, and he was restlessly shifting his bum on the seat, looking out of the car window
every so often, as if making a note of the landmarks, trying to
figure out where they were, where they were going.

Another short while, and he began slipping his hand across
Caddy's thigh, towards his trouser zip. Caddy pushed his hand
away with such force that Carlitos crouched back into his seat,
getting more and more apprehensive as the car drove on at an
increasing speed, now clearly leaving the city limits.

'You have nothing to worry about . . .' Caddy spoke, unexpectedly, without actually looking at Carlitos, 'your boss, or anything.
I'll make sure of it. I just want to ask you a few questions. Let's get
to somewhere quiet, peaceful. I like the fresh, open air.'

Carlitos was not entirely satisfied, but he shut up. There was nothing he could do. Not for now. He'd just have to wait and see. Caddy veered right off the road and parked on a sandy stretch of open land dotted by spiky trees, grizzly bushes and barren knolls. He produced the photograph of Pepsi again and showed it to Carlitos, 'Now take a good look at this boy. Are you sure you haven't seen him. Maybe in the last couple of days?'

'No. I swear . . .' Carlitos stopped mid-sentence, a canny look coming into his eyes. 'Well, maybe I have, maybe I haven't. How much is it worth to you?'

Caddy's eyes caught fire, 'Now listen, you dirty little pip-squeak. If you try playing any games with me, I'll . . .'

'Yeah! And you'll what? You better not. The boss will get you if you hurt us. He is a . . . he is in the . . . He's a . . .' he stopped himself, either because he couldn't think of a convincing lie to come up with, or because he felt he shouldn't really be saying anything at all.

Threats made Caddy angry. Threats from the powerful, whether direct or implied, he could take. They still made him angry, but he could swallow them. From his father. From the store manager he worked for at thirteen; from his superiors, in life or at work. But the nerve of this sewer rat trying to intimidate him . . . He would have to do what he had to do. He was going to do it anyway, but the boy's brazenness gave him a good excuse – no, not a good excuse, a good *reason* – to do what he was going to do, what he had to do, Taking a deep breath, he quietly got out of the car, went to the passenger door, opened it and asked Carlitos to come out. Carlitos did, suspicious, and all ready to cut loose and run, if necessary. But he didn't get the chance. Caddy pounced on the lad's neck with the alacrity of a lizard's tongue going after a fly, pushed his head against the doorpost and slammed the door against it with full force. Not caring that the boy's skull cracked the first time, he repeated the manoeuvre, twice. Alma's eyes opened wide, as did her mouth, she made as if to scream, but then didn't bother.

Caddy walked away from the car carrying a dead child under each armpit. The children were so light he could hardly feel they were there. Stopping by a mound well away from the road, he dropped them behind a clump of bushes, kicking hard with his boots until they were well hidden inside the thicket. A couple of small animals scuttled and scurried out into the oppressive intimacy of the night.

Unzipping, he began to urinate, aiming at what he thought was one eye of the girl, wide open and staring up at him from below the undergrowth, while humming softly to himself an old tune he used to hum while courting Anna.

He wasn't worried about the man, surely an adult version of the same low-life that was born in the gutter. The boy was just trying to impress, a chronic liar, like all of his kind. And anyway, who really cared about street meat. The meat vendors least of all. For every one who offs it, there are ten more around. Still, they were at peace now, the poor little misguided ones. He couldn't be angry with them any longer. They were at peace, at last; at peace with themselves, at peace with their Maker, thanks to him. He smiled benignly to himself as he shook his penis dry.

## A long-distance lorry driver

The truck driver was half-dozing, driving along the endless, naked road quivering in front of him in the heat haze of the burning midday sun, when he heard the announcement on the radio. It took him a while before it sank in.

The police, the French Embassy, and goodness knows who all were asking for information re three kids: a twelve-year-old, tallish, lanky boy with a head of dark curly hair; an eight-year-old girl with big brown eyes and longish auburn hair; and a third boy, elevenish, with messy, unkempt hair who didn't talk much but mewed every now and then.

He had found them hiding in his truck only the day before. They had got in unnoticed while he was delivering some goods to a supermarket in Avenida Francisco in Merida, about three or four days ago, just about dawn. When he stopped in the little village of El Cedral to unload some more supplies, as well as to have a leak and a rest, he saw the kids hiding behind some boxes. He was driving down south and they begged him to let them ride along, but he threw them out. He didn't mind giving rides to grown-ups. With children, you could never be sure. He did not want to be held on charges of kidnapping, child-trafficking or what-have-you.

He got on to his radio and relayed the information to the authorities concerned.

Caddy, now back in uniform to look and feel more at home, was in the Merida police station when the news came. It was broadcast on the radio and TV later on.

El Cedral . . . About a hundred miles down south. In the immensity of the continent, it was virtually next door! Caddy could hardly stop smiling. It didn't matter who the boy ended up with. As long as he knew where to reach him, he'd find a way to get even.

But he was hoping to get to him first.

He began to rub his thighs with anticipatory glee. But not for long. He had things to do. Places to go. Excusing himself as quickly and politely as he could, he all but ran out of the precinct.

On his way out he nearly bumped into a large impressive-looking man in an inspector's uniform. Both were prepared for an apologetic smile before looking away when their eyes locked. Instant recognition . . . despite change of stage, scenery, costume and light! An office and not the street. Respectability not squalor . . .

It was a weird experience. The scrap was telling the truth, after all. Or trying to tell the truth. Yes. It was a weird experience, indeed it was, a scrap telling the truth, or trying to . . .

A moment of fear, for both; then relief, conditioned relief . . . Who was going to be the first to admit, and to what? Before either chose to accuse!

Caddy walked out, the man walked in. The man who had peddled Caddy the eight-year-old girl and the mouthy boy.

# El Cedral

Pepsi was the first to wake up. They were sleeping under the awning of a rundown shop at the top end of a downhill street, from where they could clearly see anyone coming up. They were sharing one double blanket that Pepsi bought from the local marketplace the day before, along with a host of other things, including a black headscarf for Maria; two baseball caps, Gato wearing his back to front; a small radio; a camping stove; some food; and three small knapsacks instead of a biggish rucksack – Pepsi was willing to buy one for Gato, but he was still sulking about his old one and didn't want to know.

At first, Gato had insisted that he stole rather than they buy. The shopkeepers might wonder where the kids got their money from and call the police or something. 'I am very good at earning for myself,' said Gato, puffing up with pride, 'no one can catch me! I promise.'

But Pepsi did not want to risk it. It could take a lot of time . . . it was too many things . . . more chances of getting nabbed . . .

As for the shopkeepers being suspicious, 'Not if I go on my own,' said Pepsi. Maria was too sweet-looking. People might get talking to her, and that could complicate matters. Gato could be weird. Freezing suddenly, like a cat stalking a bird, if he heard a strange noise or smelt something funny. Or scratching himself at odd places at odd moments, spreading his fingers out like claws, or letting out a cat cry. 'I don't do any of it when I am earning,' Gato argued, going red, as red as he could go red with his burnt sienna skin; but Pepsi wouldn't budge. He said he could speak like a good city boy who went to a good school, and be polite and well behaved. No one would suspect him if he bought a few things and paid with good money.

The decision to make was whether to get everything from the one superstore in town, or different things from different shops; which of the two would be 'safer'.

Eventually they found an open market with a cluster of cabins and tiny hole-in-the-wall shops selling everything from cornflakes to jewellery, old furniture to live chickens. No one cared who was buying what from whom, as long as they got paid the right money. So many people were walking, talking, buying, selling, eating, drinking, all over the place, it was easy for Maria and Gato to get lost in the throng, mingle, buy something to eat and drink and generally have a good time, while waiting for Pepsi to finish his shopping and meet up with them. Gato kept to his promise that he wouldn't 'turn cat' and draw attention to himself; which was just as well, for it made Maria giggle – and the one miaowing and the other giggling would have created more interest among the public than was good for them.

Pepsi was rubbing his sleep-filled eyes with his fists when he saw somebody walking up the street that plunged downhill below them at an angle of almost seventy degrees, disappearing into a distant landscape of purplish hills dipping up and down across the horizon. He was sort of surprised, for he had looked down only a moment earlier and there was no one there. But he might have been out of sight behind one of the many trees that were scattered around. It didn't matter anyway.

Although they had heard on the radio last night that the police and the Frenchies had asked the public to keep a lookout for them, it didn't bother him much. With Maria's auburn hair hidden beneath a black scarf, and his head of heavy curls under a baseball cap, they could be any of the many kids that wandered like stray dogs up and down the streets of any town as long as they walked at some distance from each other, one on the other side of the road, and spoke no more than two at a time, for brief periods, when necessary. Although they were all three together here, two were under a blanket, and Pepsi felt under no threat.

But after a while, a strange kind of edginess began creeping up his spine. He couldn't decide why. And then he looked again at the man walking uphill on the downhill street. He didn't seem to be getting anywhere. He was continuing to walk up, but never seemed to get any higher, any closer.

And then Pepsi saw that it wasn't a man, but a boy. Hardly older than him. And he was struggling, struggling to come up, but remaining where he was, like on a treadmill. What's more – and he was sure of it, as sure as he had been of nothing in his life – the boy was trying to come up and see them, see *him*. But couldn't.

Just then he heard a flutter, just above his head. Like the flapping of large, arduous wings. He ducked involuntarily and looked up. But there was nothing there. A cold shiver in the mounting heat of the day sliced through his body like the frozen blade of an axe, as he suddenly realised what it was. It was Death. Death the Crow Boy had warned him about. And at the thought of the Crow Boy he abruptly realised who the boy was, the boy down below trying desperately to come up to him.

It was the Crow Boy.

His blood-brother.

He was trying to come up and be with him . . .

But could not.

Pepsi knew exactly what to do.

He would run down and meet up with him.

But he could not move.

Not a muscle.

Not an eyelash.

He tried to call out to him. But his voice was frozen the same as his limbs. He tried, tried again and again, to move, even a finger, just to get himself started, but could not.

Scream. Yes, that's what he should do. Scream.

Someone would then come to help him.

He didn't care if they found out who he was. Who they all were. He did not care if they got caught, taken back.

All he cared about was to get to the Crow Boy. Just as the Crow Boy was trying to get to him.

But he could not.

And then he heard Gato let out a loud, screeching catsound. He jumped up, nearly knocking Gato's eye out with his elbow. 'What the hell . . .' he began.

'Don't what the hell *me!*' said Gato, 'You should see yourself. You look like you've seen a ghost. Like you *are* a ghost. I tried to make you look at me, but you sat there like a big lump of sleeping stone. Like you were . . . dead sitting up, or something. I only became cat to get you back here from wherever you were.' These were a lot of words for Gato to speak, and he stuck his tongue out and began to pant, like an exhausted animal.

'I must have fallen asleep,' said Pepsi, trying more to convince himself than Gato.

Gato shrugged his shoulders. It was OK now that his friend was OK. No point in talking any further.

Pepsi looked down at the street, warily, half-hoping to make contact with reality, half-wanting to deny it. No sign of the Crow Boy. Nor was the street empty. It was alive with the usual signs of small-town activity in the early hours of the morning. He could see a black dog, three brown-and-white ones, and a number of people, young and old, walking uphill or downhill or going across it into the many lanes that branched off it or crisscrossed it.

How long had he been 'out of it'? He really must have fallen asleep . . .

He felt tired. Drained. Of all energy, of all thought, of all certainty. But it didn't matter. After all, he was only nothing. Nothing mattered, if you were nothing . . . His mother knew that. And he should know!

## Pressures, intimidation and threats

'I have nothing against charity,' said Mercedes Gonzales, 'but I can't see why I should be made to feel under pressure every time I go out shopping.' She adjusted her silk stole daintily round her shoulders as she side-stepped a little bald-headed boy sitting cross-legged on the pavement, back resting against a shop wall, an empty bowl in his lap, looking up with wide empty eyes at passers-by.

'Exactly!' said Donna Martinez. 'Even if his head was *shaved*, it wouldn't be so bad. But he is *bald*. Really bald. That is not natural in a child his age. His parents should have the good sense of keeping him home instead of . . . displaying him like this, openly, in the town centre.'

'That's just it. It is just their way to put . . . pressure, on . . . people. Like you and me. It isn't fair.'

'Exactly,' said Donna, 'and bald is nothing. I have seen kids that are *ill*, I mean really ill. You have only got to look at them. And yet . . .' Donna seemed lost for words.

'That's just it. What sort of parents would do that to their child. But I suppose it is just a sort of . . . threat, isn't it. To the whole of society. They could be contagious, infectious . . .'

'Exactly! It's calculated, by the *parents*. What really gets me is when they start *talking* to you. It's frightening. So absolutely frightening.'

'What's worse is when they start singing at you.'

'Exactly! The other day I was in this subway. I hate subways, but that day I just couldn't find a taxi. And a woman comes into the carriage. She had this baby in her arms. Just a few months old. And, would you believe it, she started singing. At the top of her . . .'

'God! How early *do* they start . . .' Mercedes couldn't help interrupting, open-mouthed, 'God! Almighty!'

Donna looked a bit vague for a second before understanding, 'Not the baby, silly!' she laughed lightly and waved her hand in the air, 'I would have liked to see *that*. I mean the mother. The mother started singing. I mean, *loudly, full-throatedly* singing. With the full blast of her lungs. I could see her *tonsils* from where I was. It was . . . it was so, *so* intimidating. *I* felt so intimidated, *I* can't tell you. Couldn't wait to get out . . .'

'There should be a law against it.'

'Exactly. After all, what do we honest, hardworking people pay taxes for?' said Donna as she licked lasciviously at a large ice cream cone, delicately dabbing her chin with an embroidered handkerchief after every lick.

Mercedes looked at her watch, anxiously, as they came to the west end of the newly built shopping mall, outside the foyer of a cinema complex. 'He should have been here. I am fifteen minutes late, always am, if not more. But he is always on time, waiting for me. Mind you . . .' here she hesitated, 'he is . . . he's often away at nights. But then, there are some policemen who do not get to even *see* their wives, for days. Gonzales tells me, and he should know,' her voice didn't sound quite as sure as her words.

But she didn't have to wait long. Another five minutes, and the big frame of Gonzales taking long firm strides came towards them, a look of disquiet on his handsome, if rather brutish face.

'I am so sorry to be late, sweetheart,' he said, giving a quick kiss to wife and a quicker smile to her sister, 'something unexpected came up.'

The unexpected that came up and made him late was getting info on Caddy. 'Who was that policeman who just left . . . what uniform was he wearing, which country . . . what was he doing here . . .'

After he first set eyes on Caddy walking out of the precinct, and once his initial reactions of fear and relief had settled down, Superintendent Gonzales had started getting angry . . . and angrier and angrier! How dare this man, his junior, and from out of town, out of state, take out two of his most faithful workers! He was sure he had offed them. Either during some creepy sex, like what happened to Esme and the other one, he couldn't remember her name; or out of sheer cussedness. There was no doubt in his mind.

The kids would never run out on him, not willingly. Never. Besides, Carlitos had a dying mother. He would not leave her and go off like that. He hadn't yet taken his week's ten per cent to get some food and things for her. Gonzales always delayed giving his family, as he called his children, their cut; just to keep them on their toes – or their knees, or their backsides, or against the wall, as the case may be. Conchita, Carlitos's mom, had been crying out for her cough mixture for days, not that that did her any good. If it had, Gonzales might have relented and bought her it himself. As it was, there wasn't much point to it. But her boy didn't see it like that, and would never have left her, not without food or medicine, not on the night he was expecting his cut, like he did every night. As for Alma, she was dying herself. Aids. She could no more run off than fly.

He loved them both. He loved all his charges, his family, his other family. They looked after him, and he looked after them. His wife was a happier woman because of them, and he loved to make her happy. She came from a rich family, had married beneath her, a casualty of his charm and handsome looks. But she couldn't *live* on charm and handsome looks. She needed more. She wouldn't even consider having children until she felt more secure. He could never afford those little gifts that he got for her, the new television, the digital camcorder . . . not without the help of *his* children, not on his salary. And he repaid them by protecting them, saving them from those out to hurt them, out to destroy them, out to kill them – and there were many such. Some from his own profession; others from the Good Citizens' Conglomerate or Keep our Streets Clean Campaign, or Save our Children Crusaders.

He had promised to look after this family of his, the family of his children; told them he would, given them his word. And he was a man of his word.

The report he got on Caddy was unexpected, and unsettling.

The man was here looking for three kids. The ones responsible for getting the French kidnappees free. So he meant it when he was asking about the auburn-haired girl and the other boy . . . Gonzales had heard what he was saying to Carlitos before he stepped in.

He couldn't quite figure it out. It didn't add up. And when things didn't add up, Gonzales worried. If this man Caddy was an all right, good-hearted, honest bloke, here on a sort of mercy mission to rescue lost kids and return an errant boy to his well-to-do father, why then should he snuff out *his* kids.

*Could* he be wrong . . . ? *Could* the man have taken his kids to some sort of a safe home . . . ? If he had, there was danger. The kids might talk. Would talk, in the end . . . that *was* something *really* to worry about . . .

He needed more information. More facts . . .

## Another day

Pepsi didn't want to stay in El Cedral any longer. This morning's experience, whatever it was, left him with a strange fear in his heart. He wanted to get out of there as soon as possible.

But how?

Hitchhiking was out. Stowing away in another truck was still a good option, as long as they were careful not to be found out. A bus or a coach out of town? If they sat separately, Gato and Maria together, Pepsi on his own. A train was the best bet, if there was one passing through. Walking could also be considered, if there was another village or town, not too far away, preferably one with a train station.

Pepsi was weighing the options over in his mind on their way to getting some breakfast, when suddenly Gato leapt into the air like a kitten after a fly buzzing over its head, held his paw up, and pointed to a large ten-by-thirty hoarding hanging above the shops across the road. Plastered across its surface was the face of a beautiful, sensual-lipped girl with perfect teeth and long blonde hair flowing all around her perfectly cheeked face; with a sort of faded-looking, unsmiling brunette just behind her – the one emerging from the other, as it were. It was an advertisement for a hair colour product. *Because you are worth it . . .*

'That's it,' shouted Gato.

Pepsi was normally very good at getting into Gato's mind, but this time it took even him a while to understand what he was getting at: colouring Maria's hair, black! It was true that her scarf kept blowing in the wind, revealing strands of her auburn hair.

Pepsi thought about it. With an open-headed dark-haired girl, they were less likely to be noticed. There was an outside tap at the back end of a petrol station near the top end of the town. It was closed after eight. Maria could 'do' her hair there, later at night. But it meant delaying their plans re leaving town.

At first, Maria was dead opposed to the idea of having her hair dyed, and began to cry; but got persuaded, reluctantly, when assured that it would only be temporary, and that the 'real' colour of her hair would remain unchanged.

Pepsi was still not happy about having to hang around for another day, but he too saw the advantage of it, on condition that Gato didn't go 'earning' the hair colour, just buying.

## One by one does it

Caddy could tell Pepsi from a mile off, even without the binoculars. That walk of his! No cap on the head could disguise that.
Anyone on the lookout for the children after hearing about them
on the radio, or even seeing them on television, might be deceived;
but not someone who *knew* Pepsi, not Caddy.

Neither the scarf round Maria's head nor Gato's back-to-front
cap could prevent him from spotting either of them. He may not
have been terribly bright when it came to reading, writing and
arithmetic, but he had a photographic memory for faces and
places. Not many people knew that, not even in his own profession, or they could have made good use of him for identification of
criminals and re-creating of crime scenes. He could have had a
promotion for that. But he was never very good at publicising his
better attributes, or at selling himself.

Caddy smiled to himself at the thought of Pepsi's imminent
capture: 'capture' was the only correct word for what he had in
mind, as one would capture a rogue animal – arrest was too digni-
fied a term for the boy. Extermination and annihilation came to
mind, but he wanted to proceed progressively, one step at a time,
first things first. And capture *was* the first thing. There was the
surging temptation to shoot him on sight; but now that so much
fuss had been made of the boy, and he was a known quantity
among the powers that be, he had to go with caution, one step at
a time . . . Besides, he wanted the boy to *know* that he, Caddy, had
got him, to make him suffer, beg for his life, beg for Maria's life
before he . . . took the . . . the only right and just course of action.

He tried to enter the boy's head, assess his tactics, and came
up with quite an accurate assessment: *He must have decided they
walk close enough, within sight or shout; yet apart. By nightfall
they would meet up, trickling in one by one at some out of town*

*spot.* Though why they hadn't tried to get out of town at the first opportunity, he couldn't figure out. Perhaps the boy had something up his sleeve? But there was nothing he could do about that. He could only follow his instinct, stay close to the sprouts without being seen – or rather without being identified: his civvy outfit and a commonly worn hat pulled down over his face was enough to prevent Gato and Maria from recognising him at a quick glance; but he would have to keep well out of range of Pepsi. He was sure the boy would sus him out.

He would follow their game plan. Choose one – he decided on Gato – keep him in sight, far enough, but within his binoculars . . . Wherever Gato settled for the night, the other two would join him, and he would have all three, in the dark, at a quiet spot, all to himself! He was sure of it . . . he massaged his father's gun lovingly as he conjured up the scene in his mind's eye, the little army bag containing the necessary paraphernalia resting gently on his back.


It was almost dark by the time Pepsi, Maria and Gato got together at the back of the now deserted petrol station. All going as planned. But then, the plan began to unravel.

Maria said she was too tired and wanted to go to sleep. Partly it was a ruse to avoid having her hair dyed, partly she *was* tired and sleepy.

For once Pepsi lost his temper with Maria, 'It's just because of your hair, isn't it? Isn't it? We didn't leave town today because of that! If you'd said this before . . .'

'I did, I did say . . .'

'But *then,* you *agreed.* You said . . .'

'Well, I will. I will. But not now. It will take *hours*! And if I fall asleep half-way, all my hair will fall out.'

'Of course it won't. Don't be stupid.'

'Well, I *am* stupid; I am, I am, I am . . .' Maria began to cry, Gato began to caterwaul, Pepsi sulked . . . but in no time at all, they were all asleep.

Caddy thought it took ages for the kids to go sleep. Even from his distance he could tell they were arguing about something. It pleased him. Falling out among low-life was always a good thing. It pleased him. It pleased him no end.

But he couldn't sit there smirking. He had work to do.

When he was within about twenty yards of the sleeping kids, he took off his shoes and put them in his army bag, while taking out from it a roll of broad builders' masking tape, short lengths of cut-out rope, soft tissues . . . and the little bottle of *scent!* He knew what a handful even one pair of kicking kid legs and flailing kid arms could be. With three pairs . . . he couldn't take any chances.

With the kids securely tied up, their mouths taped – and unconscious – Caddy looked around to see if anyone was about.

No one.

Not even a dog.

His shoes were back on his feet, his bag back on his back. It would only take him ten minutes to walk up to where he left his car, maybe less; a minute or two to drive back, right up to where the kids lay – he wouldn't even have to carry them to the car. Just dump them in. They would all fit in easily inside the trunk of his ancient Oldsmobile, he was sure of it.

He was about to open his car door when he felt one bony hand on his right shoulder, another on his left. He turned his head to see two men either side of him, one runty, the other runtier, each holding a gun in the hand not on his shoulder. The runty one about twenty, or less; the runtier in his mid-thirties. Caddy could have broken both their necks with one blow – if they hadn't the guns, and he had the guts.

'You should be careful not to leave your car out here. If we hadn't been watching over it, it would have been stripped naked by now.' The runty one spoke with a surprisingly friendly smile, despite tobacco-yellow teeth.

'Get in at the back, with me,' said the runtier one, 'Just open the door, slowly. Very slowly . . . Now get in, first. Slowly. That's it.' Caddy lowered his head, got in and sat down, then at the tilt of the man's head shifted his buttocks to the other end of the seat. The runtier one slid inside, next to him, gun firmly in hand.

'Hand me the keys,' the runty one held out his hand and smiled again.

Snatching the keys from Caddy's outstretched hand he got in the driver's seat with an exaggerated swagger, and smiled yet again.

## Tania and the boys

'Where *are* they? *Where* . . . ?' there was angry irritation in Tania's voice.

'Why? What are they up . . .

'Now listen . . . listen, listen, listen. Are you trying to tell me they say *I* wanted them to . . .

'OK OK OK. You listen to me. Tell them to get back here. This instant. Now! Before now!!! . . . I don't care how long it takes. I want them back, NOW . . . What do you mean they won't . . . Well, you tell Mario, if he does not want to go to the university in San Diego, it's fine by me. And tell José, if he does not want money to set up his own gym, that's fine by me too . . . Well, you tell them. Tell them I mean it, more than anything I've ever meant in my life. If they harm that kid, if . . . they are not getting a single penny out of me, ever again. Ever, ever, ever. Never.

'What! What was that? Hang on, hang on, Fox. What're you trying to tell me. Is *Julio* out looking for Andrés as well . . . You mean Romano has sent him . . . What! Oh my God, don't tell me the old fool is having an attack of conscience . . . *That* serious . . . You're making this up, aren't you? To take my mind off Mario and . . . I can well believe them thugging after Andrés, but Romano wanting him . . . I mean *wanting* him! Are you sure! It is not one of your . . . tricks, Foxy boy, is it? . . . Or one of those *stories* . . . ? Well, can you blame me! You and the truth have never exactly been best of pals in the past, now, have you?

'OK, OK. OOO KAAY. Well, I am not having that, if it's true. You've nothing to worry about. For me, or for yourself. No way am I having that. I don't want the poor bugger to be made mince of, by my gorilla brothers or anyone else; but I don't want him coming back here and lording it over my boys as the eldest and . . . Well, I will see about it when it happens.

'Anyway. You call the gorillas off, pronto, and I will see to Romano. Both his wigs are going, and I'll call the papers next time he's out on . . . No matter, nothing for you to worry about. No. Nothing. *I'll* deal with it, with Romano and Julio. You get Mario and José back. They'll come running with their tails between their legs when they hear there isn't going to be any San damn Diego or a muscle factory if they don't . . .'

## Was it a cat . . . ?

Gato claimed it was a cat that clawed at his ropes to frazzle them, make them come loose. Maria said it was Pumpkin, her little girl-dog, who had bitten at the ropes to try and free her. Pepsi said nothing and, though feeling foolish, looked around him, as if hoping to recognise one particular crow among the many that circled the air above them, or strutted about the grounds with their little black chests puffed out, pecking among the grasses for whatever food they could find . . .

The truth was, perhaps, much simpler.

Caddy hadn't made a very good job of tying them up in the first place! The kids were fast dropping out of it under the influence of his 'little bottle of scent', unable to struggle effectively or even call out to anyone, just about aware of who he was and what he was doing, so he felt under no threat from them. And he was in a hurry. Tying and binding kids out in the open made him nervous. Finally, as he knew he was going to have them in the boot of his car within minutes, and they'd be brought out only when inside Raffo's 'secure' garage, there was no need to be too fastidious about the knots, even if he had the time and wasn't nervous.

But, whatever, some time during the night, when the children began woozily to become aware of themselves and the world around them, they found that the ropes round their wrists were loose and frayed, as if something had been clawing at them, biting, pecking . . . Actually, they could easily have done something like that themselves, struggling to free themselves while still half-conscious.

Now, more or less fully awake, and with a little help from Gato's extended nails, and some wriggling and squirming, they were able to free their hands, and themselves.

But what happened to Caddy? Why did he tie them up and just leave them there?

Pepsi didn't like the feel of it. They had to get out of there. The sooner the better. But Maria was still shaky on her feet, Gato looked a bit green in the moonlight, and he didn't feel too good either. After a few minutes of indecision, they got out of there, staggered downhill behind the petrol station, hid behind some bushes, and before they could think about what to do next, rolled over in the shrubbery and were fast asleep.

## A downtown garage

'Where are you taking me?' Caddy asked after about half an hour's driving, still frightened, but not as terrified as he was in the beginning. If they had intended to kill him, they would have done so by now.

'You'll soon find out,' said the runtier one.

'Who sent you?' he was getting bolder by the minute.

'We don't know,' the runty one spoke from the driver's seat, chewing at a cheap, smelly cigar. 'Don't want to know either. The less we know the better for us. We just carry out instructions.'

'And what are your instructions?' He couldn't believe he had it in him to question his captors like that.

'A friend of yours . . .' The runty one began, but the runtier one, sitting behind the driver's seat, prodded his neck with a finger to silence him, and he shut up.

They kept on driving, and Caddy could tell they were heading back towards Merida.

Once in Merida, the car turned quite a few corners in and out of quite a few twisty, narrow streets, until they came to what could have been a lock-up shop, but turned out to be a garage. It opened electronically, they drove in.

It was surprisingly spacious inside, room enough for at least three cars, or a big truck, and a lot of junk.

Runty got out of the car, at the same time as Runtier pushed Caddy out. Runty miraculously pulled out a rope from inside his soiled old jacket, and tied up Caddy's left hand to his right foot, right hand to his left foot, while Runtier kept the gun on him.

Even Caddy's rather dull mind couldn't help sensing the irony of the situation. He had planned to capture Pepsi and take him to a garage. Now he had been captured and brought to a garage. He wondered what the kids were doing now. A surge of anger rose in his breast. That blasted Pepsi. He had thwarted him again. In some way he couldn't quite be sure of, he blamed his present predicament on him, as he did everything bad that had happened to him in recent weeks. He kicked himself too, for not getting his gun back from him. That was the least he could have done after catching up with him. Unlike Anna, he was sure the scumbag still had it as his special war trophy, even if he did not have the guts to use it. But as he was going to bring all of them with him, he hadn't thought it necessary to search him there at the petrol station . . .

Securely tied up, Caddy was shoved back inside the car.

'Stay where you are. Someone wants to talk to you. He . . . or she . . . we don't know and don't want to know, will come over here, whenever he/she is ready. It is not up to us. We get our orders on the phone, don't see anybody, don't hear anything, except what we are meant to hear.' This was Runtier's longest speech.

'And don't try anything. For your own sake,' Runty smiled, and gave him a mock-respectful salute.

Keeping the gun pointed towards the car, both Runty and Runtier walked backwards towards the garage door, and went out. The door came down and shut itself behind them.

The garage door creaking upwards woke up Caddy. He had fallen asleep, and wasn't sure how long he had to wait. But it was still dark outside.

He looked up with eyes that were quickly losing their sleep and filling up with fear; his half-swollen penis began shrinking back to normality. A huge black car drove into the garage and parked behind his car, slightly to the left.

A large, impressive-looking man, dressed in a smart, summery, expensive-looking suit stepped out of the driver's side.

It was Gonzales. Caddy wasn't surprised.

# A taxi ride

The sun was high in the sky by the time the children woke up, one by one, within minutes of each other.

Their heads were still heavy from the chloroform, and their limbs lazy; but Pepsi was so keen to hightail out of there at the earliest that he began to plan their getaway as soon as he was done jumping up and down and cartwheeling all over the place to clear his brain and activate his body.

He took out the money he had, and gave some of it to Gato, in case they had to separate temporarily during their journey, and made sure there was enough water per person, water they had filled empty soda bottles with from the tap at the petrol station. He removed the gun from the knapsack where he'd kept it wrapped up in an old shirt his father had bought him ages ago, and tucked it in the front of his shorts, knotting the same old shirt round his waist, both to secure the gun as well as to hide it from view. He wanted to be better prepared this time, the gun more accessible, if Caddy made another appearance. The fact that he hadn't searched them and taken his gun away meant that he had definitely intended to come back. What could have happened to him . . . ? Part of him wished that it was something really drastic, something final; and that he would never again bother them, or anyone else. Part of him wanted to confront him, one last time . . .

There was a train station in Uzmal, about twenty-five miles away. A local bus did go there, three times a day; but by the time Pepsi and co. got to the bus stop, the second one had just left, and the next was not due till late in the evening. 'Shared taxis' were standing around waiting to be filled up, heading to different destinations. Under normal circumstances Pepsi would have avoided such a memorable means of transport, but he was so desperate to get out of there, and one of the taxis going to Uzmal had such a kindly looking old man sitting in front that he felt it would be safe to take the risk. He approached the taxi but the driver didn't seem too keen to take them, 'It will cost you. Do you have the money?'

Before Pepsi could respond, Gato exclaimed, twitching his nose like a cat sniffing at a rival's backside, and with a voice to match, 'Sure we have money, more than . . .' Pepsi pulled him to one side, gave him a meaningful, reproachful look and was about to back away, but the kindly old man got out of the taxi and urged them to get in, all smiles and twinkling good humour, patting Maria on the cheek and Gato on the back, putting an arm round Pepsi and guiding him to the front seat where he had been sitting, getting in with Gato and Maria in the back seat. After a moment or two of hesitation, Pepsi got in and eased back in his seat.

The taxi pulled out.

## Once again into the bushes

'So what have you done to my children?' said Gonzales, coming directly to the point, as was his manner. He was in Caddy's car, sitting behind the wheel, Caddy next to him in the passenger seat. Gonzales was confident enough in himself to untie him and have him by his side. 'I care for them,' he continued, in a more thoughtful voice, 'whatever you may think, I care for them. I look after them. Anyone who harms them has me to answer to!'

'They are dead,' said Caddy.

Not that he couldn't come up with any lies, but he wanted to be brutal to this man.

At first, Caddy had been almost pleased the other was who he was. A policeman. Now a gangland thug or a government minister – that, that could have been a problem! A fellow officer – *that* he could handle, especially one on the same side of the fence, as it were, if at the other end of it. He didn't exactly approve of what he was doing, but in his own way, he too was trashing the trash. Using them as meat was, perhaps, the next best thing to terminating the lot. Or rather, *another* way of terminating them – less efficient, maybe, but more profitable. And making profit was the new way, in every walk of life, even though he himself had never developed a talent for it. A weakness on his part, rather than of the system. Anna could have a better life, Juan a better future, if only he was better at making money. Yes, it was OK the man was who he was . . . He was comfortable with it.

But that was before he spoke.

Hearing him say what he said, the way he referred to street trash as *his children*, as if they meant something to him, claiming that he cared for them, Caddy was so strangely irritated, so profoundly disturbed that he wanted to show how little *he* thought of them, and cared less what happened to them. Either that, or he was so frustrated at Pepsi having slipped out of his fingers yet again that he wasn't thinking straight; or his mind was still blurred because of sleep, or lack of it.

'Yes, they are dead,' he repeated, without trying to conceal a feeling of smug satisfaction in his voice.

Gonzales was taken aback at this forthright reply. Paradoxically, Caddy's very directness made him disbelieve him. It made him fear that somehow he *had* taken the boy and the girl to some homeless children's organisation, and didn't want him to know. If he really had killed the kids, he would have tried to prevaricate, come up with stories to explain their disappearance . . .

'Oh yeah! Next you'll be telling me you killed them and dumped them somewhere in the wild outside town, but can't remember where to save your life. Is that it?'

'Yes, well. No. Well, yes, yes and no. *Yes*, I did kill them. *Yes*, I did dump them somewhere outside town. And *no*, I won't say I can't remember where. I remember. I remember exactly where.'

In for a penny, in for a pound. Caddy was letting his hair down. All his life he had cowered before bullies. Because somewhere deep down within him he believed they were better than him. But this smooth-talking suave-looking ponce was no better than him. Peddler of sick meat was bad enough, but dung-lover too!

Gonzales took a deep breath. He wasn't going to get into a verbal with this junior man. 'All right then. Take me there. Show me.'

'Let me drive, and I will.' For once he felt a shiver of fear at the prospect; not just fear of Gonzales, but of facing up to the corpses, but it passed.

Without a word, Gonzales got out of the car, walked round the front of the car and got in the passenger side as Caddy shifted into the driver's seat.

'Why did you do it, *if* you did?'

'The kid was trying to rob me. The girl was half-dead anyway.'

Gonzales didn't respond.

Caddy drove straight to where he had taken Carlitos and Alma, stopped where he had stopped, got out, and asked Gonzales to come out and follow him.

Caddy walked over to the bushes where he had dumped the bodies of the dead kids. He moved to one side and pointed to the exact spot, inviting Gonzales to have a look for himself.

By now Gonzales had come to believe Caddy, and relaxed. Too bad if the kids were dead, he was sorry about that, but at least they weren't around to expose him to fucking do-gooders. He would find some way of getting even with Caddy, maybe even make some money out of him, but there was no need for serious concern.

Tension easing from his mind and muscles, he stood at the top of the knoll feeling on top of the world, breathed in the fresh air, expanded his chest, breathed out, and looked up at the night sky for a long moment with obvious pleasure. He had always been the outdoor type of man, loving nature, fresh air – mountains and deserts alike; but his wife preferred restaurants and art galleries and shopping centres. He hadn't been out in the open air at night for a long, long time. He remembered the weekend trips he used to make in the countryside with some of his schoolmates in a past long disappeared in the annals of lost time.

But he was here for a purpose. He had to get on with it. Make dead sure of what he was almost sure of . . .

Moving over to where Caddy had pointed, Gonzales leaned forward to have a proper look. Caddy took the gun out of his back pocket, aimed for the back of the man's head, and fired.

## Sun, sand and rocks

The gritty sand reflected the burning sun beneath their feet. The baking earth, suffused with rusty pale hues of varying degrees of intensity – subdued here, sparkling there, smouldering or fiery – complemented the near-white blue of the stark, afternoon sky above.

To their left, rocks and hills rose and fell in a bewildering maze; part shrouded with emaciated shrubbery and wild grasses, part deceptively bare, interspersed with yucca plants and prickly pears and cereus and barrel cacti and boojum trees, all fading away in the distance, down to the base of formidable mountains, some blue, some grey, some brownish black, zigzagging against the far horizon. So many shades of green, tones of purple, streaks of lime and ochre, not to mention grades of brown merging into greys and blacks, spilling out into the atmosphere to overwhelm and confuse the senses.

To their right stretched the red earth of the eternal desert, chameleon-like in temporal ripples and waves, surprised by the occasional mound.

Behind them and straight ahead ran a dirt road. The dirt road upon which the taxi spewed them out, after the kindly old man robbed them of their money and their knapsacks. In the tight space of the small taxi, Pepsi had decided against trying to pull his gun out of his shorts – couldn't have done even if he had wanted to. It all happened so fast.

Earlier on, he had got the feeling that the kindly old man and the taxi man were somehow together, but dismissed the thought. Even if true, it seemed irrelevant.

Normally the old man just sat in the taxi to give the impression that it was filling up, and motivating people to get in. When enough people appeared, he would step out to make room for the 'real' passengers. An opportunity like today didn't come up often – not in broad daylight. When it did, he remained in the taxi to 'assist' the driver. Muggings could be tricky.

Apart from what he was wearing, the only possessions Pepsi had left with him were a shirt given him by Romano, and Caddy's gun.

He felt yet another surge of revulsion for the gun, the urge to throw it away, throw it somewhere far into the vastness of space to rot. But then he thought of Caddy . . . he might need the gun after all.

Apart from still being numb with fear and stunned with shock, Maria was practically wilting away in the heat, Gato looked totally bushed. If only they had some water to drink.

## The last rites

Caddy rolled down the now naked body of Gonzales next to his children.

He took the money out of the superintendent's wallet and put it in his pocket; quite rightly – after all, the man had taken *his* money out of *his* wallet and put it in his pocket. Gonzales's clothes and shoes and whatever else he had he bundled up, and after dipping some sticks and branches into his petrol tank made a bonfire and burned the lot. On the other side of the hill, well away from the main road.

Not that there was much traffic there at that time of the night anyway, or that anyone would have noticed anything or bothered if they did notice.

He felt a different man, a new man; a new man he could be proud of. Whatever else happened in his life from then on, whether he lived or died, he had one truly great moment to cherish, to look back on with his head held high.

Yes, he had become a new man, a better man, a stronger man; a man who could do anything, tackle anyone . . . . He smiled with satisfaction, filled his lungs with the fresh night air, free from city pollution, flared his nostrils, smelt the floating fragrance of the surrounding vegetation . . . and thought of Pepsi . . . The smile disappeared, the lips pursed, the mouth tightened – twisting itself; the eyes shone with a dark light.

He had to get the bastard. It was to be his life, or *his*!

## A sleepless night

Anna turned over in her sleep and nearly suffocated little Juan with her breasts as he lay by her side. She often took him out of his cot to sleep with her when Caddy was not there. Finding it difficult to breathe Juan kicked out with his legs, getting Anna in the stomach. She grunted and, falling out of sleep, looked around her with bleary eyes. Where was she? What was this warm, fleshy bundle doing next to her? Where was Caddy?

It only took a minute to resolve the first two questions. But the last bothered her. Where was Caddy? He had promised to call, but hadn't. She was never fully at ease when he was away. What with the growing violence these days, you could never tell when a policeman's life could be in danger. Even when he was not out on official duty. Perhaps more so when he was not on official duty. He was likely to let his guard down. Not be so vigilant.

A great unease began to rise from somewhere deep inside her and engulf her entire being.

She could no longer go back to sleep. Too much tossing and turning might wake little Juan. Getting out of bed she went and stood by the window looking out, hoping to see Caddy's short squat figure making his way to the front door.

But of course that was not possible.

She had to take her mind off the dark thoughts that began to gather like rain clouds over her heart.

Switching on the light she picked up Jane Austen's *Sense and Sensibility* and started looking for the page she had left it off at. The receipt for half a dozen eggs and a loaf of sliced bread that she was using as a bookmark had fallen out. She turned the pages this way and that, but could not remember where exactly she was. Irritated beyond reason, she threw the book away on to the bedside table, but it hit a reading lamp standing on it, making it tilt, shiver for a brief moment, then fall. She didn't bother to put it back up, and went over to the window again to look out.

## A black kind of sea

Pepsi said the best thing to do was to stay where they were. It was a road, and though not the one connecting main towns – the taxi had driven over to a by-road to rob the kids and spew them out – there was bound to be someone coming that way, at some time. But Gato said they should go and look for some water, at least some succulent plants. To their left, among the rocks and the shrubbery, there was a good likelihood of a stream, maybe even some edible roots and plants. They could rest under the shade of some bushes or something, and come back to the road when it was a little cooler, when the sun went down.

Pepsi felt that the misadventures and fiascos of last night and that day had dented his authority, at least in his own mind, and he did not want to push his opinion too strongly. Besides, he could see the sense in what Gato said, as long as they did not stray out too far, or they might get lost, and that would be the end of them.

They broke away from the road and headed to their right. Pepsi was getting more and more concerned about Maria. She seemed in a daze and, though putting one foot in front of the other, it did not look as if she knew what she was doing or where she was going. At first Pepsi was happy that she had not burst into tears and started crying. But now he wished she had, got hysterical, kicked up a tantrum, or *something*. He tried to talk to her, but she just kept on putting one foot in front of the other, eyes staring straight ahead, and wouldn't say anything.

The worst had just begun.

Pretty soon after they started their walk, they realised they were in the same endless desert this side of the road as the other. The hills and the greenery looked as far away as ever, no matter how much they walked – in fact, or illusion, they all appeared to recede further and further, the further they walked.

For ever and ever.

And ever.

And ever.

And ever.

Maria's feet faltered, she let out a squeaky gasp, and collapsed on the scorching sand.

Gato didn't even seem to notice, and carried on walking at the same dull, listless pace at which he was before, dragging his toes in the sand.

Pepsi tried to call out to him, but could hardly get the words out.

And then the world started to swim before his prickly dry eyes until it tired of swimming, let go of itself, and got sucked into an eternal and eternally black sea of nothingness . . .

## Some legal and other considerations

Tania rewound the tiny cassette and played it again. It was a conversation between Jim – Jim McPherson and Romano. Jim was a close friend of Romano, his confidant and lawyer. Six feet four, eighteen stone; a gargantuan, barrel-shaped, ginger-haired expatriate Scotsman who had settled here after some very dodgy dealings back home, if the rumour factory was to be credited. He was the one man who knew more about Romano than anyone. Anyone besides Tania, of course. She wouldn't have been surprised if he even knew about his Fridays . . .

It wasn't often that Romano spoke to Jim in any detail on the phone. Just made an appointment and talked to him face to face.

There wasn't much detail in this conversation either. Not much was said, basically just an appointment made; but there was a hint at an enquiry re the possible fallout from a hypothetical adoption by a hypothetical friend with a reputation at stake.

So Fox was telling the truth. She had come to believe him anyway – there was usually something different in his voice when telling the truth and when lying, but you could never really be sure with him. Anyway, if proof was needed . . .

She turned the tape player off, sat back in her chair and looked at her two mousy brown sons playing in the back garden outside the French windows. *And* she had seven brothers to look after. Seven costly, high-maintenance brothers.

She thought of Pepsi.

He wasn't a bad kid, poor sod. Life had dealt him a bad hand, that was all. But it wasn't her fault, not her responsibility. A thoughtful furrow appeared, and hovered uncomfortably over her pale brow.

## A vision, or not . . .

Pepsi had no idea of time or space as he lay baking in the sun-hot oven of his surroundings.

And then he began to see things. Visions, the Crow Boy would call them. Was it like this in the sweat lodge that he had told him about . . . ?

But how could *he* have visions. You needed to be an Indian to have visions. And a very special Indian at that.

But the conditions were right. Nearly. The Crow Boy had said that sometimes warriors would go out into the desert, naked, and starve themselves, rid themselves of all they possessed, except the two things that were truly theirs: their names, and their being; their dust, and their soul.

And then, if they were lucky, if they were blessed, they would have visions. Visions about their future, their lives, their ancestors, their tribes . . .

Pepsi was having visions of his ancestors. At least of his mother. And his sister. Could his sister be called his ancestor? Now that she was dead. The dead are our ancestors, the Crow Boy said. And his sister was dead. So she was his ancestor, even if she was younger than him. Was she?

He would have to ask the Crow Boy.

Lucky that he was here. So he could ask him. About his sister. And the visions.

He smiled at the Crow Boy. He smiled back at him.

But it was not the full-hearted full-toothed smile of old days. It was a rather tired smile. An 'old' smile. Can a smile be old? Pepsi wondered, and then laughed at the idea.

Not exactly laughed, not a real laugh, for his lips were too cracked and his mouth too dry to laugh. But still it was a laugh. A laugh in the mind.

214

'You better take care of yourself, and your things, Blood-brother, White Boy,' said the Crow Boy, flinging their knapsacks in front of him. He used to call him White Boy sometimes, which always annoyed Pepsi, for he was Hispanic, if a bit on the white side. But he didn't seem to mind today.

'Where did you get these?' said Pepsi, suddenly finding his voice – and the strength, the strength to sit up.

'The taxi driver threw these out of the window shortly after he threw you out. There was nothing in them he wanted. And it was black baggage. Evidence of a crime . . . you White Boys would say.'

What was this with him and this White Boy stuff today? Was it because he knew that he was going to ask him about his visions, and he wanted to mock the idea of white boys having visions . . . He was wondering about this when he found something greater to wonder about . . . 'How did you find me? Us? How, I mean . . . how? Here? Of all places?' He was slurring his words.

'Take some water out of your thingie and drink before you swallow your tongue. And give some to Maria, and that Cat over there.'

Pepsi felt like asking the Crow Boy to unzip the knapsack and get the bottle out for him, but the Crow Boy seemed to be looking at him as if looking through him to some distant horizon, and somehow he didn't have the nerve to ask.

But he was surprised to find how easy it was for him to get the bottle out, once he started to make the effort.

'Go easy,' said the Crow Boy as Pepsi began to gulp the water.

After he had taken some, he took it to Maria, and lifted her head up in his lap. It was only then that he noticed they were in a relatively cool, shady place, behind some bushes. How had they got there?

Soon Maria, Gato and Pepsi were sufficiently revived to wonder again, 'How did you find us here?'

'I am an Indian. A Crow.' He said with pride in his voice and his head held high, 'If that Mario and that José could track you down, and that Caddy, do you believe that I, a Crow Indian, could not?'

But in spite of his high-held head and the pride in his voice, there was something about El Cuervo that worried Pepsi. He seemed thinner; his voice, with all its pride, seemed to come from a long distance away; his black hair, thick and as long as his arm, looked unreal, evanescent; and there was something dark, something vague, something ashen about his appearance, as if he had only just emerged from the fire that burnt his house and family out.

But it was only because Pepsi was still not quite straight in the head himself. His eyes and his ears, same as the rest of his faculties, were not yet in full gear. Besides, if the Crow Boy had been tracking them since when, and through all kinds of days and all sorts of terrain, he would look a bit tired and off colour!

Or was he just a vision, too . . . part of a vision, a dream . . .

## Hot and cold

After the first high of power was over, Caddy began to assess his situation.

If the two pint-sized goons were right and they did not know who hired them, he had nothing to worry about. If they did, he was in the toilet, about to be flushed away to the mire of shit land.

His gut told him they were telling the truth. They were mere phone thugs. Nobody who saw them face to face would take on such pipsqueaky, squinty-eyed, bandy-legged matchstick men to do a takeaway job.

Anyway, it would be a long time before Gonzales's body was discovered, much less identified. He knew how slack the police could be, even where straightforward cases were concerned. With a naked body, miles out in the bush, and the only two who could connect him with the corpse, Carlitos and Alma, corpses before him, Gonzales was more likely to be linked with street kid crime, as he in effect was, than with another policeman, least of all an out-of-town policeman. The odds in favour of an early inquiry, especially an inquiry heading in the right direction, were less than minimal.

Unless the two midget hoodlums . . .

Or some connection could be established between both him and Gonzales with that garage in the town . . .

But none of it mattered now. What mattered was getting Pepsi. After all, he was the cause of it all . . .

He drove back to El Cedral, in uniform, claiming to be on official business, making enquiries.

It didn't take him long to find out that three kids of the type were seen getting into a taxi by the bus terminal. Nobody could be sure whose taxi it was, or wanted to admit being it. Any number of dilapidated little green-and-white VW Beetles scurried about all over the place like giant-sized, mutant ants so that it was impossible to distinguish between them, or their drivers.

He had two choices. One, to hang around and persist until he managed to discover which taxi driver it was; or, two, to get to the borderland of Maria's Heaven . . . and wait.

They were bound to get there in the end!

Unless any of the others looking for them got to them first.

Was this a chance he was willing to take?

He would keep in touch with Romano, his own police precinct, as well as the one in Merida, and the French Embassy.

But first he must call Anna. Let her know it was all taking a bit longer. The holiday in the cabin might have to wait.

It was at the thought of Anna, and thirty hours after the event, that the shakes set in.

He could barely manage to walk back to his car on uncertain legs. It took him for ever to unlock the door, his fingers were quivering so. Shoving a cold hand inside he twisted open the back door and managed to slide inside.

Hugging himself with both arms he began to shiver uncontrollably, from the ends of his hair to the tips of his toes.

## Some old mates

'What now!' said Gato looking up at the Crow Boy from his elbow and knee position on the ground, and then repeated the 'now', this time drawling it out in a long, nasal, catlike miaow.

'There's an Indian, a white Indian,' said the Crow Boy, smiling a faint smile, so unlike his usual wide-open grin, 'lives a few blocks from here, a few yucca blocks. And he has what any true Indian wants these days – a big American car!' His smile broadened, 'He will drive you, us, to . . . somewhere. He'd know.'

'A white Indian!' said Pepsi, eyebrows raised to almost hairline.

'His father was white, from England, some place like that,' said EC.

'How do you know him?' said Maria somewhat unexpectedly.

'I don't,' said EC and, without explaining, made as if to start walking. The others followed.

They started walking, Maria refusing Pepsi's offer to carry her. It was almost like old times. Pepsi's spirits revived. Even EC was beginning to look more like his previous self, walking with a jaunty, cocky step, whistling to himself.

A thousand questions had been wandering around in Pepsi's mind, but until then their own situation as well EC's look had prevented him from asking. Now seemed the right time. 'How is Pelon?' he asked.

EC's brow darkened again, his whistling stopped, but he answered readily enough, if in a softer than normal tone, 'He is fine. I managed to drag him out of the fire, no problem, even though he was half-dead with sleep and smoke and all the food he had eaten that day.'

'The fire at La Casita?' asked Pepsi, even though he knew the answer.

When EC didn't reply, Pepsi continued his questions, 'How is Miguel? Sarita?'

'Sarita is fine. Wears her ring through a shoelace round her neck these days. And Miguel has almost got his nose back.'

'What about Imelda?'

'Dead.' EC spoke through clenched teeth. 'Shot, shot through the belly where her kid lived. And Placko, you know he had come back, back when we had given him up as dead, well he's dead now. Ashes in the wind. And Pedro, and . . . and . . . I tried. I tried. I really tried . . .'

Pepsi got the impression that the Crow Boy's whole frame began to quiver as he spoke, like a tree through a heat haze, and it felt like he was going to dissolve, dissolve away into nothingness, when Maria uttered a little cry as her ankle brushed against a thorny bush. Pepsi turned to her and knelt beside her to check if she was badly cut or just scratched. It was just a scratch. When he looked up again, the Crow Boy seemed to be all right, the illusion of disintegration had gone.

He dared not ask about anyone else. His heart was still trying to get round the loss of some of the ones he had once loved.

## A new acquaintance

After what appeared to be an endless walk, they came to a flat, open clearing. To their right, bubbling downwards from between the huge phalanxes of black and puce, purple and slate grooves of a sharply sloping mountainside, and then more or less levelling out on the rocky terrain below, ran a frothy stream of sun-shiny water, clear as a baby's eyes, the pebbles and rocks strewn around and under its bed appearing to shiver with sensuous delight beneath its crystal flow.

Slightly off-centre within the clearance, outside a shabby, awkwardly rectangular wooden shack, stood this mile-long, half-a-kilometre wide, blazingly red, smooth-skinned, utterly swish Cadillac.

The incongruity of its brazenly flashy trashiness, the coldness of its fierce unnaturalness amid the passionately colourful, wildly abundant nature of the high desert – white and yellow, red and blue and pink, bright and misty against the green of the hills – hurt Pepsi's senses, and he shut his eyes for a deep, dark moment before opening them again to survey his surroundings more objectively. He looked at the Cadillac, found its long flowing body lines, its jutting-out elbows and razor-sharp haunches elegant beyond words, and silently took it in with dumb-struck adoration. Gato wanted to run up to it and start licking it. Maria was surprised, without judgement or evaluation.

A few metres to the right of the car and a couple of yards behind it sat a very old man on an upturned wooden box, eyes shut, arms crossed over his chest.

He was absolutely still. So still he could have been carved out of rock, the same rugged rock that shaped the chiselled teeth of the serrated sierras towering beyond and above their own insignificant dust.

Shirtless, in faded blue jeans, flared at the ankles; barefoot and with no Indian trappings of dress or body markings; the skin tanned like leather; sinewy, if a bit sagging at the upper arms, stomach flat, with no more than a few horizontal creases to mark his ninety-seven years – if EC was to be believed – he could have been any lean old man of any race or nationality, yet he looked the most Indian of any Indian there was, at least to Pepsi's eyes.

Perhaps it was the way he held himself. Perhaps it was the hair. Sun-white and left to hang loose, Crow style, flowing straight down until it brushed the earth in a long, low sweep.

The old man gave no sign of acknowledging their presence, even though he must have heard them coming.

When they were almost directly in front of him, EC stopped, and motioned with his hands for the others to stop too.

Very slowly, and still without a hint of a movement in any other part of his body, the old man opened his eyes. Just by moving his pupils, he began to study each of the children in turn. When it came to the Crow Boy, who was at the end of the line, his scrutiny stopped dead. His eyes stopped dead. The pupils dilated, burned with a sharp burst of light, then turned opaque.

His lips trembled, ever so slightly, his mouth opened and, ignoring all the others, he spoke directly to El Cuervo, 'So my time has come!' He hesitated perceptibly, then added, a question in his voice, 'But it is day . . . ?'

'Yes, it is day,' said the Crow Boy, 'And I am not come, I haven't gone.'

The old man thought this over, and a strange, passive sadness seemed to pass through his entire presence, which he held within himself as he spoke, this time to all the children, 'Come with me. Inside. Little girl, and big boys,' he said, uncoiling his long frame, standing up straight as a lamp-post and equally tall, hair trailing behind him like an integral component of some ethereal bridal gown. 'We'll find something to eat and drink for you. And, by the looks of you, you could do with some rest and sleep afterwards.'

He smiled, a smile that split his face in two, held together by a bridge of strong scraggy teeth.

Once inside, he introduced himself, 'My father was the White Sun, my mother the Red Moon; I am No Particular Time of Night. But you can call me John.'

'My father was a Mountain Crow, my mother a River Crow; I am Water Rock,' said the Crow Boy, 'but you can call me El Cuervo, or the Crow Boy, or just EC.'

'My father was a tree, my mother a cougar; I am El Gato, and you can call me Gato,' said El Gato.

Pepsi hesitated, then, 'My father is a jackass, my mother was . . . nothing. So am I, nothing. I was named Andrés, but you can call me Pepsi. Everybody does.'

No Particular Time of Night looked at him sharply, but said nothing. Maria seemed flushed and flustered and totally at a loss.

'Meet Maria,' said Pepsi coming to her rescue, ruffling her hair and hugging her to his legs.

The old man bowed gallantly, took Maria's hand in his own, leaned forward, and kissed it with utmost gentleness.

By the time the old man got together some food and some cool, fresh water from the stream, EC was nowhere to be seen. The old man didn't seem surprised and asked nothing about him. Pepsi felt uncomfortable, insecure, incomplete, but didn't say anything.

Then, after they had eaten and drunk, as suddenly as he had disappeared, EC appeared.

Pepsi smiled, relieved. This was more like the real Crow Boy. Here now, not here now, here again: elusive, hyperactive, unpredictable. His mind crossed over to their time in the old days, to the others in their set, and it hurt. He remembered the day he had plucked a daisy from the grass and given it to Imelda, on impulse, and she had kissed him, on the cheek, like a brother; but he had felt a sudden surge of some unnamed emotions rise within himself, making him feel both shamefully guilty and deliriously pleasured.

## Caddy updated

When Edmundo laughed, a shower of saliva sprang out of his mouth and sprayed anyone within reasonable distance, copiously – one of the many reasons he was discreetly avoided, even by those who cared for him, and there weren't many of those around. His nickname El Raton, the Thief, was as much irony as fact, for he managed to get caught whatever he stole and whenever – if at all he actually got to steal anything in the first place. He was also known as 'the boy'. Again with the same irony. Although nineteen plus, he still had no facial hair, and was the not-at-all proud possessor of smooth, flabby, pendulous breasts instead of a manly chest with a generously sprouting black fur, as was expected of the Machado males.

For once Edmundo was pleased with himself. *He would show them, show them all what he could do, what he was really made of!*

He lived with Anibal, his uncle. Or rather, Anibal lived with him. The house was his, his mother had left it to him. She had died after falling off the single step leading up to their door and breaking her hip. The hip never really got settled, despite three operations. Infection set in, and within weeks she was gone. Her husband and other son had been shot dead in a police ambush the year before. The only daughter had run off with the local butcher and was never seen or heard of again.

The uncle and his family, including *his* uncle, had left their rented little place in the shabbiest part of the town and come to stay with the orphan, to be with him, look after him. Everyone knew what it really meant, but not many were prepared to say it to Anibal's face. He was not a character to be messed about with.

Anibal drove a taxi, often accompanied by *his* uncle, a deceptively gentle looking old man, and a useful partner in his many unsavoury escapades.

They always made sure that Edmundo was never involved with any of their activities. Too stupid by half, and dogged by bad luck. Anibal, for all his bravado, was superstitious. Anyone under inauspicious stars had to be steered well clear of, religiously. And Edmundo was definitely it.

However, despite keeping the fat boy out of all their 'businesses', they had gradually begun to take his presence for granted, and often spoke of their gains and losses within hearing of the boy, something which they had carefully avoided in the earlier days. Even now they would never discuss anything with Edmundo at the table with them, as it were, or even in the same room. But if they were sitting out in the tiny back yard or the tinier courtyard, and the boy happened to be moving in and out playing ball with himself, or trying to fly a kite, they carried on their conversation, regardless. He never seemed to be paying any attention anyway. But he was.

Usually Edmundo didn't discover anything that really interested him, or that he fully understood. But only the other day he heard something that did interest him, and which he did fully understand. He heard that Anibal and his uncle had taken money off and dumped three kids somewhere along the desert road. He also heard they had taken three knapsacks, two green-and-black, one red, which too had been thrown out, after being checked out, some time soon after the kids.

At first he was only thinking of finding out how much the money was, and where hidden. If substantial, as he believed, then he would take it and make off somewhere to another town, and disappear. Like his sister. She was the only one who had ever shown him some consideration, even affection, however muted.

Two things happened to change his mind.

First, he heard that a policeman was asking after the three

kids. Anibal and the uncle had started going to another town with their taxi, about thirty miles east. As they were never regulars at the taxi arena in El Cedral – due to their extra-curricular activities, mostly related to small-time drug dealing – nobody much noticed their absence when they were not there; or for that matter, their presence, when they were.

The second, he saw a poster in the local supermarket with a picture of three kids on it, two boys and one girl; and beneath it, $500. He couldn't read what the poster said because he couldn't read. But he could tell numbers, and he recognised the magic symbol of the US dollar.

He could guess what it was about, but he wanted to make sure. He was in the habit of coming to the wrong conclusions, making mistakes, as everyone who knew him kept telling him. In fact, the only time anyone ever spoke to him was to tell him how wrong he was about this or that, rub his nose in his mistakes. He *had* to be sure. And to be sure, he had to ask someone. That was a problem. Not only was he ashamed to admit he couldn't read, he was not good at talking to people. Even those he knew well enough, much less strangers.

After a great deal of sweaty hesitation, moving forward and then back again, again and again, he managed to catch hold of an old woman, literally, by the sleeve of her dress with sweat-wet podgy fingers, and asked what it said on the poster, falteringly, adding, 'I have broken my glasses.' An afterthought, which he thought was really clever. It made him feel pleased with himself, more confident.

'I have left mine at home,' said the old lady in a squeaky voice, more scared of talking to him than he was of talking to her and, hurriedly freeing her arm from the fat boy's fat hand, she scurried out without bothering to shop.

More sweat, more pacing back and forth. The security guard by the door had been keeping an eye on him for some time. He knew him well, as did most people in the town. He started walking towards him with the intention of moving him out. But before he could say anything, Edmundo, abandoning his usual fear of advancing guards, blurted out his question. Adding his broken glasses bit. Somewhat taken aback, the guard decided to play along, and told him that the poster was about three missing kids, that a reward of five hundred US dollars was on offer, and that the reward money could be doubled if they were found alive and safe.

Even better than he had expected. He would have jumped for joy had he not been too fat and too lazy to jump.

Trying to look for and steal the money his uncle and great-uncle had taken from the kids was now out of the equation. Even if he could get to it, *and* get away with it, it would be chicken feed compared with US $500, with the possibility of double that. Plus he would have the great, great pleasure of landing Anibal and the old man in it. Years of neglect and abuse and humiliation would be avenged. He could hardly hold back his excitement.

The problem was how to get hold of the policeman. He did not want to go to the local police station. He had been there often enough. Held there often enough. He was too terrified even to go close to it, would never go close to it, unless taken by force, as he always was. This policeman was from out of town, he had heard that for sure, and that made him more confident, more daring . . . At least, less scared.

## A particular time of night

Moonlight streamed in through the open windows and open door of the wooden shack, illuminating the children as they slept on the far end of the floor. A deep and peaceful sleep.

No Particular Time of Night looked at the sleeping children, a wistful look in his night eyes. He was a child once – his heart was light then, as were his feet; his stomach was heavy. That was how it should be. These children had light stomachs, heavy hearts and heavy feet. That was how it should not be.

Through the open door and the open windows, he could see outside the craggy mountains looming high above the moon-pale horizon, hear the rippling of the stream, the sighing of the trees in the night breeze. He looked at the sleeping children again. At the brash car outside, a gift, a gift he could not refuse. All shapes of clay. All made of the same soul, infused with the same dust. The mountains, the breeze, the children, his favourite kettle that held his water hot for him to make his morning tea, the floor that allowed him to walk on it, the light of the stars, all, all varying shapes of clay, some stone-solid, some insubstantial as nothingness. He was proud and privileged to be among them, be a part of them.

He was wearing an eagle-feathered headdress, flared at the top; a leather dance kilt, beige, with a red strip round the waist and three red strips running through it vertically, its jagged edges reaching down to his mid-thigh, decorated with little bells held together with black feathers. A beaded necklace of predominantly white and blue colours hung round his neck. His face and body streaked with yellow, red and white paint.

He took out from somewhere a short-handled long-bladed knife with a curved edge, and sliced off three fine pieces of flesh from his upper arm, wrapped each piece up in a hand-sized bit of red leather, stitched it up, ran a leather string through it and made three necklaces, inserting his car keys into one of them. Kneeling beside the sleeping children he gently lifted the head of each and put the necklaces round their necks: one for Maria, one for Gato, and the one with the car keys for Pepsi.

Out in the open circle of the Mother Earth, standing with his feet well apart, No Particular Time of Night raised his hands high up in the air and started to sing.

| | |
|---|---|
| Bi taa wu hu hu | The earth – the crow |
| Bi taa wu hu hu | The earth – the crow |
| Nu naguna ua ti hu hu | The crow brought it with him |
| Nu naguna ua ti hu hu | The crow brought it with him |
| A hene heni aa! A heyene hene | *A hene heni aa! A heyene hene* |

He brought his hands down, covered his face, and crossed his arms over his chest.

| | |
|---|---|
| Ni nini tubi na hu hu | The crow has called me |
| Ni nini tubi na hu hu | The crow has called me |
| Nana thina ni hu hu | When the crow came for me |
| Nana thina ni hu hu | When the crow came for me |
| Ninita nau | I heard him |
| Ninita nau | I heard him |

He looked around him to see what he could see, and because it was a full moon shining brightly, high up in the clear sky, he could see everything. He saw the one world, and he saw the many worlds: the real, the illusory; the world of the living and the world of the spirits; the world of the ancestors and the world of the descendents; the tonal and the nagual and the neither. All worlds, all simultaneously opening up before his eyes. Some of what he saw made him smile, some made him laugh out loud. Some made him sad, so sad tears ran down his cheeks so hot and heavy they burnt furrows in his flesh. Some made him sing out with joy, or sorrow, some just stunned him into silence. And he saw the colours of his paint. The red. A red redder than the red of his Cadillac. The red of the blood of his ancestors, the red of the blood of the buffalo, the red of the blood of the children that littered the streets of the world like so much bloody trash. The red of life. The red of the red man. The yellow. The yellow of the sunflower and happiness and the laughter of children with food in their bellies and roofs above their heads and arms of love around their flesh. And white. The white of buffalo bones and the white of the white man, and the white of the frothing stream with the cool life-giving waters. The white of the sun. And blue. The blue of the sky and the sea and of the beads of peace.

He saw and he saw: till all the many worlds merged into one that was nothing like any of the other worlds – and it was beautiful; till all the many colours blended into each other to form colours that were new colours – and they were beautiful; till all his feelings mixed and grouped and regrouped to become feelings like none others – and they were beautiful.

His time had come.

He started collecting stones and rocks that lay scattered all over the place and making a pile of them by the stream. When he couldn't find any more on the ground, he waded into the stream and began picking out pebbles and stones and rocks and shells, whatever he could find, from the riverbed. After he had made a huge enough pile, he sat upon it with his eyes shut, not moving a muscle.

| | |
|---|---|
| Heye heye heye heye Aho ho! | *Heye heye heye heye Aho ho!* |
| Heye heye heye heye Aho ho! | *Heye heye heye heye Aho ho!* |
| | |
| Na dag aka na | Because I am poor, |
| Na dag aka na | Because I am poor, |
| De gyago mga da tsa to | I pray for every living creature, |
| De gyago mga da tsa to | I pray for every living creature, |
| Ao nyo! Ao nyo! | *Ao nyo! Ao nyo!* |

When Pepsi woke up in the morning he could see neither John No Particular Time of Night, nor El Cuervo. He made calling-out sounds, like 'Yoo hoo' and 'Ahoy' – but no response, except that Maria and Gato woke up.

All three went outside to look. At first they couldn't see anyone. Then there was a rustling sound a little further out, close to the top end of the stream. It was EC. Pepsi was so pleased to see him he ran towards him shouting, 'Hey man where have you all . . .' He stopped when he got close enough to see the look on EC's face.

Just to the right of where EC stood, in a small ditch the size of a man, lay No Particular Time of Night. He was dead.

'Get busy,' said the Crow Boy, and pointed to the pile of stones and rocks and pebbles.

When Pepsi looked blank, EC got to the pile, picked up as many stones and rocks as he could, walked up to where No Particular Time of Night lay, and gently dropped some over him in the ditch.

With the help of Maria and Gato, the old man was soon covered all over with the pile he had collected overnight.

EC sent the others back to the shack. He wanted to be left alone at the grave.

After a long moment of still silence, the Crow Boy began dancing and singing round and round No Particular Time of Night's grave, his body almost dissolving into nothingness in the flaky atmosphere, but his voice ringing out loud and clear.

| | |
|---|---|
| Ahu na he suna nin | There is our father |
| Ahu na he suna nin | There is our father |
| Ni taba tani bata hina ni | We are dancing as he wishes us to dance |
| Ni taba tani bata hina ni | We are dancing as he wishes us to dance |

| Ha ka ha sabina na he suna nin | Because our father has so commanded us. |
| Ha ka ha sabina na he suna nin | Because our father has so commanded us. |

When the Crow Boy finally got in, Maria asked, 'What happened to John?'

'He has gone home,' said the Crow Boy.

'I am going home too,' said Maria, all excited.

'Yes you are,' said the Crow Boy.

'I haven't got a home to go,' said El Gato.

'Yes you have,' said the Crow Boy, 'and you are going there. We are all going there. We are all going home. There is nowhere else to go.'

## Another start

It was another day.

'What now?' said Gato, without a cat drawl.

'Use the keys No Particular Time of Night has gifted you,' said EC, looking at Pepsi and pointing to the car, 'and drive!'

Pepsi had secretly driven his father's car when he lived there. It was mainly along the driveway, though he had gone for a little run on the spare roadster once or twice, only down the road in front and back again; but more than just the driveway.

His blood bubbled with excitement at the thought of having that flesh-smooth, wine-sparkling, red beauty beneath his driver's butt.

He plucked a huge cowboy hat off a wall and stuck it on his head, picked up a pair of night-black sunglasses from a box near a cooking stove and shaded his eyes, then headed for the car.

## El Raton and the vanishing American dollars

Edmundo needn't have worried about finding Caddy. Caddy found him. The next day.

Caddy had spoken to the security guard at the supermarket when he was asking around about the children. He had told the guard where to get in touch with him if he heard anything useful. He did, and told him about the local weirdo asking about the poster, and being wildly excited about it all. It wasn't difficult for Caddy to find the local weirdo!

Edmundo couldn't believe his luck. For once the gods were with him. Anibal could no longer say he was born under 'ugly' stars. Mother Mary had finally listened to his pleas . . .

But he was ahead of himself. All Caddy wanted to know was where the children were, might be. He showed no anger that they had been robbed nor any concern for their welfare. Anibal and the old man were away on one of their trips doing whatever they did when they disappeared for long periods, as they did from time to time, often not returning for a week or more. Caddy didn't even want to know, let alone talk of sending any search parties to look for them, arrest them, or something, as Edmundo was hoping, even insisting, in his own feeble manner. Once he got some idea where the kids were thrown out – the knapsacks on the road being the most important indication to look out for, there hadn't been any high winds recently to displace them – he was off in his car, without so much as thanking the boy, much less any talk of five hundred American dollars.

Anibal was right. Everyone was right. He *did* get everything wrong. He *was* born under ugly stars. But he wasn't down for long. He could still try to hunt for the stolen money. With the eternal optimism of the perennially stupid, he began to visualise what he would do with all that loot, and how it would change his life, finally!

## Red car, blue car

Caddy was tired of driving through the desert. He had been driving for hours. Could those thieving bastards have come this far? Not very likely, unless they were planning to go ahead to the next border rather than hitting back home. Maybe they were going across. If they were into some sort of drug-running, as the fat boy said, they *would* be going across. Perhaps he should have waited for them, tried to get to them, get them, and find out what really happened before making this journey. But if he had, it would have meant more delay. The kids could die out here. And he didn't want them to die. He wanted to kill them.

Also, the longer he left it, the more the chances of those knapsacks disappearing. In spite of the recent lull, high winds were common in the area. Besides, even though there wasn't much traffic on that road, sometimes none for days, if his information was correct, some car happening to pass by might have . . . Out of curiosity, if nothing else. Would they? Would a car driving fast enough on that road even *notice*! Unless someone was specially looking out for something. Perhaps that doggone taxi driver again, removing the evidence.

Caddy's brain was chasing itself getting nowhere. It was hot, his air conditioning was kaput, and he cursed those potbellied rich bastards who had everything, including perfectly air-conditioned cars.

Just then he saw a rich bastard's car behind him. Quite a way behind, but he could still tell what it was. A Cadillac, a bright red Cadillac. Maybe with a family in it. Going to the mountains up ahead. Or the beach further on. Lucky bastards. Little Juan would never have a car like that to cruise through the desert in, going on to . . . somewhere on the beach, or the mountains . . .

He was not going to let it go past him. He put his foot down on the accelerator. But would he be able to keep ahead of the Cadillac? A Caddy, he thought to himself, like me, and laughed. A hollow mirthless laugh. If only he was a real Caddy, a Cadillac among men.

He needn't have worried. At the rate the Cadillac was coming, it was never going to overtake him. It didn't even look particularly steady. Perhaps the man, or the woman, at the wheel – he was too far ahead to make out the driver – had had a binge the night before. Drinking, snorting, partying . . . Rich bastards, rich bloody bastards . . .

He tried to get the rich bastards out of his mind. He had other things to think about.

What if the knapsacks had been picked up, along with the kids? There would be no trail to follow then.

Quite likely.

But if so, he was still going about it the right way. They had certainly not backtracked towards El Cedral. He would have known if they had. If he failed here, he would have to go on to cross the border to the little slut's palace of garbage dumps. That is where they would be heading, he was certain.

He looked into his mirror to see where the red Cadillac was. It seemed to be getting closer. He couldn't allow that. Not if he could help it. For a brief second he thought he got a glimpse of the driver. Or rather, of a huge hat and black shades. 'Typical,' hissed Caddy through his teeth, and accelerated.

Then stopped. At that speed he wouldn't be able to spot the knapsack. Pausing for a breath, he restarted. The red Cadillac whizzed past him waywardly. 'Duck,' he shouted to himself. He had just looked down for a moment, the moment the Cadillac overtook; he had not been able to get a look at the driver, or anyone else in the car. There was no one in the back seat, and three heads in the front: two in the seat next to the driver.

'Rich kids!' he fumed, 'bloody rich kids!'

In the driving seat Pepsi was getting more confident by the minute. The desert road was vast and clear, except for a single car, erratically accelerating and decelerating, yet far enough ahead to worry about. He began to smile to himself, hum an old tune his mother used to sing to him, and imagined that he was not nothing after all. That if he could drive this elegant perfection of a machine, through the heart of this huge country, he could do anything, *be* anyone. Anything or anyone he wanted to do or be.

Stretching out in the back seat – the Crow Boy and the Cat were both in the front with Pepsi – Maria began to dream of home and Heaven. Not a sleeping dream this time. But a *real* dream. At least that is what she called it. A real dream was that which you had in your head and which always came true.

She was finally on her way home, just over and across the mountains to the right. The soft arms of her mother embraced her in a tight embrace as her father's face smiled the smile of a cat licking its lips after a drink of warm milk.

## Love discovered

It was only two days that Gonzales had not returned home or been to work or been seen by anyone, yet a mountain came and sat upon Mercedes's chest.

Something awful had happened, otherwise he would have at least called her, or somehow let her know where he was or what was going on, no matter how secret his assignment. Yes, something awful had happened, something awful and irreversible – like death.

She would never see him again. She was sure of it.

Her diamond earrings, her ruby brooch, her Persian rugs, even her handcrafted dining table and set of eight matching chairs meant nothing. Not without Gonzales. No more than the dust collecting on the handcrafted dining table and the set of eight matching chairs. She used to go fire-mad if a dot of dirt came and sat anywhere on any piece of her furniture or whatever else lay elegantly displayed in her showcase of a house, much of it courtesy of Gonzales's reluctant father-in-law. Now she wouldn't care if a thundery cloud of grime came and showered over the house and all its contents.

She had never realised how much she loved Gonzales. It was a strange discovery, as exhilarating as it was terrifying.

Kneeling before the life-size sculpture of Jesus on the cross that dominated the hallway, she crossed herself, clutching a rosary tightly within her left fist, and swore that if only he would bring her husband back from the dead, like he did Lazarus, she would never go shopping again.

## A fork, a choice

Caddy was getting frustrated. The road seemed to be leading nowhere slow. No sign of the knapsack. It couldn't be this far. He must have missed it, or it had been blown away or picked up by someone. He began to wonder whether to turn back and look again, or to go ahead to Maria's land. The indecision made him angry . . .

He could feel the anger boiling over from the top of his head and flowing down to his toes, *see* his eyes getting bloodshot, without looking into the mirror. He couldn't let the bastard give him the slip, not now, not after all he had done to him, made him do: lie to his wife, lie to his colleagues, and worse, kill a fellow policeman, even if he was a . . . whatever he was!

He nearly ran over some creature scuttling across the road, and then felt angrier still that he hadn't. His dilemma was further compounded when in the distance he saw the road fork: veering west towards the mountains, and eastwards into more of the same terrain. He began drumming his fingers on the steering wheel and whistling sorrily an old tune his father used to whistle on his fishing trips. He did not know the words. Could never bring himself to ask the forbidding old man.

A respite of sorts appeared on the horizon.

Snuggled neatly within the angle of the diverging roads was a petrol station. He could stop, fill up the car, have a cup of coffee, relax, and think about which way to take next.

## One little Indian

Caddy pulled into the cracked and dusty driveway of the petrol station and braked in front of one of the two rusty, old, lonesome-looking pumps. From the shop-cum-café set on the other side of a rudely concreted car-parking space with a garage to the left, a young Indian boy came rushing out, big grin exposing strong white teeth, shoulder-length straight black hair flapping about his infectiously cheerful, snub-nosed, moon-round face. He was bare-foot, his shorts too big and baggy for his narrow stick-like legs, his right shirt sleeve hanging loose with no arm inside, the left one ripped off leaving the arm bare up to the shoulder. He was so like one of those stinky street boys Caddy almost reached for his gun.

'Do I fill it up, mister?' his grin extended from temple to temple as he peered through the worn-out Oldsmobile's windscreen.

Caddy nodded angrily – angry for no particular reason he could be sure of; twisted open the car door, stepped out, 'And give it a good clea . . . can you?' he pointed to the boy's missing arm with his chin.

'Oh sure, mister,' the boy giggled as he spoke, 'my one hand works faster than two, my Pa says. And he's never wrong, my Pa, you bet!' You could almost touch the pride in his voice. Whether the pride lay in his Pa's infallibility or his one-handed dexterity was not quite clear. Probably both.

The shadows were slanting more and more eastwards as the sun continued its course down the horizon yet without losing any of its ferocity. Caddy removed his sunglasses and wiped the sweat off his forehead with his left thumb, fanning his face with the free hand.

'Why don't you go in and cool off, mister,' said the boy as he fixed the pump hose into the petrol hole of the car, 'have a soda or something. We have ice, to be sure. The coolest, prettiest, bluest ice you ever saw this side of the mountains.'

As Caddy muttered a response and started moving towards the semi-derelict building, the boy shouted, 'I'll have it shining like gold by the time you get back, mister.'

Caddy glanced back at the road and remembered the Cadillac. His curiosity about it had never quite gone away. Surely it would have passed this way. Maybe even stopped for a rest and a fill-up.

'Did you see a red Cadillac come this way?' he stopped and asked the boy, making his voice sound casual and disinterested.

'Sure, mister,' the boy looked up, squinting his large black eyes as he turned to look up against the sun to where Caddy was standing, 'they were here having a soda and bagels. Left only a couple of minutes before you came in.'

'Which way did they go?'

The boy pointed towards the mountain road.

Caddy's mind was made up. That was also the way to Maria's homeland, so it was the best way to take anyway.

Now *he* would overtake them! And he'd show them how it was done!

As a policeman he had a good idea of the speed they were driving at. If they had left a couple of minutes ago then, even after a good rest here, he would be able to catch up with them within an hour, at most.

But he might not stop, after all.

All of a sudden he felt lighter, cheerful; and full of energy. Looking forward to the chase was a policeman's Viagra. For any policeman. Especially Caddy.

He might even overtake them, slow down, let them go ahead, and overtake them again, and again . . .

## Imelda

Imelda was tired, a haggard, down-turned expression on her thirteen-going-on-fifty-year-old face, her hair still covered in a cloak of ash and dust, a wild look in her wide brown eyes: a look she had carried with her ever since she saw the Crow Boy trying to drag the screaming Vicente out to safety from the fire when a burning girder fell off the roof upon them, trapping them both beneath it.

Besides being helplessly in love with Vicente, she had totally depended on him to run her life, pimp for her, get her food, find her clothes, shoes . . . and he would have looked after her baby, even if it was of that bastard she had seen off this troublesome world. She almost envied him now. If only she had killed herself instead of him. But she couldn't now. She couldn't even kill herself. Not now, now that she could feel the baby inside her, feel it kick – at times she believed she could hear him breathe. And Vicente wanted her to have that baby. He did not want her to get rid of it. A sin, a grave sin, he said. And now that he was gone, this baby was all that was left to remind her of him. Even if it wasn't his, he had always said he would look after it like it was his. And in a way, it was his. After all, if he had not introduced her to Juarez, it would never have got into her belly . . .

With the Crow Boy gone too, there was no one in the whole world who would look after her. And the baby. What was she to do? She hadn't eaten in . . . she couldn't even remember since when. Not properly, nothing except what she had scraped off the street where someone had dropped a stinky burrito with a few beans in it. Not that she was feeling particularly hungry. In fact, when she thought about it, she wasn't hungry at all. In fact, the very thought of food seemed to make her want to puke, not that she could puke, with nothing inside her, except the baby, and she couldn't puke him out. Could she?

She remembered her mother, Justina, selling *three dishes* (anal, oral and vaginal sex) behind market stalls at night and then coming home to their crumbling shack by the open sewer in no man's land behind the old tannery in the old town in the morning to a beating by her boyfriend Roberto (not Imelda's dad) for not bringing enough money back and squandering it on glue. Her clients were mostly poor themselves, peddlers, loaders, brickies, and couldn't afford to pay much, even if they wanted to, which of course they didn't; but Roberto wouldn't understand.

One day he picked up a big rock and sent it flying full force across Justina's head, killing her on the spot. He made Imelda hold the body while he cut it up with a rusty old axe and threw the pieces one by one into the meandering sewer. Then, to console himself for his loss, he had sex with Imelda. She had often wondered what it would be like to lose her virginity, or what life would be without her mother. That day both her questions were answered more or less simultaneously.

She continued to live with Roberto, supplying him with his *three dishes* for her upkeep. Then one day Roberto upped and left, and Imelda's cosy little world collapsed. Roberto had treated her well, never beat her, never made her sell herself to others . . . She didn't know what to do now or where to go. Offering her three dishes to one man on a regular basis was one thing, having to peddle them in the open market scared her. She was not exactly a child, Roberto often reminded the child, but still, she didn't feel quite up to dealing with the adult world all on her own.

And then Vicente came along.

Imelda got a family of friends and learnt the meaning of love.

Now Vicente was gone. So were the others. Some dead, others scattered. After the fire.

It was as bad as when Roberto left.

Worse.

It was as bad as when Mother died.

She remembered.

She had forgotten about her mother's death. In fact she had

never thought about her mother, up until now. Alive or dead. It was as if she had never existed. Everything seemed to have been wiped clear out of the grooves of her brain.

Now it all came back to her as if it was happening now, before her eyes; as indeed it did, all that time ago. She could see, touch, the chopped-up limbs of Justina. She could feel them coming alive. Each separately; each with a life of its own.

She began to kick out with her hands, as if she were trying to fight off an invasion of killer bees, screaming and shouting, turning round and round, like a dancing dervish, screaming, shouting, whirling round and round, kicking away with her hands, fighting off killer bees.

A door opened out into the blackness of the night and a man stood framed within it, barefoot and in his boxer shorts. He saw the screaming Imelda dancing around virtually at his doorstep. After a moment's hesitation he rushed out, put his arms around her and, ignoring a couple of other doors and windows that had opened, he more or less dragged the girl inside his house.

The man was Marcos, Marcos Pollini: the security guard whose wife had had a baby girl and who had promised to help Pepsi, if he needed help.

The Crow Boy had told Imelda that if ever she was in trouble, to go to Marcos and ask for help. Just as Pepsi had told him. But Imelda had forgotten about him. She certainly did not remember his address. So how she ended up there, she had no idea. It was as if someone had taken her under his wings and flown her there, flown her there and then vanished into the blackness of the night. Or maybe she had the address somewhere in the back of her mind and made her way there somehow. After all, it was an area well familiar to street kids.

## Friday the thirteenth

Romano was superstitious. Crossed himself more often than he washed himself, avoided all ladders and kept out of the way of cats even if they were not black. Friday the thirteenth was a definite no-no. Yet, and yet, this Friday the thirteenth he couldn't help himself.

Last Friday he was away for a weekend meeting of the bigwigs of his party. The Friday before that his mother was not feeling well and he had to go and see her on the pain of dying unforgiven by the one who gave him birth. He was just too knotted up inside to let another Friday go by without his foray into lust.

As he sat naked on the springy bed of the two-star hotel, like an unenlightened Buddha incapable of laughter, there was a knock on the door. He pulled a corner of a sheet to cover his middle and said, 'Enter.'

He had been promised a virgin, but he wasn't expecting one. He had been let down so often that he had given up expecting, though he could still hope.

His face lit up when he saw a swarthy, bearded man come in, holding on to the arm of a girl. That she did not come on her own but had to be brought in grasped by the arm was a good sign in itself; but the bewildered look on the girl's face, and the fact that she looked no more than twelve, was almost a confirmation that this time he had hit the jackpot after all.

He could feel the sheet rising in his lap.

This Friday the thirteenth was going to be a lucky day for him!

## A free beer

Caddy went into the shop and was about to order something for himself at the counter, looking around to see what was available, when the old Indian by the cash counter asked rather brusquely if he could first pay for the petrol.

Caddy was not best pleased by the insolence of this native, but reached for his wallet, looked at the numbers brought up by the till, and paid.

As soon as the man had taken the money, he looked straight into Caddy's eyes and said, 'Now leave, please.'

Caddy nearly burst a blood vein, 'You fucki . . .'

'Please,' the man broke in, with an unusually calm voice, even for an old Indian, 'Leave. I am going myself. Out. Into the open. Please. Here, you can have this, no need to pay,' with that he handed Caddy a can of beer, pocketed all the money in the till, locked it, and walked out, beckoning Caddy to do the same.

Caddy followed, almost hypnotised.

Once outside, the old man called out to his son, took him by the hand and started hastily walking towards the back of the station.

Caddy looked at their retreating backs with a look in his eyes, then shrugged his shoulders and walked towards his car. *Good*, he thought, *I'll catch up with the Cadillac in no time now . . .*

As he was getting into his car he felt a jolt beneath his feet, as if someone had kicked his shin or tugged at his trouser leg. He looked down . . . nothing. Shrugging off an eerie feeling he got into his car and switched on the engine.

## The coming together

They had not left the petrol station long when the Crow Boy, growing even more ashen, stretched out and held Pepsi's hand on the steering wheel with frantic urgency, 'Stop,' he almost hissed, 'just stop.'

Although there was enough room on the side of the road – an endless stretch of sandy plains – Pepsi, unaware of the niceties of driving, braked and stopped almost in the middle of the road. He had hardly managed to look at the Crow Boy with surprise and a question in his eyes, when he saw in the rear-view mirror a car driving like mad and coming just behind them.

He tried to restart and move out of the way, but only managed to put himself more in front of the other car as it made a screeching swerve.

Just as the sky-blue Oldsmobile shot into the blood-red Cadillac with a bang and a clang, the earth exploded with a thundery rumble and an almighty crackling roar. Both cars flew up in the air before being pulled back by gravity, one sinking deep into a widening, zigzaggy crack, the other miraculously landing on its wheels, still shaking and rolling along with the landscape.

Then came another explosion, terrifyingly loud, hurtling through the atmosphere like a misanthropic lightning-strike gone wild, hitting out at the world of humans with full ferocity. This was followed by several lesser booms and bangs. An amalgam of smoke and fire reared up to the skies as if hell itself was burning itself; waves of skin-blasting heat, carried by a sudden storm of hysterical winds, started rushing right up to where the two cars lay, one over, one underground. The petrol station pumps had burst into an uncontrollable, roaring, raging inferno of flames.

Even now the earth was quivering and trembling, though no more than a man in high fever.

## Earth-shattering consequences

The damage in surrounding cities was not as bad as it could have been had the epicentre of the earthquake not been so far out in the desert plains.

None the less, in one metropolis, a small, rather seedy-looking, foul-smelling, mud-coloured, two-star hotel was among the collapsed buildings. Although some of the hotel staff, minimal anyway, managed to escape, none of the guests, again not many, was able to get out in time. Their bodies lay buried in the crumbled remains, some quite unrecognisable, even if their 'loved ones' had been able to get to them, or knew where they were or what they were doing in that particular establishment on a late Friday afternoon.

## Aftermath

The Crow Boy opened the car door to his right to let in some fresh air but only got the fumes of burning petrol. He turned to look at Pepsi in the driving seat and at El Gato squashed in the middle. Both had a dazed, stricken look in their eyes, but neither seemed badly hurt. Scratches on elbows, forearms and a cut or two on the forehead were the only apparent signs of injury.

The upward thrust of the earth had minimised the forward jolt of being hit by the car from behind. Maria lay on the carpet at the back of the car. Had she been sitting upright, she might have caught her head on the seat in front. But as she was lying down, she had just rolled over on the floor without being hurt.

Caddy, shook-up and dazed, watched with horror as he felt himself being swallowed by the crackling earth.

There was a sudden, jolting thud. The car hit ground. This would have catapulted him out through the roof had he not been safety-belted: a promise he had made to Anna, and which he always honoured.

He could still see the sky above. At least the earth hadn't closed in on him. He hardly had time to breathe with relief when he saw the shadowy shape of a ragamuffin pulling at the driver's door handle.

The weird slate-coloured shape, as if made of liquid ash, looked more like it was floating in the air than walking on the ground. Caddy's heart fell to his groin. The creature was so much like one of the street creeps he had helped ease out of this world. What was he doing tugging at his car door? Had one of those low-life scum managed to escape the fires of hell to wreak revenge on him . . . ?

He let out a soprano-landing-on-the-sharp-end-of-a-javelin yell. He would rather have been ingested by the soil than so summarily confronted by this being from nowhere healthy or sane, or earthly.

The yell was heard by Pepsi, Maria and the Cat Boy who had just stumbled out of their red car. Maria was looking dazed; El Gato was looking at the car, no longer shiny and bright but covered with dust and sand and pieces of rock; Pepsi was looking for the Crow Boy and wondering where he had disappeared.

All three rushed towards the hole in the ground from where the yell appeared to have emanated.

Caddy heard the stamping of feet above and looked up. He could see three pairs of mucky, scrawny legs, but because of the angle of his car window, only from above the ankles to just below the knees. *They were coming, they were all coming. Coming to take him away, take him away to their own grisly corner of hell. To be with* them, *for ever. What greater punishment than to be with them for ever . . . for ever . . . for all eternity . . .* He was so scared now he couldn't even yell out. Or move.

## An unexpected encounter

'Get out of there, mister,' said the Crow Boy to the hunched shoulders and the head of black hair of the man in the car, 'Get out, or another shake of the earth and you'll be under a mound of rock.'

Even in his state of mind Caddy was able to appreciate the sense of it. Unlocking the door he gingerly began stepping out of the car, but covering his face with arms raised and bent at the elbows, fists turned inwards and resting on his chest. The Crow Boy thought it was to protect himself from the fallout of the crumbling, sliding hole they were in.

'Give us a hand,' the Crow Boy called out to Pepsi at the same time as Pepsi yelled, 'So there you are. We were worried about you.'

It was only when Caddy was fully pulled out of the hole, not without a considerable struggle and sliding hands and flying legs and knee-grazing of all concerned, and after Pepsi could properly smell the smell he had been trying not to smell, that he knew who the man was.

Caddy, too, saw what he saw.

## Monday night in the city – one

Tania turned over restlessly in her bed. Romano had not been home for two days and three nights. And during the weekend. This was the first time he had missed going to church with his mother – unless he was officially away somewhere. And no telephone messages either. To her, his mother, or any of his colleagues or workers. Not even to Julio in whom he confided everything. Surely something was wrong . . . Something must have happened to him on his Friday night out to 'the lodge'!

*Someone may well have beaten half the life out of him. A doped-up pimp . . . a betrayed lover . . . an angry brother . . .? Or just a run-of-the-mill mugger? Good. He deserved it.*

But even so, she was worried. Where *could* he be? In what state? He couldn't be sitting dying somewhere? Or dead? Could he?

She began to consider her options, in case.

## Monday night in the city – two

Little Juan would not stop crying. Anna carried him in her arms, rocking him as if he was four months old rather than four years.

'You're crying for your daddy, aren't you? My sweet little diamond. But he'll be back. He'll be back soon. I promise. Then we'll all go for a holiday. In Daddy's friend's cabin. It will be lovely there. I am sure it will. I wonder why he hasn't called for the last two days. He always does. Every day. It's been two days now. I hope he's all right. Don't you? My precious little flower. Let's pray, let's pray, both of us, to Santa Maria, that he's all right. Oh, come on. Stop your crying now. It is bad luck to go on crying like that. For no reason. The doctor said you were all right. Grandma took you herself to see the doctor. He says you are OK. Then why don't you stop crying? You'll wear me out. I have to be fresh, and pretty, for your daddy when he gets back home. So have you. We can't have him thinking we didn't look after you when he was out, out doing his . . . duty . . . for us, for the good of the city. He's a good man, your daddy. You should be proud of him. Real proud. I wish you would grow up to be like him. If only, that will be all my dreams come true. I won't ask anything more from our dear Lord, except that you grow up to be good, and kind and gentle, like your dear sweet dad . . .' She began to hum a lullaby in a faltering but none the less beautiful voice and, still singing, sat down on the edge of the bed and fell asleep.

## Back to Friday evening in the desert

Caddy would rather be facing demons from hell than Pepsi.

The kid had saved his life, again! It did not matter that the other creature had pulled him out, and that all had hauled him up; as far as he was concerned, it was Pepsi and Pepsi alone who had saved his life. This was worse than *sparing* his life, as he had done the last time.

He couldn't let that happen. He couldn't . . . he couldn't . . . he couldn't . . . but it *had* happened. How could he possibly avenge this double humiliation. Especially now, as he stood before him and that scurvy-ridden slut of his, and two others of their ilk, his gun in the car and nowhere to run. Or hide.

But he needn't have worried. Habits of a lifetime are hard to deny. It was Pepsi who started to run, pulling Maria with one hand, El Gato with the other, and signalling the Crow Boy to do the same.

But the Crow Boy stood his place, staring straight into Caddy's eyes. Caddy didn't move either. But not out of choice. He just could not move, held by the Crow Boy's gaze as if he were the Ancient Mariner reborn, come to haunt the sea of sand and all those who sailed on it.

Caddy felt his legs turning to stone. Or rather, to wood. Wood about to catch fire. He could feel the heat, *see* the heat. All the heat of the sun, the desert, the burning petrol station, seemed to have gathered itself in the Crow Boy's eyes and be transmitted to his wooden body. All of a sudden, a crowd of flames reared out of the Crow Boy's eyes and launched itself furiously and ominously towards the centre of Caddy's being.

## The fire grows

Caddy's body stirred, his head lifted, his eyes opened, and his brain began to collect itself, trying to figure out whether he was alive or dead.

He must have fainted in the heat. He felt as if he was on fire, or burning with fever. Maybe he was. If only Anna was here. She would make such a fuss over him. He could do with some fuss. But where was she? Where was *he*?

He sat up, put his head between his knees, brought his hands up to his hair and started to massage his scalp, thankful for a slight thunder in the air that indicated some clouds were on their way to bring some much-needed shade and cool to the scene. Or was it the earth rumbling. A replay of the earthquake. Earthquake! Suddenly he remembered. But just the earthquake, nothing more.

He tried to scramble to his feet, but his head swirled, he staggered, fell on his knees and held on to his head again. Just then, through the corner of his eye or however, he wasn't sure, he caught a glimpse of something red shining under the glare of the sun. He squinted his eyes and looked, the palm of his hand sheltering his eyebrows. There was this sleek body, beautiful, beautiful like the body of a woman, a woman made to perfection, with perfect skin, the skin of steel. He was looking at a car. A red car.

It all came to him now. He jumped up, all his fatigue forgotten, looking apprehensively all around to see if Pepsi or any of the other scum were about. None. Not even the scary boy made of frozen ash. He crossed himself and thanked Mother Mary that he wasn't. There was something unnatural about him. Something eerie. Something . . . ungodly, unchristian, unholy. Or something that made *him* feel ungodly, unchristian, unholy. But even though that creature was not here, he could still feel the heat that seemed to have entered his bones in his presence.

With anchor-heavy feet he robot-walked to the car, peeped through the window to make sure if anyone was inside. As if automatically, his hand went to the door handle of the driver side of the car . . .

He felt the soft, tender leather of the seats with hands trembling with the excitement of feeling the soft, tender leather of the seats, touched the steering wheel with the gentle reverence normally reserved for religious icons by a good Catholic like him; and then grasped the glove compartment groove with fumbling fingers and opened it without the particular purpose of opening it. Inside was a gun. *His* gun. He knew almost immediately. Knew, with the certainty with which you recognise old friends, even if you see them after years of distance, age, wear and tear.

His jubilation was tempered with heat exhaustion. Gun in hand, he turned round to lean against the body of the car. And then he saw it. Saw the billowing woman of fire, filled out and overly pregnant, her time come, shooting out baby fires. Babies, born alive and agile and active. All wavering their way towards him.

The fire at the petrol station was discharging sparks, sparks that were igniting tinder-dry scrub and bushes scattered all over the plains, not to mention the wandering tumbleweeds. Ahead of the fires, and behind Caddy and the car, the not-so-distant mountains were covered with a variety of trees. The fire could engulf the whole area in an ever-expanding lake of fire, if the sinisterly advancing, hissing, bubbling stream of flames got to them.

## Monday night in the city – three

Julio had a hunch. A hunch he had to follow through.

His boss not back from his Friday night out, and the collapse of a few buildings in the city . . . There had to be a connection. With Romano gone, *if* he was gone, his future would be secure, and he could choose to work where he wanted, when he wanted, if he wanted. He knew that in case of the 'worst' happening, there was a tidy comfort insurance for him in Romano's will. But the will could only be effective if there was a body. Or else he'd have to wait for goodness knew how long. Especially the way things worked in this bloody country: at the pace of a drunk snail climbing a mountain, and a million bloody sods wanting their pockets lined along the way. He had to find the body. Or, if he was lying in a hospital somewhere, to find him alive. He might get an extra bonus, if he misidentified the wigless figure and took him home as his uncle or something, before resurrecting him as Romano returned from some secret mission or other. There would be nothing for him but cold glances from that bitch of a wife of his for as long as the whereabouts of the boss were not known. And maybe a bullet in his head from one of her muscle-bound cretinous brothers, José more likely than not. José had always hated Julio, but more so since Romano turned down his offer to be his bodyguard instead of him.

Romano always carried with him one of his private cell phones on his Friday night outings. Julio was the only one who knew of its existence, and number. In an extreme emergency, and only in an extreme emergency, he was to reach him. He would go over to the few collapsed buildings and, using his influence and physique, mingle in with the rescue crew, if any, and call the number. If he could hear a ring somewhere . . . that would be it! Of course, even if Romano was there, the phone could be damaged. But it was worth a try.

## Back to Friday evening in the desert – again

After a moment's panic, inspiration! Obvious, really. *Take the car and drive the hell away from this hell.* Without intentionally looking for them, Caddy had already noticed, from the corner of his left eye, that the car keys were still in the ignition. Jumping inside he started the car. Or rather, tried to start the car. It made a crackling noise, and then, nothing. He tried again. Same result. Again. Then again . . . The jump up and the fall must have loosened some wire or something. Caddy, quite against his beliefs and conscience, cursed. What had this boy done to him! Forced him to blaspheme against the Lord. What next . . .

But a car of this quality should have been able to withstand the impact better. Even his battered old Oldsmobile would probably have started had it been on the road and not under it.

How on earth did these wretched kids manage to acquire this classy car? Or any car, for that matter. What had they been up to? Had they graduated from being ugly nuisances to serious crime!

He cursed again. Then hastily crossed himself, lowered his head, and asked Mother Mary for forgiveness. He remained still, silent, head bowed – and thought of Anna and little Juan. A gentle smile lit his face with a glowing light, washed away the years from his face, and he ended up looking like the little boy who was in his thoughts.

The quiet moment over, he fumbled around for, found and then pushed the button to unlock the bonnet. The fire was still well away, and might not even spread this far – there was a lot of barren ground in between and further ahead, with nothing much for the fire to latch on to – although it was sending out heat waves of alarming intensity. In spite of the extra time it might take, if he could get the car started it would still be better than trying to foot it.

## Where next!

Pepsi and Maria were sheltering in the hollow of a tree when the Crow Boy found them. El Gato was lazily stretched out upon a high yet sturdy branch of the same tree. Maria came running out of the tree followed by Pepsi holding back a yawn. The heat and the excitement had left him with a drowsy sleepiness, as if he wanted to shut out the world.

There was something odd about the Crow Boy, Pepsi could tell the moment he saw him. He looked . . . unreal, insubstantial; for a moment he thought he could almost see through his body, like through a cloud of smoke or mist.

'You must get out of here,' said the Crow Boy, almost in a whisper, 'there is a fire coming up this way.'

Pepsi didn't even notice that he said 'you' and not 'we', but he did hear his voice and the way he spoke: subdued, weary, far away . . .

A dark hand clasped itself round Pepsi's heart. Not for the first time he noticed the difference between *this* Crow Boy, the one who abruptly appeared in the middle of the desert the other day, moody, dark, puzzling – and the open, bold, wild child El Cuervo who walked unafraid on bridge railings, laughed at danger, wept for friends, raged against enemies, and lived generally as if death and destiny had no hold over him; who danced and chanted like his long-dead ancestors were still alive, dancing and chanting by his side; and who swore the blood-brothers' oath with him beneath the dark skies of those haunted woods. How long ago it seemed, as if in another life – though it was only . . . Pepsi tried to remember when it really was. He couldn't. His mind refused to take in both the now and the then at the same time. His mind refused to take in the now on its own. His mind refused to take in anything. Perhaps because he was still half-asleep. Perhaps because he was just a bundle of nothing after all, who could see nothing, understand nothing, be nothing.

The Crow Boy seemed to recognise Pepsi's feelings. Smiling, he extended his hand, palm upwards. Pepsi brought his palm down on it with a thump, repeated it going upwards and then down again. Their eyes locked, and Pepsi was reassured that this indeed was the same El Cuervo, for in his eyes was the same courage, the same concern, the same warmth – and they were the eyes of someone unafraid of both life and death, no matter in which he found himself.

Whatever it was that changed him hadn't really changed him.

'No, it won't,' El Gato's voice cut through the atmosphere. He was holding a spit-wet finger up in the air. 'The fire won't come this way. The wind has dropped, dead. When it comes to life, it will be in another direction.' From his vantage point up in the tree he had a good view of the flickering flames in the distance.

'You cannot know the wind. You cannot know the fire,' said the Crow Boy. 'Don't talk what they will do or won't do. Decide what you must do.'

It was the Cat Boy who spoke again, this time turning over on the branch and looking the opposite way, 'There must be a river flowing not far from here, out there. I can see it coming down the mountains before it cuts away from my eyes. If we cross over it, we will be safe from the fire, and from . . . him.' He pointed vaguely in the direction of where they had left Caddy and their car.

'A river . . .' Maria sniffed the air in an excited manner. 'A river! This will be the river of my home. We live on the other side of the river. After it makes a U-turn. By the bank. Nearer to the mountains. I could feel it in the air.' She was almost jumping up and down with excitement.

'How can you be sure?' said Pepsi, looking doubtful. 'Don't put your hopes too high. Until you are . . .' He fumbled for the right words.

'My papa talked to me about the river. He loved the river. *Coming down the mountains, running towards the desert,* he used to say. I know this is it. I know it. I just know it.'

'Let us find it first,' said the Crow Boy, 'and not waste time talking about it.' There was an urgency in his voice.

Anticipating that Caddy might well take their car to track them down, and keeping well away from any path that could pass as a road, staying within rough brambly patches of the desert, they began walking towards where they believed the river might be.

## A bridge too near

It didn't take long for Caddy to start up the car.

He pushed down hard on the accelerator. Glancing behind him every now and then he could see that the fire was not spreading as fast as he had feared. Not only that, ominous-looking – but in the circumstances welcome – rain clouds appeared to be gathering across the horizon. Reassured, he drove on, although a part of him was telling him to turn around. He was tired. Anna must be worried. He had got his gun back. He had frightened the guts out of the scum. *And* he had got this beautiful new car! It wouldn't be any problem for him to get a new number plate and register it in Anna's name. It would be his gift to her. A gift he wouldn't have thought possible in a million years. It couldn't have belonged to those crumb-snatchers anyway. And the one who had it in the first place would surely be in a position to replace it. So he had done well out of the situation. Perhaps he should head back home now.

But – but, but, but . . . *he* had saved his life this time, not just spared it. It wasn't just him, but *he* was part of it, and that was enough. He had not even avenged the first-time humiliation, not properly. And to add this new shame on top of that! He had to carry on, to retrieve his honour. Especially as *he* was just around the corner, somewhere. Along with that betty, not to mention the weird one. There was another, too. Or was there? His mind was still in shock, his body confused.

He couldn't have driven for long, though his sense of time, along with the rest of him, was not quite functioning normally, when all of sudden, after a slight rise along the road, he could see a river below him, barely a kilometre or so away, spanned by a bridge, a recent man-made construction, at odds with the primitive landscape.

Caddy braked with a jolt. Something hit him like a splash of cold water in the face, waking him up out of a nightmare into a clear, breezy day.

A river! *The* river. Although his map and atlas were left behind in his car, he remembered that there was a river somewhere not too far off that acted as a boundary for the little slut's country where the trash merchants were heading. *They were bound to come this way.* Unless they decided to cross over by swimming. But the river was summer-rain-swollen and if they had any sense they should make for the bridge. All he had to do was to lie in wait. Must find a place to conceal the car, though. Sticking out scarlet in the desert sun – the clouds were still hovering above the distant skyline – it would be a dead giveaway.

He took the gun in his hand, lovingly, and checked to see if it was loaded. Four bullets. Enough, if he was lucky. He had no intention of shooting to kill anyway. Just to incapacitate. Then he would take over the job manually. That was the least he deserved. That was the least *he* deserved.

He would have to be careful, though. It was a case of four womb-cursed street-damned rogues against one good citizen. He had Anna, his son, his honour and his job to think of. They had nobody to worry for them and nothing to lose.

Luckily he found a knoll, probably created by the recent earthquake, behind which he parked the car, and waited. He could see right across the wasteland, and the incoming road towards the bridge, without being seen. It was getting dark, too, and that was a help. If the clouds stayed away, it would be a moonlit night; he would be in the shadow of the dune-like rise, whereas the kids would be in the open and exposed. Feeling a bit hot and out of sorts, it occurred to him that he could turn the air-conditioner on in this car. Switching on the radio to some saucy salsa and relaxing back, hands crossed behind his neck, he began to wallow in the here and now, while his flesh quivered with gratifying anticipation of what was to come.

All he had to do now was to be careful not to be lulled to sleep with the faint humming of the air-conditioner blending in dreamily with the music. He remembered his police manual instructions to turn the radio on to some talk programme in the circumstances of a vigil, as that was less likely to induce sleep than music. But before he could adjust the tuning he was fast asleep, mouth open, like a baby, like little Juan.

## A dreamer, a dream

As Caddy slept, he dreamt a dream. It was a strange dream. An awesome dream. A dream so real it was more real than reality. A dream so dreamlike it was more dreamlike than dreams. He knew that he was dreaming what was happening and yet he knew that he was experiencing what was happening. And he was aware of what had happened before.

He dreamt that he was sitting inside the stationary red Cadillac, looking out for Pepsi and his friends.

What he could see outside the car was quite similar to what he remembered seeing just before he went to sleep, and yet different. What was a river down below was now more like a water canyon. The mountains over on the other side were much nearer, much bigger, higher, rockier, more forbidding, even shape-shifting – remaining mountains all the time yet changing appearance and form, cliff sides and high points. Perhaps it was the faint smell of smoke in the air, even smoke itself, its vapours spreading lazily and sensuously in the atmosphere, causing the scenery to appear mobile and transitory. Maybe, despite the dead wind, the fire from the petrol station was gradually bridging the barren gap and moving forwards, towards the river.

When he looked up, instead of the sky there was an enormous all-encompassing sky-sized bowl of a recently ploughed field, with vertical furrows covering it from one end to the other, interspersed with blobs of greenery which appeared to be upside-down trees. Caddy felt a sudden feeling of warmth, as if cocooned within the womb of Mother Earth. He shut his eyes tight and hugged himself, smiling gently as he looked at the sleeping face of little Juan.

When he opened his eyes the sky was back in its place again with a strong yellow nearly full moon rising from the opposite side of the horizon where the clouds still hung on threateningly. In the lemony light of the moon the landscape around him appeared to transform itself into one single living organism as it heaved and breathed and looked at Caddy from all angles with numberless unseen yet seeing eyes. Caddy did not seem perturbed by this omniscient scrutiny but revelled in it, believing every side of him to be his good side. Along with this visual experience, of which he was the centre, came the music of birds and insects and animals of all species and varieties, singing and speaking at their best and most elegant to the background humming of the entity that was the living universe.

All of a sudden there was silence. Complete and utter silence, with a peculiar sound all of its own; not unpleasant, but mysterious and awe-inspiring in an extraordinary and inexplicable manner. At the same time he felt that all the eyes looking at him also switched themselves off. Not exactly switched off, but redirected their gaze towards a different focus. Instinctively Caddy knew where, and turned his face to look that way. He saw three children emerging from the distant shadowy glow of the moon, making their way towards the bridge which was there, now, again, when it wasn't a second ago.

It was *them*!

All his previous energy and purpose which had somehow been replaced by a lethargic, dreamlike quietude, leaving him blissful, but naked and vulnerable, now returned with its usual furious passion. Grabbing his gun, he waited till *they* were within bullet range.

# A wet and cold hell in Heaven

The earthquake brought the flimsy colony of Heaven tumbling down upon itself. Luckily, the dead were fewer than they could have been. The survivors had hardly managed to comprehend the enormity of their tragedy, when a rainstorm came down upon them with the ferociousness of the righteous. The waters of the river down below, into which many of them were washed, were cold. Very cold. Outside, on the ground, it was cold too.

## The dream continues

It was not long after that the kids were within range. Jumping out of his car, overexcited after his period of a drug-induced kind of repose, he fired at them as the curly black head of Pepsi came into focus. He must have missed for he saw him and the others go into a run. As he poised his gun to fire again, he heard a snarling, hissing sound coming from behind him. He turned round to see a creature on all fours about to jump at him. Before Caddy could fully comprehend his situation, the creature – with finger-like claws raised up above his head – went straight for his eyes. If Caddy had not instinctively ducked, he could have had his eyes gouged out of their sockets. By this time Caddy could see that it was a scrawny little boy, the one who was with Pepsi only a moment ago. Hissing and snarling like an animal, the boy poised to make another lunge for his eyes. Caddy fired again. And this time kept on firing, in panic, without any particular aim, till the gun was emptied. As the boy screeched in beast-like agony and fell backwards, so did Caddy, hitting the back of his head on a stone.

The hit on the head woke him up from his nightmarish dream, and he saw himself staring at the moon. But before he could get his sense of reality back, the centre of the moon parted, revealing a huge black crow, its wingspread almost covering the entire sky.

It cast its gargantuan dark shadow over Caddy as it flew down towards him, forebodingly, getting closer and closer by the millisecond . . .

## Reality

The Cat Boy had taken three bullets, one in the left thigh, another in the right upper arm, and the third had grazed the side of his body, again right; but he was still alive. Maria was sobbing, her slight body hiccupping all over. Pepsi was kneeling by his side, holding him by the shoulders and begging him to be all right, in mumbled jumbled words that did not make much sense. The Crow Boy leaned over, picked up the wounded Cat Boy in his arms and said, 'Run, cross the bridge. The fire will be here soon.'

Indeed the leaping flames were almost upon them.

## An image, a shadow

Caddy found himself across the bridge, driving the red Cadillac on a bare road with no idea where it was leading. Nor had he any idea how he was where he was. He had no memory of getting back into the car and starting it up.

He tried to think back. He came back with only one image: that of the unnatural crow casting its unnatural shadow upon his paralysed body. And with that image came a peace, a strange peace, an unworldly peace. A peace beyond imagination, beyond belief, beyond reason, beyond comparison, beyond words. It was as if the splinters in his soul had been plucked out one by one, yet all at once.

He now knew exactly what he had to do: get home and be with his family, for always!

## A clash of opinions

Although the fire caught on to the bridge, it did not do so well on the concrete as it had done on the bushes and trees, seeming to fumble and losing its strength less than half-way across.

After getting well away from the bridge and about a kilometre or so the other side of the river, El Cuervo came to standstill, carrying El Gato in his arms like a bridegroom carrying his bride across the threshold. Turning his head this way and that, he looked around, studying his surroundings. Pepsi was doing the same.

Pepsi saw a craggy landscape, similar to a high desert, with dark brown lava mountains stretching in uneven rows not far ahead. The moonlight shone on the westward side of the solidified lava, making it glow in a glittering parade of translucent silver and gold colours, while the darker east side looked ominously menacing. Apart from some cacti and a variety of tall grass growing in tufts here and there, there was not much greenery around.

The Crow Boy saw a bluey-green mist descending from an invisible sky above and embracing all that the eye could see, all that the senses could experience. Every blink or so the mist moved around and congealed into the shape of faces: faces that the Crow Boy recognised, knew, and loved. The most prominent among them being the face of his grandfather. Sometimes the mist formed itself into whole bodies, bodies of animals, animals known and unknown, animals alive and extinct.

'Which way do we go from here?' the voice of Pepsi broke the spell. He was looking at Maria.

'I . . . don't . . . know,' she said hesitantly.

'But you said you knew. You *said* your home was this side of the river.' There was a look of frustrated panic in Pepsi's eyes.

'It is, I *know* it is. But I don't know exactly *where*,' Maria was in tears. 'How can I? It is night and . . . and . . . what do we do about El Gato? That is the main thing!'

'I *know* that. That is why I am asking. The sooner we get him to some village or . . . or whatever, the sooner we can get some help, some doctor.'

'El Gato does not want a doctor. There is no point in looking for one,' said the Crow Boy.

'Is he dead! Is he?' Both Maria and Pepsi shouted at more or less the same time.

'No. But he is out, and not feeling any pain.

'And I did not say he doesn't need a doctor. I said he does not want one.'

The Crow Boy's hands were wet with El Gato's blood. His shirt was getting soaked with El Gato's blood. In the strong moonlight the blood had a pale radiance to it.

'Has he said something?' Pepsi's voice was hopeful, excited. 'How do you know what he wants?'

'I know because I know,' said the Crow Boy, looking down at El Gato; then, turning to face Pepsi, 'Just hold him for a minute. I have to find a place.' With that he gently unloaded the Cat Boy into Pepsi's trembling arms.

The Crow Boy looked around once again, focusing his eyes on a boulder some distance to their right.

'What place? You are wasting time standing about here when we should be trying to . . .' Pepsi made one more effort to talk some sense into the Crow Boy's head.

'It is you who are wasting time talking,' the Crow Boy interrupted, 'I want him to live for a while longer,' he added, and started walking towards the boulder he was looking at.

'What do you mean "a while longer"? I want him to *live*, full stop. What are you getting at? What are you doing? Where are you going?' Pepsi was almost screaming while trying to adjust the blood-covered El Gato in his arms to a more comfortable position for him, and for himself.

## The boulder and a few stones

The Crow Boy walked up to the boulder. It was a distorted egg shape, about the length of a man, and half as wide in the middle, with a flat surface smoothed out by generations of wind and rain. He ran his palm across it lovingly, then stood beside it, upright, eyes shut and lips moving silently.

After many a twinkling of the stars, the Crow Boy relaxed, moved across to his left and pulled out a few bunches of the wild-growing, tall grass. Taking these over to the boulder he swept it clean with the grass stalks. Then, going on his hands and knees, he started picking up pebbles and stones from the earth around the boulder, going for the smooth ones. When he had a certain number that satisfied him, he placed these on the boulder in the shape of a garland enclosing the central space.

By this time Pepsi was by his side, looking at him with a mixture of wild-eyed curiosity and frustration.

Without a word, the Crow Boy took El Gato from Pepsi's arms and placed him on the boulder, surrounded by pebbles and stones. As his body stretched out on the slab, El Gato half-opened his eyes and smiled, faintly – as if he knew what was happening – then relapsed into unconsciousness.

'What the hell are you doing! What the fuck are you doing!' screamed Pepsi. 'He is alive. I saw him open his eyes. It is cold, that slab. *Stone* cold. Or haven't you heard that. He is alive. He needs to be warm, not exposed . . .'

The Crow Boy looked him straight in the eyes with his eyes, and there was something in his eyes that made Pepsi shut up, abruptly, although he wanted to carry on screaming even louder than before.

A strange voice issued from the Crow Boy's mouth:

The old men
say
the earth
only
endures.
You spoke
Truly.
You are right.

Then, to Pepsi's mounting horror and astonishment, the Crow Boy stripped the Cat Boy of his clothing, leaving him naked on the cold stone in the cold night.

'Come sit with me. See what you see. Give thanks to the Universe,' he said to the dumbfounded Pepsi.

But before sitting down anywhere, the Crow Boy searched for a suitable spot. When he found it, a few metres to the east of the boulder, he brushed it clean with the grass, as he had done the boulder; then, handing Pepsi some seeds that he must have picked out while getting the grass, he said, 'Chew on these for light. Light to see.'

He sat cross-legged on the earth, nodding at Pepsi to do the same. Which Pepsi did, but not before he got the anxiously apprehensive Maria to lie down next to where he sat, her head resting on his thigh.

## The will of God, the will of Man

Romano's body was discovered in the rubble of the two-star hotel. Julio claimed it was his uncle and took him home. He told Tania he was the victim of a hit-and-run. The family doctor issued a death certificate, saying whatever he was told to say. The priest said it was the will of God. The lawyer was called in to read out Romano's will.

The will made sure that his mother was comfortable for life. The house and other properties he owned were left to Tania, with instructions, in case of her death, as to how they were to be divided between the twins and Andrés – commonly known as Pepsi. He also left Pepsi one fourth of his monies, whether in banks, stocks and shares, or whatever. And Pepsi had the right to live in the family house for as long as he chose. There was a large bequest for the Church, and handsome donations to some organisations that looked after street children, especially stray young girls. There was nothing for the brothers, and a special clause saying that anything Tania gave to any or all of them was to come out of her share of the money/property. And he acknowledged Pepsi as his natural son.

The brothers' fury was made worse by the fact that Tania ordered them to look for Pepsi and bring him back safe and sound. If anything happened to him, none of them would get anything from her. But Julio saved them the humiliation and the hassle by saying that he would arrange for Pepsi to be found. More likely go for him himself. Which was just as well, since he had been named the trustee of Pepsi's share until he came of age, with a fixed allowance before that. For this service, and as a keeper of all Romano's secrets, Julio had been well rewarded. More than Tania knew. Among the small gifts left to him was a cigar box. And in that cigar box was a key. A key to a safety deposit box.

Tania agreed, smiling wistfully to herself. She had thought she knew every thought Romano had in his head, every move that he made in his life, every greed of his heart, every lust of his flesh. But he had more to him than she could have imagined, much less believed. Not to mention more money. Three other bank accounts in the country, two abroad. And properties that she knew nothing about, here and overseas. There was enough for her brothers, if she could keep them on a leash.

Although she did resent that Julio had been appointed as the trustee for Pepsi, in a way she was relieved. It would spare her arguments with the brothers who might well have insisted on some sort of a fiddle. And she could afford her husband's generosity to the poor bastard. He wasn't a bad kid. Better than her lot.

Although Julio had always been respectful to Tania, even when her husband was openly offensive to her in front of him, she was sure he didn't really like her. And she didn't like him. Now he was the trustee for Pepsi's money *and* he was responsible for finding him . . . There could be a problem in there somewhere. That is why she would rather have had her brothers do so. However crooked, they would not have done anything against her wishes. So she believed. She did not know of Mario's attempt to rob Pepsi.

As for Julio? He always did what Romano wanted. Faithfully. And Romano wanted that money to go to Pepsi. So perhaps it was all right! However, with Romano gone . . .

## Death in life

As Pepsi chewed on the seeds his senses began to intermingle, exchange with each other. When he touched anything, he saw it; when he saw something, he felt he was touching it. His tongue could hear, his ears taste. Time became liquid, and he had to swim through it. The air became earth-solid and he was breathing in dirt. But strangely, it did not choke him. In fact it made his body a part of the earth herself. Organic life congealed into the inorganic. The inorganic dissolved into the organic. It was a feeling without feelings. Neither pleasant, nor unpleasant. Neither strengthening, nor debilitating. Neither threatening, nor safe. Neither real, nor unreal. Simply eternal, everlasting, never present. For ever in the past. For ever in the future. Never in the present. Not the present that he had known as present until then.

Then came the light. This was the light the Crow Boy must have spoken of.

The light focused itself on the boulder, the boulder upon which lay the dying El Gato. Pepsi shut his eyes, tight, in order to see better. Without extraneous influences influencing his perception.

Surrounding the boulder was a thick, sappy mist – bluey-green, that kept moulding and remoulding itself into different shapes. Shapes like faces. Shapes like bodies. Shapes organic. Shapes inorganic. Shapes he recognised, shapes that meant nothing to him.

It was when he saw his mother that he let out a squeal of delight and was about to run up to her when he realised he could not move. Not a limb, not a muscle, not a ligament, not a tendon. He hadn't even let out a squeal of delight, merely wanted to.

A roar. A roar cut through the utter stillness of the night like a hatchet through the wedding cake of a god. It was the roar of a mountain cat: a mountain cat as sunflower-bright and moon-radiant as if made from pure gold poured into a mould and infused with life. It leapt ferociously out of the mysterious mist and landed directly upon the boulder, the boulder upon which lay the dying El Gato.

The cat swished its tail about violently in the air, while sniffing at El Gato with inflated nostrils and searing eyes of burning amber. Then it went for the neck. El Gato's body twitched, shook, rose and twisted; though whether because he was trying to escape the cat's jaws, or offering himself to her, could not be clear to Pepsi. If only he could rush forward to save him from the cat's claws and teeth. If only he could scream.

All he could do was watch as the cat devoured El Gato, bit by bit, bone by bone, muscle by muscle. Until there was nothing left of the Cat Boy. Not a drop of blood, as the cat growled a few burp-like growls of contentment, licking away at her paws.

## Life in death

Pepsi awoke with the smell of rain filtering through his nostrils. And yet there was no rain. In fact, even the clouds in the distant horizon last night had disappeared. He sniffed the air.

'It has rained out there, by the base of the mountain. Where the river takes a loop,' said the Crow Boy, 'Rained heavily, by the feel of it. The clouds must have poured themselves out.'

It was only upon hearing the Crow Boy's voice that Pepsi was reminded of last night. And El Gato . . . How could he have forgotten it! His head was heavy, and the burden of thought seemed to make it heavier. When he tried to stand up, his eyes had difficulty focusing and his body reeled round, or so it felt as he fell backwards on his buttocks.

'El Gato. What happened to El Gato?' He made another attempt to stand up and, this time succeeding, ran stumblingly to the boulder. Nothing there, except a few blobs and streaks of still moist blood. He remembered the wild cat having licked all the blood clean . . . The cat! Everything came to back to him.

'You let that wild cat eat El Gato. You *invited* it to eat him, alive. Alive! How could . . . Why? Why? Why?' Pepsi was waving his arms about in the air, half-sobbing, half-choking, looking at the Crow Boy with uncomprehending eyes. 'Why did you not just let him die? In your arms. In my arms. Warm. In peace . . . Why?'

'Because then he would have just gone back to the earth, or the sky. And he was not ready for that. Not yet.

'Now, eaten by the Cat, alive, his spirit has entered the Cat. If he was eaten dead, only his flesh would've become a part of it. Now his spirit is in the Cat. Now he *is* the Cat. Just as he always wanted. Just as he knew he was. Just as the Cat knew. That's why it came.'

'I don't know. I don't know. I don't know,' moaned Pepsi. 'I don't. I don't. I don't . . . All I know is that bloody cat, chewing, crunching . . .'

'Stop making all that racket,' the Crow Boy said softly, 'you'll wake up Maria. You don't want her to hear all this, do . . .'

But Maria had already woken, only just. 'What don't you want me to hear?' she asked with a distinct yawn in her voice. 'Is it about El Gato? But I *know* anyway. I saw it.'

'What did you see?' Pepsi was jerked fully awake with her remark and, kneeling by her side, shook her by the shoulders, 'What did you see? Tell me. Tell us. What did you see?'

'What happened. That's what I saw. I saw what happened.'

'But you couldn't have. You were asleep. Next to me. You were asleep. I know it.'

'Maybe I was. At first. But when the light came, I woke up.'

'You . . . you *saw* the light?' Pepsi was getting more incredulous by the second.

'Yes. Yes. I saw the light. A cone of light, coming from the sky. And then the angel. The angel came down, looked at El Gato, kissed his head, picked him up, folded his wings around him, and vanished into the light. I saw it. I saw it all.'

'You must've dreamt it,' said the Crow Boy.

'Maybe,' said Maria, 'but then, where is Gato?'

Even his clothes had disappeared. The Crow Boy must have hidden them in the grass, or somewhere.

## At Heaven's gate

Two days and two nights later, guided by the Crow Boy rather than
Maria, the three children arrived at the loop of the river. Maria,
excited to the point of hysteria, said that Heaven lay a couple of
kilometres to the south at an angular elevation. The other side of
the loop of the river.

Along the way the Crow Boy had been digging out roots and
pulling out grasses for Pepsi and Maria to eat. But still they were
hungry. And exhausted.

At least Pepsi was. The city boy was not adjusting too well to
the wild outside. And he was still traumatised by what had
happened to El Gato. Maria was bearing up better. The hope of
being with her family was keeping her spirits up. As they neared
the colony, Pepsi was looking forward to a good home-cooked
meal. Maria was too wound up to think about eating. Her throat
was dry, there was a knot in her stomach and her breath was
coming in quick, short puffs. All she wanted now was the loving
warmth of her mother, the affectionate embrace of her father, the
sight and sounds of her siblings, the cheery excitement of her
young uncle, the unnaturally shiny smile of Nanna's false teeth,
even the erratic fumblings of her out-of-this-world grandad, the
cold wet nose, the cuddly friendly fur of puppy Pumpkin. And did
silly uncle Nolsen manage to get back home?

All the old names and faces came flooding back to her
consciousness with such force that she could have fainted with
the sheer abstraction of them. In spite of his tiredness, even Pepsi
began to be infected with some of her enthusiasm. As the optimism filled his being, he felt different from the empty 'nothing'
that he felt when at his lowest. He thought of his mother. Like
Maria's dream about El Gato, he saw her folded in the arms of an

angel. Unlike on other occasions when he thought of his mother, this time there was no pain, rather a strange kind of eerie joy.

Coming to a gnarled old tree with the marks of age running cracks across its trunk and branches, Maria came to a sudden stop.

'There should be a bridge here, somewhere here, not far along the bank. We can get over to the other side from there,' she said breathlessly.

Which was just as well, for the river was threateningly full, almost overflowing in parts, and moving much too rapidly and tumultuously to swim across, even though Pepsi was a good swimmer and so was the Crow Boy. Besides, Maria was afraid of water. As their eyes and feet were searching for the bridge, a table went tumbling by in the turbulent waters of the river. It was followed, at odd intervals, by other household objects, torn bits of window frames, clothes, doors and other floatable items. If that wasn't enough, a human body, bloated, arms raised upwards, pursued by another . . .

What had earlier been a mere whiffiness in the air was now a distinctively grim odour.

It took them longer to get to the bridge than Maria had suggested. But scenes of hell in Heaven arrived soon enough.

## José and Mario in conversation

'So what do you say?' said José.

'I . . . don't know,' said Mario.

'Come on! Everyone'll think he's off looking for that cola boy. He lives alone. All his life was devoted to that creep. With him gone, no one will miss him. Not for a long while, anyway.'

'What afterwards? Some day someone will begin to wonder.'

'They'll think he's run off with cola boy's share. All the better for us.'

'But if he has the papers, the power of attorney, whatever, we won't be able to get hold of that money no matter.'

'Eventually. When neither he nor cola boy turn up, it'll *have* to go to sis. And anyway, at least we won't be having that bastard living it up at our expense, wolfing our food and buying whatever, spending our money . . .'

'It's not exactly ours.'

'As good as. So. What do you say? Eh? I know a place to dump the body where it won't be found in a million years.'

'I have always hated him,' said Mario.

## Maria back home

Surrounded by human and substance rubble, wrecked bodies and disembodied houses, Maria stood in stunned silence, as if carved out of air, the animated and eloquent anticipation of an hour or so ago turned into a mute void.

She was in the middle of a part-encrusted mud pool. Where her home was. Once.

The atmosphere was thick with the putrid, polluting, compelling stink of rotting rubbish and decaying matter intermingled with the odour of death and diarrhoea.

Here was a naked leg trying to make its way out of piles of filth, there a hand dragging a lifeless body over the sludge, or a head with glazed eyes looking at nothing in particular, yet carrying the pain of seeing, seeing that which nobody wants to see. Ever.

Pepsi shut his eyes and thought of his mother. She was right. He was nothing, and turned anything he touched to nothing. Even Heaven was nothing now, now that he was here.

## Two boys and a cell phone

Julio thought the best way to track Pepsi was to contact Caddy.
The phone was answered by a woman's voice he did not recognise.
Anna's mother. She told him Caddy was away somewhere, and
hung up.

Julio could think of nothing else, except to post a lookout at
the grave of Pepsi's mother. He was bound to turn up there sooner
or later. In the mean time he would think of other possibilities,
after he had had a good night out at a certain club he had heard a
lot about from José and Mario. Had they told him about it directly,
he might have been suspicious that they were trying to trick him
into going to some grubby or illegal joint. But since he overheard
them singing praises of the Flying Lobster to each other while
having beer in the kitchen, he thought it might be worth a try.
When Romano was alive, he hardly ever had any time for fun.
Even at most weekends.

But first things first. He knew of two layabout brothers of
somewhat limited mental capacity, late teens, in hiding from the
police for various petty crimes. He got hold of both and told them
to keep a twenty-four hour vigil at the grave, taking day and night
shifts. Luckily there was a poor-man's-grandiose mini-tomb
nearby. The three-foot high, seven-by-four grave, covered in
marble slabs, was sheltered by a mosaic dome, Mother Mary's
statue with baby Jesus in her arms above it, a roomy, igloo-shaped
space below. One or two persons could easily stay in there, safe in
all weathers. In return, Julio would get the boys off the wanted
list, and give them some cash. Not a great deal, but more than
they had seen since birth. They were thrilled at the offer. The very
fact that they got a cell phone all to themselves – to call Julio in
case the boy turned up – was enough to excite them beyond

measure. They were allowed to use it to call anybody they liked. It was a dream come true.

'We can even bring our girlfriends in here, show them our cell phone,' said one to the other. Tiger.

'And who are they?' asked the other. Terminator.

'We'll find some. Many. After we show them our cell phone.'

Tiger carefully folded the paper with Julio's number on it – and Tania's, in case he was not available – and hid it in the pocket of his Tommy Hilfiger boxer shorts. They were stolen from a clothes-line and put on almost immediately. He was so proud he had refused to take them off since, even though Terminator had consistently offered him his ass in return. 'Who needs your hairy hole,' he'd reply, spitting on his palms, 'when I have these two sweeties to look after my boy.'

They had called themselves Tiger and Terminator for so long they had almost forgotten their real names. In police records, too, they were named as such, albeit within quotes.

Julio scribbled the telephone numbers in a corner of the alcove as well, just in case they lost the paper, grateful that they could read numbers if not words.

'And remember to get out and disappear for a while if someone comes to visit this grave. Otherwise they will have you beaten to death and thrown to the dogs,' Julio warned them for yet another time, before departing.

But the part Julio wanted TnT (that's what they liked to call themselves as a twosome) to remember particularly well was to get talking to Pepsi, if he turned up, and keep him there, until Julio arrived.

# The Flying Lobster

Although he had to queue for more than an hour to get in, Julio was pleasantly surprised to find that the Flying Lobster was indeed a cool place to be in. Its overall impact on the numbers of drunken heads and dancing feet bobbing up and down and jumping all around in the shadowy world of night-clubbers was quite stunning, even if in the sober light of the day it might have felt rather tacky.

The main dance floor was bigger than a barn, but circular with a spiralling stairway in the centre of it, decorated boldly in a mixture of contrasting, even clashing, colours and styles: gilded but not too gaudy, with a sort of overdressed yet half-wrapped look. The floor above consisted of a balcony going round and round in another spiral reaching up to a dome-shaped ceiling, blue with twinkling star-like lights of a subdued red. A scattering of men and women, hanging about, drinking and chatting or chatting up, wandered through the balcony in an apparently random fashion, though all had a purpose or a point to their movements: either towards or away from a certain somebody. The lighting was a gentle, static, romantic glow in one area; a riot of colour, agitation and lust in the other. The music was mad and maddening, the clientele a mixture of the young and trendy with the not-so-young but classy. The DJ was with-it, quick of tongue, quick of hand, quick-witted and quirky, impressive in a deranged sort of way.

There were three arc-shaped bars that Julio could see, with good-looking boys and girls serving. He went over to one to fill up, flicking his bills in a raunchily arrogant manner he hadn't adopted in months, even years – ever since he took up as Romano's bodyguard and confidant.

'He took the bait,' Mario nudged José in the belly with his elbow, gleefully, pointing to Julio below. 'Now all we have to do is to go down and start a brawl. In the free-for-all a gun goes off, somebody gets killed. A noisy crowd of drunken people, more than half on drugs, strobe lighting, loud music, who will know what really happened? We can be out and on the road before the police even get here. They always take their time coming to disturbances in clubs. Think it's a waste of time.'

'No, no, and no again. I've told you so before. It is too chancy. With so many eyes about, anyone might see, catch hold of one of us . . . Too chancy. Wait until he staggers out drunk in the dark before you go silly-buggering your . . .'

'All right. All right,' Mario interrupted, peevishly; then, in a quieter voice, 'What if he is with somebody when he gets out? He is neat enough to pull . . .'

'We'll see to it when . . . if it comes to that,' José interrupted, peevishly. 'Anyway, it is easier to cope with one witness than hundreds.'

The brothers were seated on a ledge, in one of the near unlit parts of the balcony, the lower end of it – unseen, but with a clear view of the floor below, and of the main exit.

'What if he goes out the back door?' Mario.

'He won't. And shut up, dipstick.'

'If he does, we'll know who the dipstick is. We should call Pablo or Foxy here, to keep a lookout . . .'

'If they know anything of this, Mario, they'd announce it on the mike the next second. Their mouth-holes are bigger than the holes in your brain. So don't you tell them *anything*. Anything. Remember that. Now just shut up and trust me.'

'Like I trusted you when . . .'

'If you don't shut up I'll kill *you* before I get to Julio.'

'Yeah, yeah, yeah.'

## A family reunion

After searching in vain for nearly two days, the three children were sitting by Maria's ex-home, backs resting against a broken old desk that was half-stuck in the mud, drained, dejected, down-hearted – Maria disconsolate beyond measure, Pepsi despondent as Doomsday eve, the Crow Boy faraway and distant as if in another dimension – when two things happened almost simultaneously that were radically to transform their situation and their mood.

First, there was the sound of confident, advancing feet, and animated, dynamic voices, so different from the tired steps, defeated mutterings, distressing moaning and heart-rending bewailing that had surrounded them up until then. And, if that wasn't surprising enough, there was a ring of familiarity to a couple of those voices. At the same time Maria heard a whimpering and a swishing in the air as a wet nose rubbed against her left thigh.

She jumped up instinctively, looked down and saw a black-and-white bundle of fur looking up at her. A dog. On meeting her eyes the dog's whimpering turned to excited yaps, tail wagging as if the world was on fire and it was her sworn duty to fan it as best she could. The dog began running circles round Maria's ankles, jumping up at her and generally behaving as if a young dog had found her long-lost human.

'Pum . . . Pumpkin! Oh, Pumpkin, Pumpkin, my little girl-dog!' she was down on her knees, regardless of the mucky ground, rubbing noses with the dog and generally behaving as if a little girl had just found her long-lost dog.

'Let go of her,' said the Crow Boy. And when Maria looked up at him with disbelief, he said, 'Release her and see where she goes. Might lead you to your family.'

As Maria and the Crow Boy were busy with Pumpkin, Pepsi started walking towards the source of the voices he had heard.

Among the group of official-looking people scattered in a small area, looking around and talking among themselves in an energetic manner, were the balding young man and the woman with the crow's nest on her head: the doctors from Médecins Sans Frontières, the angels from the cave, whom they had saved and who in turn had given them refuge.

Pumpkin did lead them to Maria's family. They were all alive and, considering the circumstances, in remarkably good shape. It was the grandma who seemed the most shocked, refusing to believe that this could happen to her the second time round.

Heaven being primarily a rubbish dump, soft and spongy, the earthquake hadn't done as much damage as it could have done. Even the rainwater kept soaking in before deluging the settlement. Had it been on solid rock, there would have been far more casualties. The Zapata house being at the very bottom of the colony was among the last to go, giving them just enough time to climb up a tree not far off. Although the tree was uprooted, it was solid and floating and they clung on to it; ending up a couple of kilometres the *other* side of the river, the one that the children had taken so much time and trouble to cross over.

The woman with the crow's nest on her head and the balding young man were very impressed to hear how Pepsi and Maria had managed to get to Heaven and find her family. The woman was hugging Pepsi over and over again.

'We were so worried about you when you disappeared. So worried,' she kept saying over and over again.

The young man was crying. A much-needed release from the trauma of seeing so much human suffering.

They were here, along with some other charity workers, to look after the quake-and-flood victims, give medical assistance where needed, vaccinate against possible disease, and to provide some sort of temporary housing or shelter to the affected people.

There were some self-assembly wooden shacks sent over from Sweden, a few miles across the hills, where Maria's family could be housed, along with a few others with small children or very old parents. Some were refusing to take up the offer, at least not until they had sorted out their belongings and found missing family members, alive or dead. The rest would be taken to a refugee camp set up for the purpose.

The Blind One and the Silent One were doing fine, having found a good foster home willing to take them both.

## Of Highlands and low-life, mice and brothers

Julio found himself dancing with an arresting young girl, very different from the type he used to dream of whenever he had some time to dream, time off from Romano. She was a blond-eyed blue-haired girl from Scotland, with contact lenses and a punk coiffure, aristocratic connections and low-life ambitions: from a castle in the Highlands to the street scenes of the Americas. She said her name was Amelia, Mee for short.

Julio and Mee left for Julio's sister's house where he had a room for himself to stay when not with Romano. It was a long taxi ride from the Flying Lobster and Mee fell asleep on the way. Julio carried her softly into the house, and then to his room, making sure not to wake her, or his sister and her brood. Especially them. Laying Mee on his bed, gently, he took off her shoes and covered her up before dropping off to sleep in his TV chair.

José and Mario were woken up about four o'clock when the club was shutting down.

'*Trust me!*' hunhed Mario. 'Trust you to fuck up.'

José gave him a thick lip with his right.

They were still beating each other up good and solid when thrown out into the night by the bemused bouncers. Usually the brothers got along well together, even sharing girlfriends. Luckily, the bouncers did not notice the gun each brother had, or they could have been blacklisted and barred. At least Julio's idea of stuffing the guns in their respective underpants had paid off.

# A new house

Luis and Carlos set up their new house in a day: basically, just a room and some. Along with Bernardette and Pepsi, they had the help of two strong young volunteers from some Christian-based aid organisation. Maria wanted to 'do something' as well, but was being treated like a princess, doted upon, passed from hands to hands, lap to lap, given hug upon hug, not allowed to exert herself. The little ones – Cristiano, Angelina and Sara – ran around doing whatever they could, sometimes losing things and creating a mini-chaos rather than advancing the construction. The Crow Boy appeared tired and lost. He excused himself, saying he was not feeling well and went away for 'a walk', not returning until the whole place was set up. This was so unlike the *pro-active, taking-command-of-the-situation El Cuervo of the old days* that once again Pepsi had doubts as to his state of mind, or body.

Bedding and blankets were provided, along with some food. Apart from that they had nothing, and with the garbage and the van gone, no means to make a living. But even so, they realised how very lucky they were. First and foremost to be alive, and then to have a little house all their own: brand-new, rich with the fragrance of fresh wood. Most people in their situation, here as elsewhere, languished in nowhere-land camps for ages, rotting away like so much waste, as many perishing after the event as during. At times, more.

And, and, and . . . they had got their Maria back. How much luckier could they get!

## Of hate, greed and love potions

José and Mario were still wondering how next to get Julio 'within range': whether to wait for him next Friday at the Flying Lobster in the hope that he would turn up again, or follow him from Romano's home, where he still kept turning up to ask Tania if she needed anything, when luck came their way.

Julio himself rang Mario to ask if he or José had any idea where Pepsi might be. After all, it was the brothers who had got hold of Pepsi the last time. Mario said he would speak to José and call him back. Although pleased, there was also a note of apprehension in his voice. He was still not too keen on the idea of killing. Not just Julio. Anybody. Killing was too big a responsibility. A certain fear of the unknown, of the undone, of retribution – legal if not divine – mixed with a question of conscience, haunted him as much as the possible pitfalls of the actual doing of the deed. After all, his solo attempt to rob Pepsi of the money didn't exactly turn out as it should have. And this was no mere robbing of a skinny kid, but the murder of a trained-to-fight grown-up well-muscled man: none other than Julio . . .

José had no such worries. Or qualms. He was delighted to hear of Julio's call. *'He walks into the lion's den,'* he exclaimed, sure that that was a worthwhile quote from someone worthwhile. 'Now all we need is a little bit of your love potion,' he winked wickedly at Mario.

'What, what d'you mean?' said Mario with the air of someone who knew what the other meant, yet not quite sure what he meant.

'You know! Your love potion. What you use to get your . . . ladies,' he winked again.

'I can get ladi . . . girls any way I want,' Mario said sulkily. 'I only use it now and then, for some extra . . . But what has that got to do with Julio. Surely you don't want me to . . .'

'That's exactly what I *do* want. Ask him to come over to the club. Then spike his drink, like you . . .'

'I am *not* fucking him?' Mario showed a set of strong white teeth.

'As if. We *soften* him up. Lead him to the car, like you . . . well, you know. Then, instead of driving him to our place, like you . . . We drive him to where I want the body dumped. Shoot him there. Leave him there. Simple. See? Am I a genius or am I?'

'He is not a little girl, the type I . . . He is a big guy, he might not . . .'

'Double the dose. Two tablets instead of one. Even three. Though that might be too much. I want him to have some idea of what's going on. Anyway. Pick up that phone. I want tonight for I just can't wait. On the other hand, that might appear too . . . too . . . too something. Tomorrow. Make it tomorrow night.'

'Six?'

'No, dipstick. We want it to be dark when we whisk him out. Late as late can. When everyone expects drunks to be helped out by their friends. Make it nine.'

'Nine is not that late.'

'We'll keep him talking for a while. Any later will appear suspicious.'

'We can say we're going to a movie first.'

'Whatever. As long as you have him there tomorrow night.'

'That I will,' grinned Mario, confident for once. Then, face clouding over, 'Are you sure they will let us in, after . . . after last time?'

'You leave that to me. Chances are they won't even notice. Otherwise, at most a couple of American greenbacks.'

## A new home

'Why don't you boys stay with us?' said Bernardette to Pepsi and the Crow Boy. 'We would never have got our daughter without you. Now you are like our sons.'

'Yes, yes,' echoed Luis and Vivecca simultaneously.

'We have three lovely girls,' Bernardette continued, 'and only one son. Now we will have three beautiful sons as well.'

'Oh, please, please stay,' said Maria, clinging on to Pepsi's shirttail.

'I am strong, and still young,' said Luis, 'I can always find some work. I'll make a living somehow. You don't have to worry about that.'

'If the Lord has kept us alive after this tragedy, he won't let us starve now,' said Bernardette.

'You can always help me around with something.' Even Carlos seemed excited by the prospect. He had always felt a little left out in the house because of his age and gender.

Pepsi was sorely tempted. He looked at the Crow Boy to read his response.

He was again struck by El Cuervo's appearance. He looked ashen grey, and the fire in his eyes was no more than dying embers.

'I am tired. Time to return. But you should stay, Pepsi. I think it is a great idea for you to stay. At least till you grow up some more and decide where you want to go from here.' He seemed to be talking like an old man with an old man's voice.

Pepsi felt a growing weight on his heart. There was something not quite right here. 'All the more reason to stay. If you're tired. At least for a while. Like you are telling me. Till you feel better.' Then, a surprised afterthought, 'Return where?'

The Crow Boy was silent for a moment. Then, with a dark look, a distant expression and a shaky voice, 'Nowhere. Everywhere. I am not quite sure yet.' With that he started towards the door, 'I am going for some fresh air now. See you later.'

Pepsi felt left out. Somehow he could feel that he was losing his friend. And he did not even know why.

Tears began welling in his eyes, and he too walked out so as not to be seen crying. Especially as he could think of no really good reason as to why he felt like he felt. Not really, except that a certain indeterminate fear was coursing through his blood like a toxic virus. He could hear the aggravated beating of his heart pounding his chest, as if it were drumming out some dreaded, deadly message of incalculable distress.

## Another family reunion

Caddy found himself in front of his house without being quite sure how he got there. It was about two in the morning, and the street was dark, except for a dusty lamp glimmering half-heartedly at the far end of it. He parked on the opposite side of his house, but stayed inside the car, head bent, collecting his thoughts. Eventually he stretched out his hand to get to the door handle, turned it, pushed open the door and came out.

Looking for his house keys in his pockets, he briefly stopped in the middle of the road and looked up at the sky, searching for the moon. But the moon was low on the other side of the horizon. Its light, although making the sky glow a lemony blue, only made the street darker with long, black shadows of the tall, narrow houses that stood shoulder to shoulder in a row, like half-starved prisoners of the Big City that enclosed them with all its grim opulence. Although he could not see the moon, its memory came back to him from back in the high desert and flooded his being with the kind of peace known only to saints and fulfilled lovers, not for the first time.

The Caddy that tiptoed into his house, careful not to wake the sleeping family, was very different from the Caddy who had left the same house just a few days ago. There was no conflict in his mind, no rage in his heart, no furrow on his brow. It was the Caddy that Anna always believed he was. Like a child deep in sleep, eyes softly shut, mouth half open, unconcerned with the clamour and commotion of the adult world that surrounded him in all its chaotic splendour: at once tragic and comic, pathetic and powerful, earthy yet ethereal.

He soft-footed it to the bedroom. Anna was sleeping on her right side, as she often did, left arm bent at the elbow, pressing little Juan to her breasts in a motherly embrace. Just as she would hold him to herself when he was sleeping with her. He stood there looking down at them, a flickering smile playing on his lips. He leaned over, gently, and stroked the wild abundance of Anna's rich, dark hair, running his fingers through sleep-ruffled strands. After little Juan's birth she had gradually become a heavy sleeper, otherwise she wouldn't have slept at all. She stirred a little, languidly, a near smile on her cheeks, as if having a pleasant dream. He wanted to kiss her, but knew *that* would wake her up. He then rubbed little Juan's exposed cheek with the palm of his hand and stuck his forefinger into his open mouth. Little Juan suckled at it, and made a few kiddy noises in his sleep. Anna pulled him closer to herself.

After a long, long moment, he entered the other room and looked at his sleeping mother. Safe in the knowledge that his family was safe and well, he went into the little alcove behind a door to the left of the living room where he kept his police things – gun, bullets, batons, uniform, any paperwork – well away from little Juan's reach.

His uniform was hanging in its usual corner: washed, ironed and in spruce condition, as Anna always saw to it that it was. He lingered for a moment looking at it, affectionately, almost as if it were a person, a friend, before taking it off the hanger and laying it on the table, ready to wear. Sorting out the underwear and socks, he checked to see if his boots were all clean and shiny.

Taking off his clothes he went to the bathroom, shaved, showered, rubbed himself well dry with a crisp white towel, and looked at himself in the mirror. He was pleased with what he saw. Away from home cooking and running around like he had been recently, his ring of belly flab had nearly disappeared. His body looked almost taut. Yes, he was pleased with what he saw.

Out of the bathroom and back to his little alcove.

Slowly, carefully, as if performing a sacred ritual, he began putting on his uniform.

## No date rape, this

José kept driving, and driving . . .

'Where *are* we going?' Mario was losing patience. He wasn't terribly pleased anyway, with Julio's head in his lap. He had wanted to sit in front, but José said he'd better stay with Julio who was stretched across the back seat. *Best not take any chances. Any movement from him, and clobber him on the head with this,* handing him a baseball bat he'd plucked out of the boot.

Julio was aware of what was happening, as in one of those half-awake nightmares, but was unable to stir a limb or to dispel the feeling that he was in some sort of limbo hell. And the more he pushed his mind to move himself, the more rigid his body seemed to become.

José braked to a sudden halt. Julio's body jerked outwards and upwards, Mario's lurched forwards and downwards, bringing his mouth to within kissing distance of Julio's mouth.

'Jesus,' muttered José. 'Christ,' shouted Mario. 'Shit,' screamed Julio, but no one heard him.

'Jesus,' repeated José, 'I think I have missed the place!' 'Christ,' repeated Mario, 'What d'you think you're doing! Trying to kill us all.' 'That'd be two better than just killing me,' thought Julio.

'I have missed the turning. Shit,' said José.

'What turning?' snarled Mario, 'We've been on a straight desert stretch for the past one hundred and thirty-seven years!'

'I didn't know you could count up to one hundred and thirty-seven.'

'I am the one going to college, or didn't you know.'

'And I am the one making sure you have enough money to do that. And have some fun along the way. So shut up and listen. You see that little knoll with a funny tree on it? The turning I am

300

looking for was before that, a dirt road of sorts. To the right. I am sure of it.'

Mario muttered something inaudible, and took out his frustration by pulling Julio by the hair this way and that to get his head back where it was before the hard brake. Julio was not enjoying it one bit.

José turned round and started back, this time driving slower and looking constantly to his left. They passed some old ruins, left to rot in the sun and wind – and, as now, the desolation of the night. Neat little piles of bricks in regular little squares, behind an erratically flowing river. Who could have lived in them? Once, so long, long ago. Mario's mind began to wander. Strange he hadn't noticed these on the way up. He conjured up an entire civilisation, with pretty girls wandering around in sarong-like dresses, singing songs to their beaus; men working the soil, making pots; women weaving, dancing in the moonlight . . . He imagined one of those girls in his arms, swearing everlasting love for him, love that would overturn the rules of time and space, love that would be there for him, even in the here and now. The hazy light of the moon provided a grand backdrop to his fantasy, the never-ending ever-changing sand was the eternal stage on which the drama of his love would be played out for all mankind to see. How jealous José would be. José, who did not have to drug his girls for sex. José, who could click his fingers and make any of the brothers do whatever he asked. Not because he was cleverer or better-looking or had more money. Mario would have understood better if any of those reasons applied. But José could, just because he could. And it was always a source of resentment. But also of conceit. For out of all the brothers, José chose him to be his lieutenant. And *he* would choose José to be his best man at the wedding. His wedding. His wedding with this girl from long, long ago. This girl who wore a sarong, had lips like red roses, eyes like a doe, hair like a lion's mane, chaste as Mother Maria, and who sang like angels on their night off. José would be so proud of him then.

Mario was so lost in his imagination that he quite forgot the passage of time or distance. He came to himself as once again the car came to a halt. This time more of a staggering halt than a sudden one like last time. It must have been quite some distance and quite some time for by now Julio was becoming more and more aware of himself and, more importantly, of his body, his muscles. José had been back and forth on the same road, and turned into any path that remotely resembled a road track.

'Shit! Shit. SHIT!' José cried, 'I think it is no longer there! Gone . . . Vanished into nowhere . . .'

Mario didn't respond. Partly because he was still having difficulty relating to the hostile world of present rationalities after his sweet flirtation with another, more amenable and fantastic world, hand in hand and lip to lip with one of its most beautiful representatives; partly because he had no idea of what José was on about.

'Wha . . . what is not there?' Mario at last.

'The riverbed. The riverbed where I was planning to dump the body. Part of it ran into a grotto type something. No one would have found him there.'

'He isn't dead yet,' Mario snapped. Then after a moment, 'And we *have* been past a river.' He remembered this, in spite of his reverie, because the idyllic village of his dream in-laws was near that river, 'I don't know exactly when or where, but only . . .'

'That was a river, stupid. *I* said a riverbed. A *dry* riverbed.' José snarled.

'*This* is the rainy season,' Mario sneered back. 'Even dry riverbeds fill up. *Now* who's stupid!'

For once José was dumb-struck. Julio could have almost laughed. At the same time the gravity of the situation hit him straight in the guts. *They were going to kill him and dump his body out here somewhere.* Somewhere in his heart he had already known this, but now, for the first time, the fact became starkly naked before him, like sunlight beating directly into one's eyes.

Anger and fear brought new life to his limbs, but he realised he would have to wait for an appropriate moment to attempt an escape. He was at a strict disadvantage in his current situation, and any false move could lead to an earlier action on their part, an action leading to his premature demise. He continued to lie motionless, unpleasant though his position was, with his neck cushioned by Mario's fat thighs.

'If you are so clever,' José finally found voice, 'then why don't you come on over and drive?' José opened the driver's door with a violent push and jumped out of the car, banging the door shut and stomping his boots heavily on the thickly sanded ground.

'OK, so I will. So I will,' said Mario as he kicked his door ajar and heavy-footed out into the open air, letting go of Julio's head, unceremoniously, before banging his car door shut more ferociously than José. Julio's head fell on the seat with a thump. Good for him, for it gave a further, positive, jolt to his consciousness.

Soon the brothers were involved in a noisy altercation outside, punctuated with pointy fingers stabbing ribs, and tensely flattened palms shoving chests.

Julio saw his chance. Slowly stretching his arms, he grasped the backs of the front seats with each hand, and fumblingly edged his feet forward, attempting to get into the driver's seat. An attempt in which he succeeded, if only after a few knocks on his knees and elbows and a bump on his forehead.

Turning the ignition key, he switched on the engine, pressed hard on the accelerator and zigzagged his way out of there before the wide-eyed open-mouthed brothers could bring themselves to believe what had happened.

## A meeting of friends

Pepsi was feeling strangely out of sorts. Of course it had to do with the Crow Boy leaving, but there was something more to it. Something beyond mere sadness and emotional distress. It was physical. His body seemed to be relaxing. Not in a nice restful way, but as if it were giving up its tensions and intentions of being alive, his zest for life draining away. He felt like curling up, lying down, and going to sleep.

Fighting against this feeling, he decided to go and look for El Cuervo who still hadn't returned since he had gone out earlier. The day had run through its appointed course, and Pepsi wanted to bring his friend back before the night was too late into itself.

The light of the sixteenth night of the moon was strong, the rough, uneven ground beneath his feet distressed. Pepsi was still looking for the Crow Boy when the Crow Boy found him. Without a word spoken they sat down side by side beneath an arrogant-looking, ancient tree, resting their backs against its calendered trunk. Deep, dreary shadows of the crooked, half-naked branches of the gnarled foreboding tree danced menacingly around them in the rising breeze.

## Tania's dilemma

Julio arrived at Tania's place to return José's car and to explain what had happened. The brothers had already contacted her by cell phone and given them a garbled version of their situation. Something about taking Julio for a drive, and him beating them up and dumping them in the middle of nowhere.

Tania had to choose which version to believe. She loved her brothers. Deeply. She was suspicious of Julio. Always had been. And she never really understood him. Why should an apparently sensible young man, healthy, good-looking, devote himself so wholeheartedly to a creep like Romano? The concept of simple loyalty was not entirely alien to her, but she found difficulty in relating it to Julio. What was he up to now?

However, the more she thought about it, the more her brain leaned towards believing him. Why would the brothers take Julio for a ride in the first place? And even if they did, why would Julio beat them up? She *could* see why the brothers would want Julio out of the way. This was just the type of damn fool thing José could dream up. The fact that there were two guns in the side pocket by the driver's seat of José's car lent further credence to Julio's story. On the other hand, Julio looked a bit wobbly on his feet and sounded slurry in his speech. Was he given alcohol and drugs? Did he take them himself? That could explain his weird story . . .

On the face of it, she reserved judgement and called up Pablo and Fox to find the boys, based on Julio's account of where they could have been, and what the brothers told her. She had sense enough not to involve the police.

Julio offered to go with them. Tania hesitated. But then agreed. After all, if all he had done was to dump the brothers somewhere, and then come over to tell her about it, he couldn't be that much of a danger.

As Julio waited for Fox and Pablo to arrive, Tania said she'd make him a cup of coffee. On her way to the kitchen she cast a sideways glance at Julio. His long hair, usually kept in a pony-tail or greased back and tied in a knot, was now loose and hanging around his face and shoulders in a curly mess: black as the night, black as his eyes, usually sharp and alert, now drowsy and dreamy. His rugged face had a tired, exhausted look about it, vulnerable even. His broad mouth twitched, his chubby lips trembled in an embarrassed quiver as he tried to smile back at her for her offer of coffee, gratefully; while huge hands ran strong but restless fingers through the unruly mass of his confused hair. The cleft in his chin took a sudden plunge and got deeper, more mysterious.

Tania felt a stirring in her insides she hadn't thought possible. Certainly not in connection with Julio. Perhaps, with the Catholic guilt of being a married woman now gone . . .

## The unexpected

'How are you feeling now?' said Pepsi, looking sideways at the Crow Boy.

'How are *you* feeling?' was EC's rather unexpected response.

'Not too good, now that you ask,' said Pepsi, 'Just tired, I suppose.'

'You are dying,' said the Crow Boy.

## Back to Caddy's house

Five gunshots and two screams shattered the stolid silence of the gloomy street. Many neighbours heard them, two called the police.

The local police arrived at Caddy's place, followed by an ambulance. A quicker response than normally exhibited by the respective and respectable services, as they knew it was the home of a police officer. They found both the women alive. Amazingly. The old one despite having been hit twice.

It was surmised that Anna woke up when Caddy fired the first shot at the boy's head. She attempted to shield her son. Her movement caused the second bullet to get her shoulder instead of her head. In the mean time the old woman, awake and terrified, came screaming in. She was on the floor by the bed. Caddy, distracted, instead of taking another shot at Anna, shot the mother once, and then again, as she might have kept coming at him, both times missing vital organs. He then shot himself in the heart.

The papers were told that a criminal, whom Caddy arrested some years ago and who was just released from prison, had 'inflicted his revenge' upon Caddy and his family. A photograph of the man was printed with the name Pancito beneath it. The man had, of course, been arrested 'almost red-handed'. The photo was of a homeless vagrant, dead. Pancito was the name of officer Pepe's dog.

The old woman later died in the hospital through loss of blood. Anna was discharged within a week. Her mother came to stay with her.

Having lost her son and husband at the same time, one at the hands of the other, she lost touch with reality. Little Juan killed in her arms . . . his blood all over her, her blood all over him . . . She was told of her mother-in-law's death, but didn't seem to take it in. She only knew that Caddy was away in the country somewhere trying to find and help some poor street kids. On his return they were going for a holiday at a friend's cabin: peaceful and beautiful, by the mountains or the sea, she couldn't remember. Little Juan would love it. She had told him so many times about it, and would tell him again once his grandma brought him back from the local shop where she had taken him to get him some sweets.

The doctor said Anna should be back to normal once the trauma wore off, but in the mean time she needed regular care. Her mother was more than eager to provide it.

She really cared; being away from the bully husband and the grubby house was just a bonus.

## The cat claws

The two boys still sat under the weird old moonlit tree, shoulders touching, breathing synchronised, eyes staring meaninglessly into all the nothing that surrounded and held them gently in its embrace.

'Yeah, yeah, yeah,' said Pepsi after a short pause, in response to the Crow Boy's *You are dying.*

'You *are* dying,' repeated the Crow Boy, softly. 'Your life spirit is packing up to leave your body.'

'Whaa . . . Whaa . . . What are you trying to say!'

'I am not *trying* to say anything. I *am* saying. You are dying. Your body is . . .'

'Yeah, yeah. I heard that. You may not be, but I am *trying*, trying to understand. Explain.' Pepsi tensed, moved his back forward, away from the tree trunk, eyes looking directly into the Crow Boy's eyes.

'You are dying, in order to keep your vow. Your blood-brother vow. The vow to be with your blood-brother to meet his ancestors, now your ancestors.'

Pepsi thought this over, 'Are you playing Indian with me?'

'No play.'

Pepsi thought some more. 'Does this mean you are dead?'

'I managed to take out many from the fire before I burnt. Don't tell me you didn't know?'

Pepsi knew then that he knew. Deep in his heart he knew. Had known from the start. Or had he? Was he just pretending now that he knew then . . . ? His mind was getting confused. Things were getting a bit fuzzy. He tried to rest his back against the tree but missed the trunk and fell over backwards. It could have been a rather thuddy fall, but it was light. He hardly felt his body touch the ground. Was this what dying was like?

'How come you are here then? Alive. Or so it seems.'

'I came to fulfil my blood-brother vow. To help you with your life mission: taking Maria to her Heaven. Now your life mission is complete, I have to live my death. With my ancestors. And you have to follow me. That was your pledge. If you had died first, I would have followed you. To your mother, your Jesus, whoever, wherever.'

Were they in story-land? The country of myths and fables? What was happening?

He didn't seem to care. All was fine. All was as it should be. As it was meant to be. The Crow Boy was right.

He had been sure of only two things in his life. Of the fact that he was nothing. And that he had to get Maria to her Heaven. Now that Maria was safe in her Heaven, with her mother, it was time for him to be with his mother. For nothing to melt into nothingness.

'So that's it, then? You are going to give up that easy?' said the Crow Boy, heavy sarcasm in his voice.

Pepsi looked up with surprise. He had thought the Crow Boy would be pleased. 'What do you expect me to do then?'

'Fight. Fight for your life. Life is not nothing. Neither are you. Fight. You are worth it. Life is worth it. My ancestors tell me. If you let yourself go this easily, it means you think of yourself as no better than Caddy and his lot think of you and me.'

'You want me to dishonour my blood-brother vow? Is that how low *you* think I am?'

'Sorry. I didn't mean it like that. I should have told you first. I have released you from that vow. If I release you, you have no obligation to honour it. In fact, you are obliged to honour my wish to release you.'

'What if I do not wish to be released?'

'The choice is mine. If you had gone first, the choice would have been yours.'

'So it is all right then? Nothing happens? You die, I live?'

'Not as simple as all that. I can release your spirit. Only you can release your body.'

'How do I do that?'

'Cut your other wrist. Not the one from which our blood flowed together. Then I will suck out your blood, *my* blood, from there back into my own. Your blood, and your body, will be free after that.'

'If I don't cut myself, will you?'

'No. I cannot do that. Only you can. Or someone other than me.'

'And if I don't and no one else does either, what will happen then?'

'Then you will die. Your life spirit will gradually pack up itself and leave your body behind. Dead.'

'Good. I am happy with that. I would rather be with you. Your ancestors. I have always wanted to meet your grandfather. He must be a super man.'

'But you won't. I have released you. You will not be with my ancestors. Or with me. You will float in a limbo of emptiness. Neither with yours, nor mine.'

'Why would you do such a cruel thing to me!' Pepsi cried out in a rush of sudden pain that seemed to attack him out of nowhere.

'I won't be doing it to you. You will do it to yourself. If I release you, as I have, I will always be with you, if you choose to live. For I have released you to live your life. But if you choose to die, that means it is you who have rejected me. Rejected my decision. I want you to live. I want to see you alive. Young, free, beautiful. I will see you whenever I think of you. And it will make me happy to see you. But if you die now, I will lose you for ever. And you will lose me for ever.'

'You mean if a boulder falls on my head now and I die, we will lose each other for ever?'

'No. Of course not. That will be a death *given* to you. Offered to you by Destiny. As a gift. But if you *choose* to die, by doing nothing to live, then, then you will have refused Destiny's gift of life. Then we will lose each other.'

'Quick. Hurry up,' said the Crow Boy, 'Time is running out. All this talk has taken more out of you than I'd have thought.'

But Pepsi could not run a deep enough cut through his wrist. The sharpest objects available were dried-up tree twigs. Even his nails had been clipped smooth by Bernardette . . . Neither he nor the Crow Boy had the strength left to run back about two miles to Maria's place and get a knife or something sharp. And would anyone there let him cut his wrist?

Pepsi was desperately trying with his teeth, but his bite lacked intensity. Was it the power of suggestion or was his life force really fading away that fast?

The moon covered itself up with a thick duvet of black clouds and went for a nap. Neither boy could even see to look for anything sharp, even if something pointy had overflowed here from the river along with the household debris.

Just then two keen, green eyes glowered in the darkness and a yellow body sinuously glided forward towards the boys, tail held high in the air.

It yawned, showing huge teeth, pale and jagged, growled, then with a sudden but gentle blow of its front right paw on Pepsi's left wrist, clawed a gash along the side of it. As the Crow Boy lowered his lips to the blood, he lifted his right hand and began stroking the back of the Cat Boy, who had seated himself down between his friends, licking his bloody paw, happiness smiling broadly all over his face.

## Julio's new position

It was a week after Julio's abduction and he had just been to the grave of Pepsi's mother to see if the TnT were still alive and aware of the world around them. They were.

Yet again, he reminded them of all that was expected of them. They remembered all right. Even they were not stupid enough not to realise they had never had it so good. Julio had brought them a new radio. Even a CD player. Lots of food and fruit. New designer clothes were promised. Hugo aftershave, Calvin Klein perfume for men, and whatever else . . .

On his way back he thought of looking up Tania. She was happy to see him and suggested that since her damn fool brothers were always up to some silliness, she would like it very much if he stayed over in the house to 'keep an eye' on things, as he did with her husband. Of course, she realised he now had money of his own and did not need a job; but as a favour . . . if only for a short while . . . she was sort of afraid to be on her own, suddenly. From having both him and her husband in the house, to no man now, the brothers being all over the place . . . never to be trusted . . .

Julio looked around him. This place had been his home for such a long time. He did not want too much out of life. He was happy with what he had. It would be nice to keep having it for some time more. At least for now. If Pepsi turned up, Tania would need some extra help. He would stay. At least till Pepsi turned up.

'At least till Andrés turns up,' said Tania gratefully, 'that is fine. Fine. Thank you Julio. Thank you.'

## A promise - no matter what!

Pepsi woke up the next morning, feeling dizzy, with a dull ache in his head and heart. *Where's EC*? was his first thought. He had a strange dream last night. He wasn't even quite sure what it was. But it featured the Crow Boy. And the Cat Boy. The Cat . . .

'Your friend left last night. But you should stay. Must stay,' said Bernardette, interrupting his thoughts.

'OK,' said Pepsi, shrugging off his thoughts – they were far too uncomfortable to pursue, unsettling beyond belief – and accepting what Bernardette said. 'I will stay here. Thank you so much for asking me. I have never had a proper family before . . . I will make myself useful. Help you build a proper house again. And whatever else.'

'You don't have to do anything,' said Luis, 'You have already done for us more than anyone could ever . . . You've brought us our daughter back, Maria, we'd given her up . . . I don't have words, there are no words . . .' he stammered. Tears began to well up in his eyes and he averted his face.

Vivecca was old enough and wise enough to see that all was not quite as well with Pepsi as he would have them believe. There was a sadness in his eyes, a sense of loss in his voice, and almost an indecipherable, indescribable 'incompleteness' about him that even her years of life and experience could not properly fathom.

'Are you sure you are happy to stay? Because if . . .' she began, but Bernardette interrupted, 'Of course he is happy to stay. He's been Maria's friend for so long. He knows she'll be sad to see him go. He's not the type to give up on his friends, is he?'

It was probably not the right thing to have said, for it made Pepsi's heart even heavier. Of course he knew now that the Crow Boy would always be there for him, somewhere – and even the Cat Boy – but it would never be the same again.

Once more it was Vivecca who noticed the melancholy looming over the boy's aura adopt a darker shade.

'Don't cut me short, girl,' she turned towards Bernardette. 'Let the lad speak for himself. Come, Pepsi kid, tell your grandma: are you sure you are happy to stay?'

'Yeah. Sure,' and then he remembered another reason for his sadness, a reason he could share. 'It is just that the anniversary of my mother's death is coming. And I promised to visit her grave every anniversary. Actually, more regularly than that, when I am in the city; but at least on her anniversary, no matter where I am.

'So I think I will have to go away for some time. But I will be back.'

Maria, who had so far been snuggling against her father while holding her mother's hand, looking as dreamily contented as if she were in child heaven, suddenly tensed. 'You will come back? Won't you? Won't you?'

'Of course I will. I don't have anywhere else to go. Do I?'

'What happened to your wrist?' said Carlos, who was sitting next to Pepsi.

'Let go,' whispered Pepsi. 'It's nothing.'

'Can I come with you?' asked Maria. 'Then we can both return together. Now we know the way . . .'

'Of course not,' said Pepsi before either Luis or Bernardette could speak. 'You've only just met your family. And you must be exhausted.'

'But so are you,' said Bernardette, 'Why don't you wait for a few days, rest, enjoy yourself. Then, maybe . . .'

That dilemma was soon resolved. The balding young doctor was returning to headquarters for more supplies. He said he would take Pepsi more than half-way there, then put him on a coach going right up to the city *and* give him more than enough money for the return fare; maybe even bring him back himself or arrange for another party to do so. 'I will give him a cell phone and my number. He will be able to reach me anywhere and let me know where he is or whatever.'

'You promise you will be back,' said Maria, letting her tears roll down her cheeks like an unending chain of dewdrops.

'I promise,' said Pepsi, 'I promise. Once I have seen my mother, told her all the exciting things that have happened to me, prayed for her and asked her to pray for me, I will be back. I promise.'

And, as he jumped into the jeep, he yelled out, 'I promise.'

'No matter what!' shouted Maria.

'No matter what!' he shouted back . . .

*Author's note*
*Despite some actual rituals and songs, this book does not claim to*
*present an authentic account of any form of Native American culture,*
*tradition or beliefs.*

## A BLADE OF GRASS
### Lewis DeSoto

Märit Laurens, recently orphaned and newly wed, farms with her husband Ben in an Edenic setting near the border of South Africa. But when guerrilla violence and tragedy visit their lives, Märit finds herself in a tug of war between the local Afrikaaners near the farm and the black workers who live on it. Frightened and confused, she turns to the only person who can offer her friendship – her black maid, Tembi. Märit stubbornly determines to run the farm with Tembi's help, until the encroaching civil war brings out their conflicting loyalties and turns their struggle into a desperate fight for their lives.

Lyrical and profound, this exciting novel offers a unique perspective on what it means to be black and white in a country where both live and feel entitlement.

**International Book of the Month Club Choice in the USA**

Lewis DeSoto was born in Bloemfontein, South Africa, and emigrated to Canada in the 1960s. An artist and writer, he has been awarded the Books in Canada/Writers Union Short Prose Award. He lives in Toronto and Normandy. This is his first novel.

£8.99  ISBN 1 904559 07 7


## GOOD CLEAN FUN
### Michael Arditti

A young boy discovers the ambiguity of adult affection. A camp comedian cracks up on stage. A picture-restorer learns to accept her husband's true nature. A prisoner confronts the unbridgeable gap between 'town' and 'gown'. A travel agent tastes the mysterious power of the Internet. A honeymoon couple take an unconventional route to love.

This dazzling first collection of short stories from an award-winning author employs a host of remarkable characters and a range of original voices to take an uncompromising look at love and loss in the twenty-first century. These twelve stories of contentment and confusion, defiance and desire, are marked by wit, compassion and insight.

**'The diverse, urbane stories here *are* good, some of them are fun, and others are far from clean, depicting frightening excursions into dangerous territory'—Shena Mackay**

Michael Arditti was born in Cheshire and lives in London. He is the author of three highly acclaimed novels, *The Celibate*, *Pagan and her Parents* and *Easter*.

£8.99  ISBN 1 904559 08 5

## UNCUT DIAMONDS
### edited by Maggie Hamand

'The ability to pin down a moment or a mindset breathes from these stories . . . They're all stunning, full of wonderful characters'—
*The Big Issue*

£7.99
ISBN 1 904559 03 4

Vibrant, original stories showcasing the huge diversity of new writing talent in contemporary London. They include an incident in a women's prison; a spiritual experience in a motorway service station; a memory of growing up in sixties Britain and a lyrical West Indian love story. Unusual and sometimes challenging, this collection gives voice to previously unpublished writers from a wide diversity of backgrounds whose experiences – critical to an understanding of contemporary life in the UK – often remain hidden from view.

## ANOTHER COUNTRY  Hélène du Coudray

'the descriptions of the refugee Russians are agonisingly lifelike' —review of 1st edition, *Times Literary Supplement*

£7.99
ISBN 1 904559 04 2

Ship's officer Charles Wilson arrives in Malta in the early 1920s, leaving his wife and children behind in London. He falls for a Russian émigrée governess, the beautiful Maria Ivanovna, and the passionate intensity of his feelings propels him into a course of action that promises to end in disaster. This prize-winning novel, first published in 1928, was written by an Oxford undergraduate, Hélène Héroys, who was born in Kiev in 1906. She went on to write a biography of Metternich, and three further novels.

## THE THOUSAND-PETALLED DAISY
### Norman Thomas

'This novel, both rhapsody and lament, is superb'—
*Independent on Sunday*

£7.99
ISBN 1 904559 05 0

Injured in a riot while travelling in India, 17-year-old Michael Flower is given shelter in a white house on an island. There, accompanied by his alter ego (his glove-puppet Mickey-Mack), he meets Om Prakash and his family, a tribe of holy monkeys, the beautiful Lila and a mysterious holy woman. Jealousy and violence, a death and a funeral, the delights of first love and the beauty of the landscape are woven into a narrative infused with a distinctive, offbeat humour. Norman Thomas was born in Wales in 1926. His first novel was published in 1963. He lives in Auroville, South India.

## ON BECOMING A FAIRY GODMOTHER
### Sara Maitland

'Funny, surreal tales
. . . magic and
mystery'—*Guardian*
'These tales
insistently fill the
vison'—*Times
Literary Supplement*
£7.99
ISBN 1 904559 00 X

Fifteen 'fairy stories' breathe new life into old
legends and bring the magic of myth back into
modern women's lives. What became of Helen of
Troy, of Guinevere and Maid Marion? And what
happens to today's mature woman when her children
have fled the nest? Here is an encounter with a
mermaid, an erotic adventure with a mysterious
stranger, the story of a woman who learns to fly
and another who transforms herself into a fairy
godmother.

## IN DENIAL  Anne Redmon

'This is intelligent
writing worthy of
a large audience'—
*The Times*
'Intricate, thoughtful'
—*Times Literary
Supplement*
£7.99
ISBN 1 904559 01 8

In a London prison a serial offender, Gerry Hythe,
is gloating over the death of his one-time prison
visitor Harriet Washington. He thinks he is in prison
once again because of her. Anne Redmon weaves
evidence from the past and present of Gerry's life
into a chilling mystery. A novel of great intelligence
and subtlety, *In Denial* explores themes which are
usually written about in black and white, but here
are dealt with in all their true complexity.

## LEAVING IMPRINTS  Henrietta Seredy

'Beautifully written
. . . an unusual and
memorable novel'—
Charles Palliser,
author of
*The Quincunx*
£7.99
ISBN 1 904559 02 6

'At night when I can't sleep I imagine myself
on the island.' But Jessica is alone in a flat by a
park. She doesn't want to be there – she doesn't
have anywhere else to go. As the story moves
between present and past, gradually Jessica reveals
the truth behind the compelling relationship that
has dominated her life. 'With restrained lyricism,
*Leaving Imprints* explores a destructive, passionate
relationship between two damaged people. Its
quiet intensity does indeed leave imprints. I shall
not forget this novel'—Sue Gee, author of *The Hours
of the Night*